BLOOD LINES

Also by Angela Marsons

Detective Kim Stone series
1. *Silent Scream*
2. *Evil Games*
3. *Lost Girls*
4. *Play Dead*

Other books
Dear Mother (previously published as *The Middle Child*)
The Forgotten Woman (previously published as *My Name Is*)

BLOOD LINES

D.I. KIM STONE
BOOK FIVE

bookouture

Published by Bookouture

An imprint of StoryFire Ltd.
23 Sussex Road, Ickenham, UB10 8PN
United Kingdom

www.bookouture.com

ISBN: 978-1-78681-099-1
eBook ISBN: 978-1-78681-098-4

This book is dedicated to Beau David Forrest
whose life was tragically cut short.

If ever a true angel walked amongst us, it was he.
His spirit is with us always.

PROLOGUE

Drake Hall Prison – present day

Doctor Alexandra Thorne sat at the square writing table that separated the two single beds.

She had claimed the second-hand piece of furniture for herself.

Cassie, her cellmate, barely possessed the ability to read or write and had no use for the makeshift desk.

The stupid woman had once placed a pile of clothing on the right-hand side of the table. One look from Alex and the pile had been swiftly transferred to the bottom of the bed.

Alex felt the right leg of the chair wobble as she pulled it beneath her. Damn cheap furniture was as inferior as the people around her.

Had she been at her office in Hagley her legs would have slid beneath a mahogany desk. Her backside would have been caressed by the tan executive chair. The deep pile carpet would have cushioned her feet. Her eyes would have rested on expensive paintings amongst the luxury for which she had worked so hard and so richly deserved.

But that had all been taken away from her.

She was holding a Bic biro that had been signed for and a sheet of A4 lined paper that looked as though it would tear if she bore down too hard.

But facing forward to the stark white wall she could convince herself she was in any hostel or dirt cheap hotel room. Not that she'd ever stayed in such a place but she could extend her imagination that far. The lingering aroma of cheap perfume mixed with body odour added to the illusion.

She crossed one leg over the other beneath the table. She was in no rush. She would savour writing this letter and the effect it was sure to have.

There were many people she could blame for the direction her life had taken. And yet she blamed only one. A person that had not been far from her mind since the last moment they had spent together.

Alex resented the fact that no one had seen the value in her experiments. Given longer she would have been able to add a significant finding to the mental health community. Her only mistake had been in choosing poor subjects who had inevitably let her down.

A small voice reminded her that she had been foolhardy in allowing her fascination with a certain detective inspector to distract her from her goal.

But now it was time for them to reconnect.

A frisson of excitement coursed through her as she put the pen to paper and wrote the two words that would change everything.

'Dear Kimmy...'

CHAPTER ONE

Kim Stone heard the footsteps behind her. She didn't turn. Her pace quickened in time with her heartbeat. The proximity she couldn't determine. His steps had fallen in sync with her own.

She stumbled.

He paused.

An ordinary pedestrian would have continued normally and passed her or quickened their pace to assist her.

He did neither.

She righted herself and continued. The footsteps resumed but were now closer. She didn't dare look back.

She quickly assessed the local area. At 11.30 p.m. there were few people around the trading estate through which she'd taken a short cut.

As she'd travelled deeper into the belly of the estate the sound of the sparse Sunday night traffic had become even more distant. The street lights from the road no longer cast any light in her direction.

To her left was a row of small units, no bigger than garages. To her right was an alleyway that ran between a steel fastener company and a food processing plant. The width was no more than five feet but it headed back towards the main road.

She turned into it.

The footsteps followed.

She increased her pace, focussed only on the lights at the other end. Running was not an option. In four-inch heels it would be like a toddler trying to take its first steps.

The footsteps behind were now faster.

As she neared the halfway point she upped her pace again. The sound of her blood thundered in her ears.

The footsteps stopped. A hand grabbed her short black hair from behind and slammed her against the wall.

'What the—?'

Her words were cut short as a fist crashed into her mouth. Her bottom lip exploded.

A hand covered her mouth.

'Don't fucking scream, bitch, or I'll fucking kill yer.'

Kim tried to shake her head to say she wouldn't but the back of her head was jammed against the wall. The knobbly bricks bit into her scalp.

He looked to the right and to the left and back at her. He smiled. 'Ain't nobody gonna hear you anyways.'

Kim guessed him to be an inch short of six feet giving him a two-inch height advantage.

She tried to kick out but he used his body to force her against the wall. His erection strained against his trousers and rested against her stomach.

She fought down the nausea and tried to wrestle her arms free. He laughed and pinned her harder. With his full weight against her torso her arms and legs flailed uselessly.

A blow to the temple caused her vision to blur for just a second.

She shook her head and looked into a face she knew to be mid-twenties. His expression was triumphant and amused.

'Listen, darling, we're just gonna have a little fun—'

'Please… please… don't… '

'Oh come on, you whores are all the same. You know you want it.'

He leaned down and licked the side of her neck. The feel of his tongue on her skin sickened her. She bucked against him. He laughed and did it again, biting the skin beneath her ear.

'Oh yeah, you just love it, eh slag?'

She struggled against his bulk again but his body imprisoned her against the wall. His right hand reached down to his zipper.

'Darlin', tonight is your lucky night.'

Just the words she'd been waiting to hear.

She snapped her head forward hitting him square on the nose. Blood spurted immediately. She took the advantage to knee him in the balls and grab his right wrist. She turned it until something snapped. He howled in pain and dropped to the ground. His free hand travelled between his groin and his nose.

Two sets of boots came from each end of the alley. Bryant and Richards got there first, closely followed by Dawson and Barnes.

'Thanks for showing up, boys,' she said as Dawson secured the man's feet.

'You okay, guv?' Bryant asked.

She nodded and turned to Richards who was carrying a small medical bag.

'Swab my neck here,' she said. Just in case he played hard to get. His saliva had been deposited on her neck and now belonged to her.

Richards ripped open the cotton bud and rolled it around the area she'd indicated. He turned his attention to her lip. 'Let me take a look—'

She turned away and wiped the blood with her sleeve.

She leaned down to the scumbag responsible for seven rapes in the last three months. No physical trace had been left on six of the victims, but with victim number seven he hadn't pulled out quick enough, giving them a DNA sample to work with.

That last line about 'lucky night' he'd used with all of them and had been all she'd wanted to hear before making her move.

His eyes were full of pain and hatred. She smiled in return.

'Looks like it was my lucky night, after all, matey boy. And someone should have told you that withdrawal is not a safe method.'

Dawson and Richards covered their amusement with sudden coughing fits.

His ankles had already been secured and, as they tried to do the same with his wrists, he screamed with pain.

She smiled as she walked away. Oh yes, her work here was done.

CHAPTER TWO

Burger wrappers littered the four desks in the Halesowen CID squad room. Kim had collected the takeaway on the way back from the sting.

Only Dawson was still eating: a flurry of some description. The plastic spoon scraped at the cardboard container before he was satisfied it had been defeated.

'Cheers, boss,' he said.

'Everyone's notes up to date?' she asked and was rewarded with three affirmative nods. The details of the case lay in their notebooks.

'If you're finally ready, Kev, it's time for the wipe and you get to do it.'

'Hang on, why him?' Bryant asked.

'Because he got to me in the alley first,' she said, throwing Dawson the roll of kitchen towel.

Although it was after midnight Kim had insisted they all return to the station. After a high tension job like that it didn't work well to go straight home. The adrenaline and excitement still coursed through the body. There had to be a 'come down' period allowing the levels to return to normal.

This was decompression.

The case was solved and the seven women who had been sexually assaulted would sleep easier knowing their rapist was no longer out there.

Dawson ripped off two sheets and began to wipe the board clean. It was a ritual at the end of each case to erase it. To enjoy the satisfaction of wiping it all away. Every swipe across the board signalled that another scumbag was off the streets. She enjoyed the symbolism of the exercise.

Tomorrow they would complete their statements and continue with the interview process; tonight was the time to enjoy the results of their work.

She pushed herself up from the spare desk and started to gather the takeaway wrappers. Bryant offered an impressive yawn just as her phone began to ring.

She saw Woody's name and stepped out of the squad room into the dimly lit general office.

'Sir?' she said into the phone.

'I did ask for an update the minute the operation was concluded, Stone.'

'Just about to call you,' she said, pulling a face. 'Martin Copson is in custody right now and—'

'Well, I know that, Stone. I've already spoken to the Custody Sergeant. I don't have all night to wait around for your call.'

She frowned. Well, if he already knew why was he bugging her now?

'Jack also told me that your face is quite colourful.'

She groaned. Damn Jack on the front desk. Now she knew what was coming.

She braced herself.

'I thought we agreed that Stacey was going to be the decoy with you and the others supporting?'

'Did we really agree that, sir?' she asked, innocently.

'Do not play dumb with me, Stone. You know full well that we did.' He sighed heavily. 'She is a police officer as well as a young woman. You have to let her do her job.'

'Of course, sir,' she protested. 'Just a simple misunderstanding.'

The line fell into silence, and Kim made no effort to fill it. She continued to walk around the dark office without speaking. If he'd thought for one minute she was going to let the twenty-three-year-old try and entrap a vicious, brutal rapist he didn't know her as well as he thought he did.

She had thought she might escape the rebuke. Her boss was now on annual leave, but he couldn't resist one last check-up before he took his granddaughter away for a few days. And by the time he came back it would all be forgotten.

'We'll discuss it on my return.'

Or maybe not.

'Need me to check on anything while you're gone, sir? Water your cat? Let your plants out?' she offered, generously.

'Oh Stone, I would not trust you, of all people, to feed or water anything of mine. Thank you for the offer but my cleaner has it all in hand. And don't forget to keep the superintendent informed on a daily basis while I'm away.'

'Yes, sir,' she said, rolling her eyes.

'I heard that eye-roll, Stone,' he said and paused. 'It'll give you two the chance to umm… bond in my absence.'

Kim opened her mouth to retort, but her boss had already ended the call with a chuckle in the background.

Kim sighed and strode back to the office, but stopped a couple of paces out.

'Honestly, Stace, you should have seen the boss in those high heels. She—'

'What, Kev?' Kim asked, stepping into the doorway. She leaned against the door frame.

'Please… continue,' she urged.

He shook his head. 'Nah, nah, I'm done now. I can't even remember what I was going to say.'

Bryant, who could read her better than anyone, stifled a smile.

Kim folded her arms. 'Really? Bryant, throw Kev the shoes.'

Bryant reached behind and did as she'd asked.

Kim tipped her head. 'Stacey is more of a visual person. I'm sure she'd appreciate the demonstration.'

He looked from her to the shoes and back again. 'You don't really want me to—?'

'You started it,' Kim said.

He looked around the room for support. Stacey raised one eyebrow, and Bryant sat back in his seat.

'Bloody hell, you pair,' he said, removing his shoes and socks.

He forced his feet part way into the shoes while using the filing cabinet for support.

'Aww… shit… ' he said, trying to take a step without letting go of the cabinet.

It reminded Kim of someone trying to ice-skate for the first time who was loath to let go of the side.

'A fiver if you can make it over here,' Bryant said, taking the note from his pocket.

Dawson smiled. 'Ha, for a fiver of yours I'd wear them all day.'

He suddenly threw one foot in front of the other and half staggered and half fell across the office.

To Kim it appeared he'd just stepped off a really bad zombie movie. His arms were stretched in front either for balance or to break his fall.

He fell against Bryant's desk and held out his hand.

'Fair's fair,' Bryant said, slapping the note into his palm.

Dawson turned to her, imploringly.

'Take them off,' Kim said, smiling.

'Damn, I was just starting to like him, too,' Stacey said.

Dawson handed Kim the shoes. 'Seriously, boss, respect.'

She slung them beneath the desk. 'Okay, folks, time to call it a—'

Her phone sounded from the desk. She frowned as she picked it up.

'Stone,' she answered, shortly.

As she listened to the voice on the other end she could feel her frown deepening.

'Okay, got it,' she said, ending the call.

She sighed heavily.

'Okay, scrub that last instruction, for one of you anyway. Time to get the straws out 'cos control room just handed us a body.'

CHAPTER THREE

A quarter-mile out Bryant was guided by the blue fireworks that lit the night sky. Such a pretty announcement for the horror that lay beneath, Kim thought.

There had been no straw pulling back in the squad room. Bryant had sent the kids home to bed and jumped in the car beside her.

The traffic slowed, and Kim pictured an officer at the crossroads guiding traffic away from the crime scene.

For every one that acquiesced without questions there would be three motorists demanding an explanation and then double that for the ones trying to get a look.

The area known as Colley Gate sat on the A458 that linked Halesowen and Stourbridge. Although traffic reduced at night the road never quieted completely. The main road gave way to side roads that led to the infamous Tanhouse estate.

Kim had responded to many calls on Tanhouse. By the 1980s the resident community had been plagued by drug abuse, burglary, vandalism, car crime and violence. Much of which had emanated from the three tower blocks. Kipling House and Byron House had been demolished in 1999, and the last remaining tower block, Chaucer House, had been renovated. A man was stabbed the week the project was completed.

Kim remembered the off-licence that had been attached to one of the tower blocks. Such was the level of crime he had refused to open his doors at night and had served customers through a hatch in the window.

They reached the outer perimeter which was flanked by three squad cars, two officers and half a dozen cones.

She opened the window and thrust out her ID and her head. The officer raised a cone and waved her through.

'Here we go again,' Bryant mumbled as he killed the engine on the Astra Estate. She stepped around Keats's van and assessed the scene as a warm drizzle began to fall. The autumn day had been bright with a temperature in the late teens and was still in double digits in the early hours of the morning.

The car, a one-year-old Vauxhall Cascada, was parked in a lay-by that fronted a row of shops on the main road.

Of the nine properties only three were not boarded up: a Chinese takeaway, a post office and a launderette.

Opposite, but within the cordon area, was a pub that had, thankfully, emptied a few hours earlier. She could live without the live audience.

As she approached the vehicle a familiar voice met her ears.

'Oh goody, my favourite detective. How are you, Bryant?'

She snatched the blue slippers hanging from the hand of the diminutive pathologist and offered him a look in return.

'Bryant, you'll be rewarded in the afterlife for your—'

'Keats, I'm waiting,' she said.

'Oh Inspector, you're just no fun anymore.'

She'd never been any fun, she thought, as she bit back a hundred acerbic retorts that came to mind.

The pathologist weighed in at around twelve stone, wringing wet, and the top of his head just about reached her chin. That alone was enough to keep her tongue in check.

'Victim is female, late forties to early fifties, smartly dressed, with a single stab wound: lower torso, left side.'

Kim nodded and headed around the side of the car.

A young bespectacled male stood in her way. She was instantly reminded of Harry Potter.

She stepped to the left. He followed.

She stepped to the right. He followed.

She briefly considered picking him up and throwing him out of the way when the voice of Keats found her again.

'Detective Inspector Stone, please meet my new assistant, Jonathan Bullock.'

The misery of the kid's school days flashed before her like a film.

The trainee pushed his glasses further up his nose and squinted as though his approaching middle finger had surprised him. He held out his hand and opened his mouth.

'No, no, Jonathan,' Keats said, stepping forward quickly. 'It's best not to make eye contact or address her directly. Like most wild animals, she's unpredictable.'

Kim stepped around him to the front passenger door.

White suits surrounded the vehicle. One dusted the door handle; another was taking the last couple of photographs of the car's interior.

They moved away and gave her the nod.

The first thing that hit Kim was the smell. Copious amounts of fresh blood brought a metallic smell wafting towards her. As pungent as it was she found it preferable to the sickly sweet smell that accompanied decaying blood.

She turned her face to the side and took a generous gulp of air. She turned back and began her appraisal from the top. The crime scene photos would assist her later but her initial priority was to commit the scene to memory. Her senses would never be as keen as they were right now.

The woman's hair was dyed a classy chestnut brown. A hint of grey at the temples signalled touch-up time. The stylish cut landed an inch below the jaw. The forehead was smooth with just the hint of lines that would have stretched and contracted during animation. They would deepen no more, Kim thought sadly.

Her face was still holding on to the remnants of make-up applied at the start of the day. It had worn and faded since the morning and a small smudge of mascara was visible beneath the left eye, perhaps an absent rub at the end of a long day; driving home, when her appearance mattered a little less.

Her eyes were open wide and the lips slightly parted. A layman might say she looked surprised but the dead usually looked that way. Once the heart stopped beating the muscles dropped and returned to rest without retaining the memory of the last known expression. The finality of death lived in the eyes. Had they been closed she would have looked peaceful – serene.

A pearl earring was centred in each earlobe.

Around her throat was a simple gold chain with a small heart-shaped ruby resting against her skin.

A powder pink cashmere cardigan tucked neatly beneath the collar of a plain white shirt.

Kim's gaze continued down. She paused and turned.

'Keats, anybody touch this woman?'

The pathologist came to stand behind her.

'Only me to establish the wound site. And that's exactly as I found it.'

She nodded and continued her assessment. She pushed aside the cardigan to see the full extent of the wound. A crimson stain coloured the whiteness of the shirt. A single tear in the fabric denoted the site of entry.

Kim lowered the cardigan and continued.

Her lower half was clad in quality black trousers. Her feet were encased in court shoes that were stylish but functional. A Burberry handbag sat in the foot-well of the passenger side.

She reached in and removed it as Bryant reappeared beside her.

Although there was no official pairing in her team the two of them often worked together. Her boss liked it that way.

Bryant provided damage limitation. He possessed manners and social skills. It worked well. She hadn't needed to tell him to seek out the person who had found their victim. He had known. And during the conversation he would have shown the correct level of empathy and consideration. She had automatically headed for the victim; luckily for her she couldn't offend the dead.

'Chinese guy, closing up for the night found her, guv,' he said. 'He didn't see the car pull up.'

Kim nodded. 'Okay, get details of as many customers as he can remember.'

She looked around and assessed the surroundings. 'Find the pub owners and do the same. Someone must have seen or heard something.'

He turned away, and Kim continued interrogating the handbag.

Although she didn't carry one, many of the general contents appeared to be present. She glanced back into the car to the hands-free apparatus. An expensive smartphone was still present.

Kim felt rather than heard a figure sidle up beside her.

'Go on then, Keats, what do you know?' she asked.

'I can confidently confirm that she is dead.'

She raised an eyebrow.

'Did you know that long ago, when science was in its infancy, there were some very interesting methods of testing for death.'

Kim waited.

'Among them were tongue and nipple pulling, tobacco smoke enemas and insertion of hot pokers into various bodily orifices.'

'Not great if you're a heavy sleeper,' Kim observed.

'Thank goodness for the invention of the stethoscope, I say,' Keats murmured.

'Okay, so how about telling me something I need to know,' Kim pushed.

'I'm guessing a five to six-inch blade, one stab wound, almost immediate death.'

Kim had guessed that much. There was no blood on the woman's hands. She had not reached for the wound.

Harry Potter approached and pushed his glasses further onto his nose. 'A carjacking, Inspector?'

Keats shook his head and mumbled, 'Oh dear, I told you not to—'

'It's okay, Keats. Let the boy speak,' she said.

Keats spoke around her. 'Walk away, Jonathan, while you still can.'

He ignored his new boss. 'I'm just saying that's what it looks like. I mean it's a nice car and… '

'It's still here,' she said.

Keats groaned and walked away.

'The perp could have been disturbed?'

Her tongue was charged and ready to fire when his long swallow and the memory of his last name stopped her.

She nodded towards the passenger door which was still open.

'Firstly, don't ever use the word "perp" and secondly, take another look.'

He did so as Kim continued to speak to him.

'All her jewellery is in place. Even that Rolex on her wrist. Her phone is still there, and her purse is still in her handbag. You see anything else?' Kim asked.

He shook his head.

'Seat belt is off. The car is parked straight, and she's turned slightly to the left. Anything now?'

His mouth had fallen open slightly but still he shook his head.

'The car is fitted with OnStar,' she said, pointing to the three-button control panel. The button on the right was red and marked 'SOS'. Any activation would have been received at the Vauxhall command centre in Luton, and the police would have been informed already.

Realisation dawned in his eyes. 'It was someone she knew?'

Satisfied he'd learned something it was time to drive it home.

'Listen, if you want to be a detective be one, otherwise focus on the job you're here to do. Us investigators don't take kindly to being told how to do our job.'

He nodded, swallowed and touched his glasses all at the same time. The kid was a multitasker.

It was a lesson he needed to learn quickly and she'd done it privately. Another SIO might not have done. He would have been humiliated into understanding. And yet the redness in his face as he'd turned away remained in her mind.

'Oh and Jonathan… '

He turned.

'You doing your job well helps us do ours.' She smiled. 'Got it?'

He smiled in return, nodded and walked away.

She turned back to the handbag. She took out a tan leather purse containing notes and coins, a dentist card with an appointment for the following week, a cheque book holder and a small cosmetics bag.

She took out the driving licence.

'Okay, Deanna Brightman, let's see what we are going to find out about you.'

CHAPTER FOUR

He felt the hatred surge around his body at the sight of her.

She put her leg to the ground and tipped the powerful motorbike to the right. Her left leg swung around with ease and yet there was a weariness to her body as she pushed the machine under the garage door.

He cared nothing for her fatigue.

He had been here when she had left at 9 p.m. and he was here when the single headlight had turned into the street at almost 2 a.m.

And for the whole time one single question had looped around his brain.

Take the helmet off, he instructed, silently. *Let me see that face. Let me see the cold, selfish bitch that you are.*

Although he had never met her, he knew her. She had saved people from the devil and now the devil lived inside his head.

Just one question – he wanted to ask one question – before he unleashed the rage that was now aimed directly at her.

The childhood abuse that had shaped him was because of her.

The voice in his head was because of her.

His powerlessness to break free was because of her.

The filth in his soul was because of her.

The question finally burst through his lips – no more than a whisper:

'Why didn't you save me?'

CHAPTER FIVE

Kim let herself into the house quietly, not sure who she was hoping not to disturb. The only living thing in her home didn't care that it was after 2 a.m. and was already at the door wagging its tail.

'Hey boy, how're you doing?'

She picked up the post and rubbed Barney's soft black head with her spare hand. As she passed the sofa she reached over and touched her usual spot. It had a Barney-sized patch of warmth.

A small voice reminded her that one of her first rules after collecting Barney from the dogs' home had been 'no sofa'. If she recalled correctly that had lasted about thirty-five minutes.

The 'no feeding by hand' and 'you sleep on your own bed' rules hadn't fared much better.

'Show me,' she said, as he walked at the side of her.

He ran ahead to the kitchen and sat in front of the treat cupboard.

Barney was partial to the teeth cleaning chews. She took out the box and counted. 'Yeah, right,' she said, putting back the box. There had been seven left earlier in the day and now there were six. Charlie from two doors down visited Barney while she was working, and took Barney back to his house when she was away from home for long periods. Since losing his wife of forty-four years the two of them provided company for each other. But despite her gentle reminders about Barney's weight Charlie continued to spoil the dog rotten.

She opened the fridge and took out a carrot.

She would swear he did a dog shrug as he took it to his usual chewing spot on the rug.

She could hear his teeth crunching through the vegetable as she filled the coffee machine with water. It would drip through the coffee grounds while they took their nightly walk and be perfect for her return.

Thankfully, the humid, sticky heat of the summer was behind them and the late September temperatures were stuck around the mid-teens. Perfect.

She leafed through the post as Barney continued to do battle with the carrot.

A gas bill, a bank statement and a third envelope that caused her to frown.

It was plain white with her name and address neatly written on the front. She couldn't remember the last time she'd received a handwritten envelope.

The postmark was Staffordshire. She didn't know anyone in Staffordshire.

She tore open the envelope with a curious expression. Immediately Kim could see through the thin paper that the single sheet was handwritten. The bemused expression froze on her face as she read the first two words.

Her fingers loosened the paper as though flames were leaping out at her. The single sheet fluttered and landed on the breakfast bar.

Her eyes were still locked on those first two words. And they could only have come from one person.

Kim stepped away from the breakfast bar and paced.

Suddenly she was transported back to the previous year and her first meeting with the sociopathic doctor, Alexandra Thorne.

Kim used the word 'evil' very sparingly, even in her job. It was too general, too easily applied to people who did bad things but, in the case of Alex Thorne, the description did not do the woman's despicable nature justice.

They had met during an investigation into the murder of a convicted rapist, and Kim had been on alert straightaway. Persuading anyone to believe ill of the beautiful, enigmatic and charming woman had been an impossible feat, even for her. It had taken every ounce of determination she possessed to uncover Alex's foul, sick experiment, and she had almost lost her mind in the process.

There had been a moment during their battle that Kim had almost slid into the darkness: when Alex had thrown the worst memories of her childhood into her face, exposed all her vulner-abilities. She had been tempted to let go. And yet she had just barely managed to hang on. Only the willpower to expose the true depth of evil that lived inside the woman had kept her from oblivion.

Most people thought her encounter with Alex had been just another case, and there were times Kim tried to tell herself that too. Occasionally it worked.

She reached for the sheet of paper without looking and scrunched it into a ball, as though even reading the words would take her right back to that moment.

She launched it towards the bin. It bounced off the lid and landed in the corner.

She had survived one battle with Doctor Alexandra Thorne.

She was by no means sure she was capable of doing it again.

Her thoughts were interrupted by a scream that chilled her blood.

CHAPTER SIX

Barney reached the front door before she did. She nudged his barking frame out of the way and stepped outside.

Kim heard the words, 'Get the fuck off me,' screamed from her left.

She ran to the end of the drive as bedroom lights began to illuminate the street. Curtains twitched and front doors opened but no one made a sound.

Kim looked in the direction of the scream and saw a dark form leaning against the lamp post. A shadow rounded the corner at the end of the road and disappeared from sight.

A low groan sounded from the figure as it staggered two steps forward.

'Yer fucking bastard,' it shouted before falling to its knees.

Kim reached the figure in seconds and put a hand on her shoulder.

'Hey, are you—?'

'Get the fuck off me,' she screamed, violently shaking her away.

Beneath the lamplight Kim could see that the girl was late teens with hair that was a short mixture of blonde and green. She wore heavy make-up, especially around the eyes, one of which was already starting to swell. That would be a corker tomorrow.

'Did he take your bag?' Kim asked.

The girl gave her a filthy look.

'Bitch, you wanna get away from me before I kick the shit out of yer?'

Kim took a closer look at her. Two of her knuckles were grazed and red. A mark was beginning to show on the right side of her jaw.

Kim briefly considered going after him but knew he'd be long gone.

'Did he hit you anywhere else?' she asked.

The girl snarled in her direction. 'I ain't gonna tell yer again. I'm fine. Now fuck off.'

Kim took a step back and was about to do just that. Being helpful was not a natural disposition for her. But something caught her eye.

'You're bleeding,' she said as a perfect line of red started travelling down the girl's neck.

'I'll live,' she said, wiping absently. 'Which is more than can be said for that fucker if I ever see him again.'

'You could need stitches,' Kim said.

'Lady, I'm warning you… '

Kim held up her hands in defeat. Some people didn't want to be helped. 'Please yourself,' she said, turning around and heading away. In the last few hours she'd entrapped a serial rapist and attended a horrific, bloody crime scene. The day had been long enough as it was.

She shook her head at the girl's prickly attitude. She headed back towards her home. She had no doubt the girl could take care of herself.

Two more steps and she heard a sickening thud behind her.

She looked.

The girl was in a heap on the ground.

Kim groaned out loud as she turned and headed back.

CHAPTER SEVEN

'What the hell… ?' the girl cried, catapulting herself to a sitting position.

'Calm down,' Kim said, placing a steadying hand on the bony shoulder.

The girl shrunk from her hand and looked at her properly. Her eyes narrowed.

'You're the bitch that wouldn't back off when I—'

'I'm the bitch that carried you back to my home when you landed in a heap on the floor, tough girl,' Kim snapped.

The girl looked at her dolefully.

'What's your name?' Kim asked.

'Gemma,' she spat, sitting up and swinging her legs around.

'You're a prickly little thing, aren't you?' Kim asked as she gathered up the antiseptic wipes she'd used on the girl's knuckles while she'd been out cold.

'Was it really worth putting up such a fight for your bag?' Kim asked.

The kid had got herself pretty well banged up.

Gemma looked around pointedly. 'Easy for you to say.'

'Fair enough,' Kim conceded but she could have been hurt much worse.

The girl's hand moved to the back of her ear.

'It's just a plaster,' Kim explained. 'Leave it on until tomorrow.'

Gemma rolled her eyes. 'What the fuck? You a nurse?'

'No, I don't think you need one of those. I think the passing out was more shock than injury, but if your head hurts—'

'Fuck me, lady. Give it a rest.'

For a petite girl with little meat on her bones she packed a whole lot of attitude.

Kim hid the smile inside. There was a familiarity to the girl that she recognised.

In her experience attitude was like a second skin: grown to keep something out. Normally, it didn't just appear for no reason.

Kim could see her looking around for her shoes.

'At the end of the sofa, and your coat is hanging by the door.'

Gemma was on her feet in seconds. Her feet burrowed into the grubby trainers and she strode towards the door.

Kim made no effort to stop her. She had only reacted to the situation because she'd been there. Her duty as a responsible citizen had been fulfilled.

'Listen, if you can identify him, give us a description of the man—'

'Us?' she said, turning. Her eyes were filled with loathing. 'You ain't a fucking pig?'

Kim bit down her irritation. 'I am a police officer and—'

'See ya,' she said, grabbing her coat and heading out the front door.

Kim's shot of irritation turned to amusement.

Oh, how she loved the tough kids.

CHAPTER EIGHT

14 December 2007

Dear Diary,

Well today I finally did it. I still can't believe how simple it was. Months of fantasising about the moment and it was so much easier than I thought.

I still can't choose the moment that the fantasy became a plan. It just kinda happened. One moment I was thinking wouldn't it be great to do such a thing and without me realising it had changed to when.

All day I held my secret close. There was a moment I wanted to tell someone, to share the excitement, the anticipation but I didn't. Because I wanted it all to myself. It was mine.

She was mine.

By the end of the day every one of my senses had been lit by a fuse. It's ignition travelling every inch of my skin. I couldn't have stopped if I'd tried. My body and mind cried out for the satisfaction of which I'd dreamed.

And the first part of the plan worked.

It was awesome. I was awesome.

I know it was the smile that did it. It's a smile perfected over the years.

I have a good-looking face. I know this. People stare and I smile. For that I use my practised performance smile. The one that has got me through life. It has got me everything I wanted. It has got me out of trouble. I am told it is beguiling.

Personally I prefer my real one. The smile that feels natural on my face. The one that says I'm winning. My favourite smile.

The execution of the plan was painful in its simplicity. I offered to walk her home, smiled, looked down and then up again, a question in my eyes.

She hesitated.

My smile turned tremulous.

She nodded.

Result.

There came a point on the journey when there was a choice. Not about what I was doing. That was never in question. It was left to her house and right to mine.

She wanted to go left. I did not.

No one heard her scream.

CHAPTER NINE

'Okay, people, let's get to it,' Kim said, joining her team in the squad room. 'Stace, are the crime scene photos printed?'

Stacey nodded and rose. She stepped towards the whiteboard and taped them on. The first was a headshot. The other displayed a broader view of the car's interior.

Kim waited for Stacey to sit back down before she began.

'Our victim is Deanna Brightman, forty-seven years of age and Deputy Director of Children's Services at Dudley Council.'

'Single stab wound, boss?' Dawson asked, standing up and staring at the photo.

Kim nodded.

'Tidy,' he said, sitting down.

And just like that the investigation took its first breath. The board had a name and a picture. This woman would hold all of their attention until they found out who had taken her life. The pictures on the board provided a focus. Few of her victims remained just a name.

'No defence wounds and the seat belt removed.' She turned towards Stacey. 'Body slightly—'

'Someone she knew?' Dawson piped up.

Kim narrowed her gaze in his direction. 'Thanks for that… Stacey,' she said.

'Oh sorry,' he said, grinning across the desk at his colleague.

Kim liked to tease the information from her team instead of hand-feeding all the time. It was her hope that one day they would all lead their own teams.

'Looks that way,' she confirmed. 'No attempts to make it look like a robbery.'

Kim continued to stare at the photo for just a second longer, a half thought playing in her mind.

'It's almost emotionless,' Stacey said suddenly.

Kim nodded. She had wondered if anyone else would pick up on what she'd been thinking.

There was no rage. No anger. No multiple stab wounds to send a message. No frenzy of a hand that couldn't stop.

It seemed functional.

'Well, someone wanted her dead and she is; so I'd say that's enough emotion for us,' Dawson offered.

Kim couldn't really argue with his point. There had been enough feeling for their killer to plunge the knife in and take away her life. And yet, something about it bothered her.

She refocussed her attention. 'Kev, post mortem is at eleven and then I want every patron of the Chinese takeaway and the pub opposite the lay-by interviewed.'

'Aww… boss,' Dawson said. 'I thought maybe while the cat was away the mice…'

'Kev, the only cat you need to worry about is right here,' she said, raising one eyebrow. Woody's holiday was no excuse for anything less than their best or for approaching the mountainous task of securing statements from both the pub and the takeaway with reduced vigour.

Admittedly, interviewing every person from both locations was an impossible task but if they aimed for one hundred per cent and achieved ninety-five she'd be reasonably satisfied. Aiming for eighty per cent and achieving less would mean a whole bunch of missed potential witnesses.

And right now there was little else to be done. So far they had a respectable middle-aged woman with a single stab would. The people they really needed to see were the people closest to her.

'Boss, is it worth appealing for witnesses instead of—?' Dawson asked.

'No,' she answered.

'But while it's fresh?' he pushed.

'Not at this stage, Kev,' she said, patiently.

An appeal so early would bring hundreds if not thousands of calls that would all have to be dealt with immediately. It would also mean divulging details of the case that she wasn't ready to release for public consumption. The family had been informed barely eight hours earlier.

'Stace, start checking to see if there's any reliable CCTV in the area.' Kim knew it was unlikely. Expensive surveillance systems had been replaced with dummy cameras following vandalism and theft of equipment. Metal shutters were cheaper. But it only took one camera image so was worth checking all the same.

'On it, boss,' Stacey said.

Kim sometimes likened the beginning of an investigation to a single rose. One by one they picked off the petals around the edge until they got to the heart of the case.

And it was time to pick the first petal.

'Bryant, get your coat. We're off to see the family.'

CHAPTER TEN

Doctor Alexandra Thorne waited patiently at the visiting centre for her solicitor to arrive.

She took the time to analyse her surroundings and realised there were worse places she could have been incarcerated.

Drake Hall was situated in Staffordshire and had provided accommodation for female munitions workers during World War II. In the 1960s it had been a male prison, changing to a female one in the mid-seventies. In March 2009 it had been redesignated from semi-open to closed. Having changed from an open to a closed prison it had a fairly relaxed environment and the regime had pretty much stayed the same, allowing prisoners free movement inside the fence.

The facility had a capacity for 345 inmates shared amongst fifteen houses with mainly single rooms and a few double rooms. Alex was thankful she had been assigned to a double. Her plan relied on it.

A form appeared around the side of the coffee machine, and Alex fixed a smile to her face. He looked well, she thought, as he strode forward smiling. He had more to smile about than she did.

His fifty-three-year-old body was slim and well-toned. She idly wondered if he would like to compare his gym facilities with hers.

She had instructed the law firm Barrington and Hume, and she had the benefit of being represented by Mr Donald Barrington himself. And so she should, she thought, for the money she was paying.

She stood and shook his hand, pleased that she could operate on his level as far as attire was concerned. His pinstriped Savile Row suit easily matched her Chanel sweater and Dior trousers. Drake Hall allowed prisoners to wear their own clothes.

'How are you, Alexandra?' he asked, trying his best not to look uncomfortable.

Alex lowered her eyes. 'Bearing up, Donald.'

A little sympathy never hurt anything. She reached across and touched his hand lightly. 'Thank you for putting me in touch with Melvyn Trotter. He's very good.'

Donald nodded as he placed his Asprey briefcase onto the table.

Donald had recommended Melvyn Trotter, a private detective, and he had cost her a fortune, just like the man before her but, unlike Donald, Melvyn had already started providing results. Donald had yet to prove his worth and only an appeal followed by a 'not guilty' verdict would do that.

'We have a trial date: nineteenth of November.'

Alex hid the anger that coursed through her. Another six weeks in this damn place because of one simple error in judgement.

It wasn't that she couldn't cope with incarceration – she could cope with anything – but she didn't want to. She missed the three-storey Victorian house in Hagley. She missed her sporty BMW. She missed good food and occasional sex with good-looking strangers.

'And what's the plan?' she challenged, wondering if he possessed any strategy at all.

For her there was only one available option: 'Not Guilty' followed by immediate freedom and return to her previous life. She tucked the blonde hair behind her ear. It was longer than she liked but there was no way she was getting a prison trim.

'We are all doing our best, Alexandra,' he said, placating.

'I would hope so, Donald.' Though it didn't look like he was breaking much of a sweat. And a strategy did not appear to be resting on the tip of his tongue.

She considered the cost of the Queen's Counsel defence. Her savings were taking a beating, but they would be easily replenished once her liberty and good name were restored.

She would consider selling her beloved BMW Z4, but only if it became absolutely necessary.

'You must realise, Alexandra, that the conclusion to this is not foregone.'

Alex understood that and hoped he was not angling for extra money. The glare from the diamond encrusted cufflinks was hurting her eyes.

'But you are the best, aren't you, Donald?'

He smiled in acknowledgement, showing perfect, gleaming teeth.

'We have a couple of challenges ahead of us. The first is the fact that Ruth Willis will again testify against you. I can't tell you how that hurts our case.'

Ruth Willis had been a promising research subject in an experiment she'd planned since completing her PhD in Psychiatry.

The boundaries of conscience had always fascinated her, not least because she didn't have one. As a sociopath she was born without the ability to feel remorse, meaning she could commit any act and feel no guilt. It also meant she could not form any attachment to another living thing. She had learned very young that her feelings did not work the same way as normal people. She had access to the primal emotions but not the 'higher' ones. She would never feel or understand love in any form, and that was perfectly fine by her.

She could easily cause some poor unsuspecting fool a lifetime of torment and feel not one moment of empathy. This shortcoming had not impeded her life in any way but she had become fascinated by people ruled by conscience. She had selected various patients to partake in her experiment; they remained blissfully unaware.

Ruth Willis had been her first. She was the victim of a brutal rape at the age of nineteen, and she had entered Alex's sphere a few years later, following an attempted suicide upon discovering her attacker had been released.

Alex worked with her for months, manipulating her emotions until finally taking her through a visualisation exercise that had resulted in Ruth following it to the letter and killing her attacker.

Perfect, that was exactly what Alex had wanted her to do. She'd had no doubt that Ruth would commit the act. Her interest was more in how Ruth would feel afterwards, and the stupid bitch had still felt guilty. After the horror of his attack and the permanent impact he'd had on her life she'd still felt guilt for snuffing out his.

The complexity of human emotion was a constant source of puzzlement and amusement to Alex.

She already had a plan for Ruth.

'What if Ruth Willis did not testify against me?' Alex asked.

Donald sighed in the face of the remaining challenges. 'Even without Ms Willis we'll still have the testimony of the detective inspector.'

'Unlikely,' she muttered.

'I'm sorry.'

'Nothing.'

She had known from day one that even the best legal team in the land couldn't get her acquitted from a charge of conspiracy to commit murder. Even OJ's team would have struggled, which was precisely why she'd taken out her own insurance. She'd been right to make her own plans. Her legal team had given up.

She rose, thanked Donald and left the room.

If her plan came together, as she hoped it would, Ruth would no longer be a problem and the inspector would be a gibbering wreck in Grantley, right alongside her mother. But not before she'd afforded herself some light entertainment at the woman's expense.

The first time they had come together Alex had been intrigued by the darkness that emanated from the police officer. It was a blackness that she had wanted to explore, to expose.

And she had.

She had already taken Detective Inspector Kimberly Stone to the edge of sanity once, and she was sure she could do it again.

This time she knew exactly which buttons to press and how hard. She would not be distracted by her own fascination again.

This time there would be no mistakes.

CHAPTER ELEVEN

The house was double-fronted and lay behind a tall row of trees that separated it from Mucklow Hill traffic and the road leading from Halesowen into Quinton.

White pebble gravel gave way to a red-brick driveway. No unsightly oil stains marred the perfection. Perfectly symmetrical hanging baskets hung from brackets either side of a heavy-looking dark oak door.

A white Range Rover took the first space in a three-car garage. A green sports car sat beside it. A red Vauxhall Corsa that, if judged by its dents, had lost more than one fight, was outside, exposed to the elements.

'Is that poor knacker playing hide-and-seek?' Bryant asked as he brought his own Astra Estate to rest beside it.

'It's not theirs,' Kim said, confidently. Even a runaround would not bear so many scars.

'Best guess?' Bryant asked.

It was a game they always played when visiting the homes of the wealthy.

'Between one and a quarter and one and a half,' she said.

Bryant nodded his agreement before lifting a lion's head and dropping it, twice.

The door was answered almost immediately by a short, plump woman in her mid-forties. Her hair was a helmet of tight curls that greyed at the temples. Red-rimmed eyes shone from a plain face.

Kim held up her identification as Bryant started the introduction. The door was pulled back for them to enter before he had finished.

The vast space of the hallway was emphasised by oversized stone tiles alternating in contrasting colours of brown and cream.

With so many doors Kim waited for further instruction.

'They're in the lounge,' she said, pointing down the hall.

'And you are?' Bryant asked, looking down into a face that fell a good foot lower than his own.

'Anna, part-time housekeeper.'

Kim headed towards the door she'd indicated as Anna disappeared to the back of the house. The woman appeared to be treading softly so as not to disturb the settling grief.

Three people were present in the room that was darkened by the closed curtains.

'Mr Brightman?' Kim said, stepping forward.

He nodded and made to stand, but Kim indicated for him to stay seated.

He looked as though he might topple over at any moment. His complexion was still devoid of all colour. She could imagine that it had simply dropped from his face on hearing the news and couldn't yet find its way back.

She sat in the seat opposite and only then allowed her gaze to sweep the rest of the room.

The woman that sat beside him looked so similar to the dead woman that Kim had to stop herself from gawping.

'I'm Sylvie, Deanna's sister,' she said, catching Kim's glance.

'Forgive me, the resemblance is—'

'It's okay, officer,' she said, with a half-smile. 'We always have that. Deanna was the younger. Just by one year.'

Kim couldn't help thinking about the face of the woman in the car. The comparison of the deadened muscles, the dormant skin, the glassy eyes and the slackened mouth. This almost exact replica held the animation that her sister would never have again.

Sylvie's hair was a couple of shades darker than the chestnut hue of Deanna, and her nose slightly wider.

'My daughter, Rebecca,' she offered. Only the name had been required to complete the picture. The woman's beauty had clearly been passed on to her child. Long black hair hung loose and glossy down the girl's back. Her green eyes were emphasised by black eyeliner.

At the sound of her name she lifted her head, positioned a smile, and then dropped it again back to her phone.

If there had been tears they'd been shed before the eye make-up had been applied.

'We are sorry for your loss, Mr Brightman,' she offered.

He raised his head and acknowledged the words that meant nothing to him. He sat forward in the centre of the sofa. He was dressed in a crumpled white shirt and black trousers. The man had not even attempted bed or getting changed from the previous day.

'I know this is difficult but we do need to ask you some questions,' Kim said.

'Of course,' he whispered.

'You've already been informed of the circumstances of—'

'It was a carjacking, wasn't it?' Sylvie interrupted.

Kim frowned and shook her head. 'No, it was not.'

Both Mr Brightman and his niece looked her way with surprise but Kim kept her gaze on the face of the husband. His heavy dark eyebrows lowered. 'It wasn't… ?'

'No. This wasn't a random act of violence, Mr Brightman. In fact, we believe your wife knew her attacker.'

Sylvie gasped with horror and moved an inch closer to Mr Brightman. Rebecca swallowed deeply and slowly returned her gaze to the phone, although Kim could see from the corner of her eye that the girl was pressing no buttons.

Kim continued. 'Can you think of anyone who had any issues with your wife, Mr Brightman?'

Confusion and horror went to war on his face.

Sylvie's chin jutted out. 'Now, wait a minute, officer. Deanna—' Sylvie stopped talking as Anna entered the room.

'Err… family business, Anna,' she said, nodding towards the door.

Anna ignored her. 'Would anyone like a drink: coffee, tea?'

Everyone in the room shook their heads, and Mitchell Brightman offered Sylvie a look for her rudeness as the housekeeper left the room.

'Mr Brightman,' Kim said, looking only at him. 'I need you to really think about it. Anything at all that might help us. It might just be something small.'

'I honestly can't think of anything. Deanna was not a confrontational person. She wouldn't upset… '

'What about that scandal at work?' Rebecca asked, looking at her uncle.

Kim sensed a bristle of irritation as the girl spoke. He didn't look at her.

Kim did.

'What scandal?' Bryant asked.

'That little girl who died on that estate?' she said, scrunching her perfectly plucked eyebrows.

'Hollytree?' Kim asked.

Rebecca nodded.

Kim looked back at Mitchell Brightman.

'Was she involved in that case?'

Kim had seen the news reports. Trudy Parsons was a three-year-old girl who had been on the 'watch' list of Child Services for most of her short life. Her mother had a drink problem and was quite receptive to giving Trudy up when she was unable to care for her. Except, she'd got herself a boyfriend who didn't like to hear a child cry.

In a fit of rage, while Shirley Parsons was at the off-licence, he punched the child so hard in the head that she never regained consciousness.

The court case had been heard the previous week, provoking an outpouring of anger that social services were totally to blame on this one.

Mitchell Brightman nodded. 'It wasn't her case, but Deanna was in charge of the whole department.'

Sylvie shook her head. 'You can't think someone would blame Deanna for what that evil bastard did?'

Kim shrugged. It was something to consider. How involved in the case had she been? Was there someone from the family that she would recognise? Allow into her car?

'Mr Brightman, can you tell me why Deanna was out driving late last night?'

Again Sylvie edged forward. 'She was—'

'Sylvie, please… ' Mr Brightman said and then turned to Kim. 'Deanna went for an Italian last night with a couple of colleagues. It was a birthday treat arranged for one of the girls as a surprise. She phoned at around six and said she didn't really feel like it. I told her it would do her good,' he said. Kim could hear the irony in his voice.

'Why?' Kim asked. 'Why did you say it would do her good?'

He paused and gave it some thought. 'I don't know really. It's just what you say, isn't it? She'd been a bit quiet since the court case.' He shook his head. 'That poor little girl. But there's never any fanfare for the ones they save.'

Kim understood that all right. It was no different for the police. People were only interested in the ones that got away.

'And she was due home?'

'Eleven, half past,' he said.

Kim wasn't sure what else she was going to get from Mr Brightman while Sylvie was around. She seemed determined to answer most questions for him.

She stood. 'My colleague will just ask a few more questions while I get a glass of water, if that's okay?'

She nodded towards Bryant. He knew what to ask.

She headed out of the room and followed the direction Anna had taken after letting them in. She passed a sauna room on her left and a utility room on her right before finding herself in the spacious kitchen.

The white cabinets were stark and sterile. The ultra-modern kitchen seemed at odds with the warm personality of the house. Kim saw everything reflected in the cupboard doors. An extractor fan hovered above the hob encased in a central island.

The housekeeper had her back to Kim as she stepped in to the kitchen. There was no movement as she stared out of the window.

Kim coughed.

Anna turned and wiped at a tear on her cheek.

'I'm sorry,' she said, quickly. 'Is there something you need?'

Kim stepped further into the room. 'Just a glass of water.'

Anna reached into one of the top cupboards and took a glass. She filled it from a water filter and held it towards her.

'Thank you,' Kim said and glanced over her shoulder.

The sink was filled with soapy suds and crockery was draining on the stainless steel unit.

'Isn't that a dishwasher?' Kim asked, glancing to the left.

Anna nodded. 'Never use them. You have to clean off the stuff first and there's no machine I've seen yet that comes with elbow grease.'

Kim had to agree. She had one and never used it for the same reason.

'So, you've worked for the family for… ?'

'Almost a year.'

'Are you here every day?'

Anna shook her head. 'Three mornings.'

Kim paused. 'Mr Brightman seems very nice.'

'He is.'

'Any children?' Kim asked, realising she'd seen no photos that weren't just the two of them.

Anna shook her head. 'She would have made a great mother. She was a wonderful aunt to Rebecca.'

Kim was surprised. The girl didn't look particularly grief-stricken.

'Did they spend a lot of time together?'

Anna suddenly turned towards her. 'Inspector, when are you going to ask me the questions you really came in here to ask?'

Kim smiled at the bluntness of the statement. Good, she liked it when cards were on the table.

'How was the marriage?' she asked.

'Strong,' she answered immediately. 'I can tell you now they loved each other very much.'

'No issues?'

'I wouldn't say that. Every marriage has their ups and downs but they seemed to have worked through some stuff and were coming out the other side.'

'What about Sylvie?'

'What about her?' Anna asked.

'How was their relationship?'

'Complicated.'

'Go on,' Kim urged.

Anna seemed uncomfortable. 'It's strange because they were close as anything. It's been just the two of them since they lost both parents as teenagers. They only had each other. And yet there was a weird kind of rivalry between them too. Neither seemed to want the other to have the upper hand; when Sylvie's husband died Deanna practically moved into Sylvie's house. Made all the funeral arrangements, everything. Got quite upset when Mitchell asked when she was coming home.'

Kim stored the information away.

'And Rebecca?'

'Not a bad kid from what I've seen. Not that she comes here all that often but she tends to keep shtum around her mother. You'll have noticed that Sylvie controls every conversation.'

'Tries to,' Kim corrected.

The woman's mouth twitched slightly.

'Well, thank you, Anna, you've been very helpful and if I could just ask—'

'Here's my full address. And my phone number, and if you want to know I was at a Sally Morgan event at the Wolverhampton Grand. Just to save you some time.'

Kim took the paper and put it in her pocket. 'I like efficiency,' Kim said, smiling. 'And I didn't even have to ask.'

'I watch the telly, officer,' Anna said, seriously.

Kim thought about commenting on real police work being nothing like the television shows, but changed her mind. Such revelations always prompted disappointment.

The meeting had been fruitful, Kim thought. Anna knew a lot about the family unit and the nuances within it, and Kim was not surprised. It was why she had opted to talk to the woman.

Domestic help often became invisible to the occupants of a large home. And so learned a lot. The good ones didn't gossip.

'And, Inspector, if there's anything else you want to know, just ask. I'll tell you anything that will help you catch the bastard. Deanna was a lovely woman. She didn't deserve this.'

Kim nodded her agreement and filed away the offer of help.

With the weird undercurrents in this family she had a feeling she was going to need it.

CHAPTER TWELVE

'What do you think?' she asked Bryant as they left the property.

'Strange dynamic, if you want the truth,' he answered.

'So, where were they last night?'

'Husband was home in the study, working late. He's currently prosecuting a kid from Hollytree for armed robbery of a Pensnett petrol station. His star witness is now only "pretty sure" it was him that did it.'

'He's a Crown prosecutor?'

'Yeah, they didn't get that house on the back of his job.'

And Deanna had been a civil servant too, Kim noted.

'Where were Sylvie and her daughter?'

'Both at home: Sylvie watching television and Rebecca in her room.'

'Hmmm… '

'That's how it is now, guv. You're lucky to get a grunt out of your kids at the dinner table. And if you insist on no phones it's like you've just shared her baby photos on her Facebook page.'

Kim looked at him questioningly. A lot of detail.

He smiled. 'Just saying.'

Bryant's daughter, Laura, was now safely ensconced at Loughborough University studying a few 'ologies that Kim couldn't quite remember. But she was a good kid.

'What about the housekeeper?'

'Sally Morgan show in Wolverhampton.'

He nodded. 'The missus wanted to go to that but it was sold out. Or so I told her,' he smirked.

'You're kidding?'

He shook his head. 'The weekly dance class is all she's getting from me.'

'Bloody hell,' she said.

'You're surprised I told her a harmless little lie?'

'No, I'm more surprised you keep giving me this kind of ammunition to use against you.'

He thought for a minute. 'You're right. So, what next?' he asked, changing the subject.

'I'm going to call the others to see how they're getting on with the folks from the pub and the takeaway. You take us towards Deanna's office in Dudley.'

She took out her phone and paused. 'Bryan… '

'Yeah, guv?'

She continued to stare at the phone and then shook her head. 'It doesn't matter.'

For a moment she'd been tempted to tell him about the letter she'd received from Alex, but then changed her mind.

To tell him would be to attach a much higher importance to it than the letter deserved.

She wiped it out of her mind and put her thoughts to work and Deanna. And what exactly might have happened at the Italian restaurant last night.

CHAPTER THIRTEEN

Alex watched as the juvenile party took place. Melanie Jackson was being released after serving two and a half years for dealing heroin. Alice Tromans had been allowed to make a celebratory jelly. Alice Tromans, who was four years into a ten year stretch for a string of armed robberies, had been allowed to make a jelly.

How bloody fabulous.

Unlike these pathetic creatures Alex had no intention of spending the full term of her sentence in this hell hole. With good behaviour her twelve-year sentence would be reduced to seven or eight. Still not happening, she mused, as her gaze rested on the person integral to the next part of her plan.

The guards had agreed that the small house kitchen was too small and had allowed them a party in the visitors' room. There were no streamers decorating the barred windows that ran the length of the wall. There were no balloons hanging from the stained tiled ceiling and no party favours on the fixed round metal tables that filled the room.

Although the party was for Melanie, Tanya Neale took centre stage as the pathetic little gifts were unwrapped and exclaimed over. A packet of Haribo, a used hairgrip and a crossword puzzle book.

As though sensing her attention Tanya turned and stared right at her. Alex held the hard gaze without fear. Nothing inside these walls frightened her.

'What you lookin' at, bitch?' Tanya called, in a sing-song voice. Every pair of eyes in the room fell upon Alex. Alex smiled.

Tanya looked around at her posse and stood. She sauntered towards Alex with a menacing stare. Despite her diminutive stature the woman was solid muscle and commanded the respect of every person around her.

Alex remained leaning against the vending machine, her arms crossed casually across her breasts. Tanya stopped one foot away from her. Alex towered over her by a good ten inches.

'I said, what you lookin' at, bitch?'

Alex shrugged and said nothing as she looked down onto the woman's greasy blonde hair. A thin scar ran from the edge of her right eye, down her cheek and ended at the tip of her mouth.

Home-made tattoos, fashioned with a pen and a biro, decorated her fingers near to the scarred knuckles. The right hand spelt 'fuck' and the left spelt 'off' with an exclamation mark on the final finger. Because punctuation mattered, Alex mused.

Tanya grabbed one of her own breasts and fondled it. 'You after some of dis, bitch?'

Alex was unsure why this woman in her mid-thirties reverted to gangster slang every time she opened her mouth. She almost laughed out loud, but she checked herself. Now was not the time. The entire room had stilled and was watching a possible drama unfold. Alex could feel the tension as women turned in their chairs hoping for the distraction of a fight. The fight would last only minutes but would entertain them for days.

All background chatter had stopped. A guard watched from the corner of the room. Any altercation between the two of them would be logged for the intelligence officers. It didn't suit Alex's purpose to have anything between the two of them reported.

'Maybe later, sweetheart,' Alex responded. 'We'll just have to wait and see.'

Alex walked around the woman and away from the vending machine.

Thankfully, Tanya let it drop and returned to the party. As she sat she said something and the group laughed. A couple glanced back in her direction. The background chatter resumed. Something else would now be needed as the topic of conversation for later.

From the corner of her eye she saw the exchange had been witnessed by Natalya Kozlov. Alex turned to face her. Natalya would like nothing more than to see Alex get beaten to a pulp. Not today, Natalya, Alex's eyes communicated. Natalya offered her a hateful stare and turned away.

Cassie, her cellmate, placed two coffees on the table. 'I still can't believe she killed three men?' she said, glancing towards Tanya.

Alex nodded and sipped the coffee. She could, and she knew the reason why. The private investigator recommended by her lawyer had compiled a dossier of all the inmates on her wing. She knew who was doing time for what, their family status and their record since being in the prison.

No one in this place held any challenge for her. Within minutes she had analysed Cassie and treated her accordingly.

The woman was a visual introvert prone to agreeableness. She was a typical Type B personality, living her life with a low-level of stress. Working at a steady pace, creative in nature, reflective.

It had been easy to read Cassie. The picture of herself and her two girls that she sobbed over every night. The sketch pad and monthly art magazines brought in by her mother.

Offering friendship had established an instant connection. Manipulators always understood the weakness of their targets. Cassie's had easily been her oversentimentality, resulting in a loneliness that cried out for a special friend.

To gain her trust Alex had used a technique called mirroring. It began with matching mannerisms: a scratch of the nose, crossing the legs. It communicated to the subconscious that you were alike and promoted instant trust.

Next she had initiated small talk to see which personality type she was. It was a technique used by marketers to define motivators. Cassie had instantly fallen into the Yellow category, which dictated she was driven by pity. Green was for the details people. Blue for familiarity, and Red for competitive.

Alex had listened for hours to Cassie talking about her girls and their perfect life together. And never once had she reminded Cassie of the fact she was in prison.

Slowly Alex had teased details of the prisoners that her outside contact could not get for her. But it had been slow. Cassie had sometimes been overcome with guilt for telling tales.

Eventually, Alex had begun to withdraw that friendship leaving Cassie confused and bereft. Intermittent Positive Reinforcement caused an unpredictability that prompted a subconscious craving for positive attention: Cassie had begun chasing her for a positive reaction.

And she had given it.

And then Cassie had told her everything.

Many things she'd been told had helped her refine the methods of attack, and Tanya Neale was no exception. She knew what she liked, what she didn't like and, more pertinently, what was important to her.

Cassie was still watching the woman. 'You know, I've been here twenty-seven months and I've never even spoken to her once. I'm way too scared.'

Of course you are, Alex thought. Cassie was a gentle soul who had made bad choices after getting hooked on meth. She was a poster girl for the system. She'd used her time in prison to get clean and had joined every club and work group she could manage. Her parole hearing was due in a week.

Cassie fidgeted as she watched the silly little party. 'I can't wait until that's me. Just a few more days and then I'll be back with them.'

Hmmm, probably not, Alex thought, while nodding her agreement. Unfortunately for Cassie, she was an integral part of the next stage of Alex's master plan. A subject of which the spineless little fool was unaware.

Melanie Jackson was Tanya Neale's cellmate and would be leaving the prison any day now, meaning that Tanya, the most feared inmate in the prison, would have a cell to herself.

Alex tightened her palm around the sachets of salt in her pocket. It was time to start the game.

CHAPTER FOURTEEN

Kim led Bryant into the office of Children's Services in St James's Road, Dudley.

They stepped into a wall of sombre shock.

The office was open-plan with desks sectioned into cubicles by chest-high barriers that appeared to serve as cubicles on the outside and pin-boards on the inside.

A few heads raised in their direction as they headed towards a glass office in the top left. Kim caught a few sniffles as she passed.

The office still held the nameplate and title of Deanna Brightman.

A woman in her mid-thirties with short red hair rose to greet them. 'Lorna Fisher, Deanna's Personal Assistant,' she said, offering her hand.

Kim took it and introduced them both.

The woman glanced down at the desk. 'I've been asked to clear up,' she said, shaking her head. 'But I just… ' She tried to blink the threatening tears away. 'Please excuse me, officer. I'm still trying to process what's happened.' She nodded beyond the glass. 'We all are.'

Kim understood. It wasn't the news you expected to be met with when you rolled into work. Changing deadlines, increased workload, impromptu meetings – yes. Murder of your manager – not so much.

'I don't even want to be here,' she said, honestly.

For a moment Kim wondered whether she meant at work, or here, in the office of the dead manager – amongst her personal effects. Kim could see a framed photograph of Deanna and Mitchell dressed for some kind of black tie event. There was a stress ball, not unlike the one Woody kept on his desk, except this one had an emoticon face. A square coaster with a cartoon of Shrek and Donkey sat to the right of a meerkat decorated mouse mat.

'There's an interim manager due later today,' she said.

'You can't step in?' Kim asked. As Deanna's assistant this woman probably knew more about the job than anyone.

Lorna shook her head. 'Not my bag, Inspector. Some people were born to make all the tough decisions and others were born to support the people that make the tough decisions. Deanna was the former and I am most definitely the latter.'

'I hear you,' Bryant mumbled.

'Did she make all the decisions on the Trudy Parsons case?' Kim asked, gently.

Lorna swallowed. 'Believe me, we all still have nightmares about that little girl.' She shuddered. 'It doesn't matter whose desk it was on. As a department we failed,' she said, truthfully.

Kim couldn't help but like this woman. She appreciated people that didn't try and duck responsibility or point fingers around the compass. By the same token Kim didn't agree with individuals being held out to dry for such tragedies. She understood better than anyone how children could fall off the radar. Her own mother, whilst mentally unstable, had been adept at subterfuge and misdirection when it came to hiding the truth from an overworked social worker.

'And Deanna's involvement?'

'Minimal. We have meetings, of course, and individual cases are discussed and assessed but Deanna was front and centre when it all hit the press. And she didn't shirk the responsibility or try and shift the blame on to—' Her words trailed away as she looked from her to Bryant and back again.

'Wait a minute. You don't think Deanna's death is linked to that?'

Kim noticed how the second 'd' word stuck in her throat. She shrugged. 'We have to explore all avenues of enquiry. A lot of people were very angry at your boss.'

'I suppose,' she said, doubtfully. 'I think we all assumed it was some kind of carjacking gone wrong.'

Kim wondered if the whole world had been listening to Bullock, Keats's trainee, last night. Every single person had assumed that someone was after Deanna's car.

'Another avenue we'll be exploring,' Kim stated. She continued, 'can you tell me a little about Deanna?'

The work persona often differed greatly to the home persona and she preferred a fully rounded view.

Lorna smiled and tears gathered in her eyes. This time she made no effort to blink them away. 'You probably hear this a lot but she was a lovely person. She expected people to work hard but was quick to spot if someone was working too hard. We've all had the training, of course. Work-related stress is rife in this career choice but she didn't need a training course to be told how to spot the signs. She just kept her eyes open.

'She would find ways to help and support the team whether it be a quick coffee away from the office, a night out to bond or a new initiative for addressing the work–life balance. Not necessarily the methods listed in the *Managing a Team* handbook but she understood people and worked with individual personalities. I suppose I'm saying she didn't manage by numbers like a lot of people here.'

Kim was beginning to get a clearer idea of the woman. The more Lorna spoke the less idea of motivation for her murder there seemed to be.

'I mean, she wouldn't even give up that old phone, in case people wanted to get in touch with her,' Lorna said with a sad smile.

'What old phone?' Kim asked. Deanna's smartphone had been in the car.

'A really, really old Nokia that the network couldn't transfer the number from when she upgraded. It was the phone she'd used as a case worker years ago and had given it out to parents and relatives. She wouldn't get rid of it. She was worried that someone might call for help and the phone would be dead. She transferred it to a pay and go and kept it with her at all times.'

'Did she still get calls?' Bryant asked.

'Sometimes,' Lorna said, looking thoughtful. 'Although she did mention two days ago that she appeared to have lost it somewhere. She thought it may have slipped out of her pocket at the salon.'

This additional phone was something they would need to follow up on immediately.

'Do you have the number?' Kim asked.

Lorna shook her head. 'That phone was long gone from the system by the time I started working for her. I only ever used her new number. It wasn't a number she gave out anymore.'

Bryant took out his notebook and scribbled something down.

'There was a celebration last night?' Kim asked.

Lorna nodded.

'Did they happen often, these nights out?' Kim continued.

Lorna thought for a minute. 'We probably found a reason once a month to go and have a bite to eat. Someone's birthday, someone leaving, someone starting,' she said, wryly.

'And last night?'

'Oh that was Amanda's birthday. The big four oh.'

'And was there anything there that happened out of the ordinary?'

Lorna frowned. 'You mean to do with Deanna?'

Kim nodded, feeling that was pretty obvious.

Lorna began to slowly shake her head.

'Absolutely nothing at all, Inspector, because Deanna wasn't even there.'

Kim sat back in the chair and looked at Bryant and knew he was wondering the same thing as her.

Where the hell had Deanna Brightman been?

CHAPTER FIFTEEN

'So, where the hell was she?' Bryant asked for both of them as they got in the car.

Kim didn't bother answering. It was something they would have to find out.

She took out her phone and dialled Stacey.

'Stace, see if you can find out anything about a second mobile phone. Apparently Deanna had a Nokia for old contacts.'

'Okey dokey.'

'And do a quick check on Sylvie Drummond, her daughter, and the part-time housekeeper, Anna Mills. Lastly, check for anything obvious on the Trudy Parsons case that was recently in the news. Although the little girl died last year the court case might have stirred up something, and Deanna was front and centre shouldering most of the responsibility.'

'Got it, boss,' Stacey confirmed.

'Any news from Kev?'

'Nowt yet. He's tracked down a couple of witnesses who live within spitting distance of the pub. He's on his way to Keats and will goo back to the pub once he's done.' Stacey paused. 'He's pissed off, boss.'

Kim was not surprised. It was a mammoth task to track down every person who had been in the pub and the Chinese takeaway. And that was his job.

The second she ended the call, her phone rang.

'Detective Inspector,' said a familiar voice.

'Keats, are you actually ringing me by choice?' she asked. 'Much as I know you might be missing me, Dawson is attending the post mortem of—'

'You might want to pop along. I may have something to show you.'

'Keats, I wish I could say I've had a better offer but I haven't so we're on our way.'

An invitation from Keats had to mean something, surely.

She bloody well hoped so.

CHAPTER SIXTEEN

Ruth Willis had spent most of the day trying to outrun the feeling of anxiety that had woken her up an hour before the 7.30 unlock time. It had accompanied her every move along with the gnawing ache to understand it. If she understood the cause perhaps the rolling in her stomach would go away.

Normally she was not overly attentive to the mood amongst her fellow prisoners at Eastwood Park. Intensified emotions hit troughs and peaks throughout the year like a tide, swelling around bank holidays, Christmas, family time. Abating once they'd passed. A sense of relief that another 'occasion' had come and gone. It travelled the air like an invisible current. Pent-up frustration passing from person to person, a recipe for trouble.

Presently there seemed to be a restlessness amongst many of the inmates, a nervous energy that vibrated from their bodies against the restricting walls, floors, ceilings and back again. Not so with her.

Unlike most of the inmates she didn't have a calendar on the wall marking the days until her release. She didn't torture herself at her loss of liberty as each day passed.

She had taken a life, and she was paying the price.

Ruth had been careful to keep her head down since her incarceration the year before. She had five years to do, and she hoped to do them without incident. She would leave prison three weeks before her twenty-seventh birthday.

She had gratefully accepted the decision of the court when reducing her sentence once the manipulations of Alexandra Thorne had been uncovered.

As usual any thoughts of Alex brought a mixture of emotions. She hated that she had been nothing more than a pawn in Alex's game. She hated that Alex had managed to manipulate her darkest fantasies about murdering her rapist. She despised her own weakness in carrying out the murder and taking the man's life. She could not bring herself to feel sorry that the man was dead. He had changed her life for ever. But he'd had a mother who now missed him – who'd done nothing wrong.

She felt proud that she had faced the pure evil of the woman across a courtroom and told her story. Every bit of it and left it to a jury to decide.

And yet, pathetically, there was a part of her that missed the bond she'd thought they'd had.

Alex had a way of reeling you in. Her beauty and charm when directed your way were both gratifying and overwhelming.

Ruth had begun to study psychology and manipulation in an effort to learn more about her own weakness and vulnerabilities. Many times she had shaken her head in wonder as she'd read perfect examples of a dozen techniques Alex had employed to gain control of her mind. Ruth likened her own consciousness to an empty car that had been parked and ready to drive. And Alex had switched on the ignition and done exactly that.

Ruth now knew one of the first and most important tactical principles of undetected mind control was finding a victim with a goal over which to exert a subliminal influence.

Oh, and there'd been no shortage of that in Alex's world. All of her victims and patients had wanted only one thing: to heal.

Their relationship had become like an abusive marriage. Alex had showered her with praise and affection when she had performed and then withheld it when Ruth hadn't quite measured up.

She had engineered their sessions so that Ruth had been constantly trying to please her. She hadn't always agreed with everything Alex said but had nodded accordingly, not wishing for the nice Alex to depart.

And yet, even though she knew just how evil the woman was, Ruth still longed for those days back.

She had felt that Alex was the only person in the world that had understood her. It had been the two of them against the world. She had shared more with Alex than she had with her parents.

It reminded her of the film, *The Matrix*. What was wrong with total ignorance if you were blissfully happy? So what if I'm not really eating steak? I'm enjoying it anyway. She sent up a silent prayer that Alex was at Drake Hall and not here at Eastwood Park.

'Ruthee,' said a voice from the door.

Ruth's initial surprise was replaced with pleasure as Elenya tentatively entered Ruth's cell, holding out a book.

The woman was two years younger than Ruth, hailed from a small town in Ukraine, and was serving three years for her part in an armed robbery with six members of her family. Like her, Elenya wanted to do her time and get out, unharmed. Only two weeks ago Elenya had admitted that she couldn't read or write, and Ruth had agreed to teach her. Elenya was grasping the English language tremendously and, in truth, Ruth was enjoying teaching her.

'Come on in,' Ruth said, moving along the bed.

They sat together with their backs against the wall.

'I finish chapter two on my alone,' Elenya said.

'On your own,' Ruth corrected with a smile.

Elenya frowned. 'Yes, I say that.'

Ruth motioned for her to open the book.

This was exactly what she needed to lift that uneasy feeling.

CHAPTER SEVENTEEN

Kim never minded the trips to the morgue. None of her fears lived here.

All she saw was the cold, hard metal and its simplicity. Of course, she understood the purpose of the facility but both she and the pathologist were doing the same thing. They were both seeking answers from Deanna Brightman. He was picking apart her body, and she was picking apart her life. They were both searching for clues.

Dawson was standing against the metal sink furthest away from the body around which Keats was moving deftly.

Although he nodded in her direction, Kim could see that he was a little miffed that Keats had called her to tell her about the hair when he had been the detective assigned to the post mortem. As a major development in the case, Kim would have been more than miffed if he hadn't.

She understood Dawson's hunger for responsibility, for his own investigation. She understood it because she had been filled with the same enthusiasm to prove herself. However, she had trusted her commanding officer to know when the time had been right.

She had yet to see if Dawson had the same trust in her.

'Where's your mini me?' Kim asked Keats, looking around the space that hid nothing.

'Sent out for coffee,' Keats admitted.

'To the canteen?' Bryant asked.

'No, sergeant, further. Much further.'

'Bit of a pain?' Bryant asked.

'Very bright, very curious and very talkative. My silences don't need filling.'

'I hear you, Keats,' she said. 'Some of us work better alone.'

'Ahem,' Bryant interjected.

Kim smiled and ignored him. 'What have you got?'

'Stomach contents sent off to Toxicology. Not a lot in there, so she hadn't eaten for a while.'

Kim knew the whole digestion process of food being broken down and reduced to a liquid pulp could take anywhere from twenty-two hours to two days. Normally only two hours were needed for food to pass from the stomach to the small intestine.

Fortunately, the stomach contents were not needed to assist with assigning a time of death as they already had a pretty accurate note of that. Keats would still send off the limited contents, along with ocular fluid, to reveal any drugs their victim may have ingested during the hours before her death.

So, wherever she had gone last night, it hadn't been for food.

'Recent sexual activity?'

'Not obviously,' he said, stepping towards a tray at the foot of the trolley.

'This is what I thought you might like to see.'

She squinted at it and frowned.

'Look closer. It's in there.'

She took it from him and held it up to the light.

A single hair was contained within.

Finally, Dawson moved towards her and took a look. She was unsure if he'd been waiting for her to coax him out like one would do with a moody child. If so, he didn't know her as well as he should have done.

'With follicle?' she asked Keats, hopefully.

He nodded.

They would be able to get a full DNA profile. The hair shaft alone did not contain nuclear DNA but it was often useful to police in cases of drug use. It acted as a secret diary and had tripped up many people professing abstinence.

'Where was it?'

'Just inside her cardigan.'

Kim felt the excitement start in her stomach. The hair was from someone who had managed to get pretty damn close to the woman. Now all they needed was a suspect.

'Anything else?' Kim asked.

He shook his head.

'Relatively straightforward. Single stab wound, the measurements of which will be on the report you'll get later today.' He paused and peered over his glasses. 'So, Inspector, looks like a pretty simple case for an officer of your calibre.'

Kim offered him a look before turning to leave. In her experience there was no such thing.

'Oh, one last thing, Inspector. There were no hesitation wounds on the body at all.'

Kim paused at the door. Often such marks were found as the killer gathered courage for the fatal wound.

That told her their killer had not been nervous at all.

CHAPTER EIGHTEEN

Alex carefully placed the beaker of water on the bedside cabinet and clutched the two sachets of salt in her closed palm.

The lights went out.

Cassie put down her Sophie Kinsella novel and turned onto her back. With no real window to the outside world the cell was immersed in total darkness. But Alex knew Cassie's movements by heart. She would now be staring at the ceiling willing her eyes to droop and discard this day.

'You know, Alex, the closer something gets the more time seems to stand still,' she murmured.

'I know what you mean,' Alex agreed, wishing the stupid cow would just go to sleep. Tonight was the night.

'It's like, I know I'm going to be with them in just a few days, but each hour is like a week.'

Alex smiled in the darkness. A person with a conscience might feel a touch of guilt for what was about to occur, but not her. She'd been lucky enough to have been born without such an encumbrance.

'It's really strange but this place has been the turning point I needed. I'm twenty-five years old and I've got a lot of life left to live. I'm clean now, and I can go home and finally take care of my children properly.'

'Hmm,' Alex murmured. *Of course you can.* Alex gently ripped the top of both sachets and emptied the salt into the water.

'I'm sorry,' Cassie said. 'That was insensitive of me.'

'It's fine,' Alex answered. 'I'm happy that you have your children to go home to.' She glanced towards where she knew her one photo was taped to the wall. She didn't need light to recall that a handsome man and two fair-haired boys looked down on her. She could recall their features perfectly.

'You never talk about them, do you?'

No, Alex didn't talk about her husband and two sons. It was enough that the photograph did all the work for her. It was a beautiful photo of her family who had been killed in a car crash four years earlier. The story was heart-stoppingly sad. It was poignant that they had been on their way home from buying her a huge bouquet of flowers for Mother's Day. It was poetic that the bouquet had been strewn across the bodies of her two dead sons. It was emotional that in her husband's pocket was a locket engraved with their intertwined initials.

And it would have been all of these things had it been true. The photograph was from a catalogue, and she'd never been married in her life. The photograph had served her well in a previous life. It had adorned her desk, pointed subtly towards the chair that had been used by her patients. Family gave the perception of kindness, of stability. It had worked.

Alex shook her head in the darkness. 'It's still too painful.'

'I'm so sorry, Alex. It must be terribly—'

'It's fine, honestly,' Alex interrupted. The pity in her voice was gratifying but also irritating. She just needed the gullible idiot to go to sleep.

There was another photograph that remained hidden inside the plastic cover of a paperback book. And that photograph did have meaning for her. It was of a little girl and a little boy: twins. And it would be the catalyst that would bring Kim back into her life.

She pushed that delicious thought away. For now, she had work to do.

Alex turned on her side, indicating that the conversation was over. She lay there counting and reached seven hundred before the slow rhythmic sound of Cassie's breathing changed.

Alex slunk beneath the covers and retrieved her tool of choice: a paper weight, stolen from the library. She closed her hand around the object that was solid and heavy in her hand. She took a deep breath and counted. On three, she struck the paperweight into her right eye socket. The pain shot through her temple into her forehead and all through her nose. She gritted her teeth to prevent herself from making any sound. The initial impact subsided quickly and was followed by the immediate swelling around her eye. In a few minutes the bruising would already be starting to show. Perfect.

She slid her hand beneath the waistband of her pyjamas and rested to the right of her belly button. She pinched the skin between her thumb and forefinger and squeezed hard. She repeated the process in two other areas until the pain stung her eyes. Even in the darkness she could visualise the three red patches of flesh on her skin.

Slowly she sat up and turned so that her legs were over the side of the bed. She reached for the glass of water and quickly drank half. The result was immediate. She bent over and vomited on the floor.

Cassie stirred.

Alex repeated the process.

'Alex, what's wrong? Are you—'

'Help!' Alex screamed. She banged her fists on the door. 'Someone please help me, quickly.'

Cassie shot up in bed, instantly awake. 'Alex—?'

Alex banged and screamed.

'Help, someone; please, get her off me.'

Cassie jumped out of bed. Alex heard Cassie's foot slide in the vomit.

'What the hell… ?'

'Someone help… '

Alex could feel the confusion emanating from her cellmate. She was barely awake, standing in a pool of vomit, with a crazy woman screaming for help. She had no clue what was going on.

She didn't have long to wait for an explanation, Alex thought, as the sound of footsteps thundered along the corridor.

The door was thrust open by a red-faced plump officer named Beckett. The lights went on.

'Jesus Christ, what happened?' the second officer asked looking straight at Alex's swollen eye.

Alex backed away from Cassie, who stood bewildered in the middle of the cell.

'She just started attacking me for no reason. I was sleeping and I woke up and she was standing over my bed.' As if the black eye was not enough Alex pushed down her pyjama bottoms. 'She hit me so hard in the stomach I vomited.'

The guards looked from one to the other.

Cassie was shaking her head vigorously. 'I didn't, honestly, I swear I didn't do anything. I was asleep and I heard—'

'Please, you have to get me away from her. I'm terrified,' Alex said, clasping her arms around her torso. 'She's gone mad. Please, just get me away from her.'

The plump guard touched her gently on the forearm and ushered her out of the cell. 'Come with me, I'll take you to medical.'

Alex allowed herself to be guided down the corridor. Twenty feet away from the cell Alex pulled her arm out of the grasp of the guard.

'You people placed me in a cell with a fucking lunatic. My expensive lawyer is going to love this. Now, I want to see the warden, immediately.'

CHAPTER NINETEEN

Dawson pulled in to the car park next to the pub and sat for a moment. The boss had dismissed them an hour earlier, after a quick catch up briefing. He had tried to hide the fact he was still smarting from Keats's blatant undermining of his authority, or lack of it, during the post mortem.

Dawson knew he had never given the pathologist any reason to distrust him with the information but, as was the case with most people, they preferred to deal direct with the boss. Which was fine if he wanted an easy life, but he didn't.

There were times he wondered if his boss trusted him. He knew there were days he irritated her by questioning everything, but if she really wanted him to stop she would have told him so. Objectively, he knew he was a pain. He could hear his own voice pushing when a decision had been made, and he often pissed himself off, but there were times he just didn't agree with the decisions she made.

Stacey always seemed to be the golden girl. She always managed to uncover some kind of nugget in her data mining that pushed their cases along. He respected her abilities and he liked her well enough but sometimes he felt like the last kid to be picked for the football team.

Sometimes he wanted the boss to notice him.

Which was why he was back here at the pub hours after everyone else had gone home. Maybe there was someone from last night in again tonight. Someone who spent many nights in the pub.

He loosened his tie, even though it would make him look no less like a copper than if he'd walked in wearing his old uniform.

'Hey mate, got a sec?' he heard as he approached the door.

He turned to see a kid in his late teens or early twenties wearing an Adidas track suit. The lower half of the boy's face was covered in acne. Dawson immediately felt his pain. He'd had the same problem. And he'd been fat.

'Yeah, mate,' he said.

'Got a quote for the *Dudley Star*?'

Dawson looked him up and down. 'You're joking, right?'

He smiled cockily and offered his hand. 'Bubba Jones, trainee crime reporter.'

Dawson ignored the hand. 'Bloody hell, mate. Even Frost has more tact than that.' He frowned. 'And where is Frost?'

'Chasing a story up in Manchester. You know her?' he asked.

'Oh yeah,' Dawson said.

'Isn't she awesome? I've been shadowing her for a few weeks, since I left Uni.'

Dawson wasn't sure 'awesome' would have been the first word out of his mouth to describe the reporter so he left it there.

'Is Bubba your real name?' he asked, frowning.

The kid shrugged with that ridiculous smile still plastered to his face. 'It's my pen name, and I think it'll get me noticed.'

Dawson considered offering his opinion on that one and then decided against it.

'So, you wanna chat or what?'

'What,' Dawson responded, trying to step past him.

'Huh?'

Dawson couldn't be bothered to explain. 'I don't want to chat; now get out of my way,' he growled.

'I could help you, man. Get the word out, maybe an appeal or—'

'Get out of my way, mate,' Dawson said, nudging him aside. He really didn't have time for this stupidity.

He stepped into the bar and a wall of excited chatter. He had no doubt at the topic of conversation.

If there was something here, he'd find it. It was time to prove his boss wrong.

CHAPTER TWENTY

Kim took her cup and wandered into the garage. Barney followed closely behind.

She leaned against the countertop and surveyed the mess on the floor. Some people chose to unwind on a breezy autumn evening by sitting on the patio with a glass of wine while watching flowers or branches or something. Some people allowed the dusky birdsong to pull the grime of the day from their skin. She chose to stand in her garage and stare at an explosion of bike parts.

Thoughts of the case were spinning around in her head. Something about Deanna Brightman's death was not making sense to her. She had seen murder victims with a single stab wound before. And every time there had been a clear direction of travel for the investigation: a domestic violence situation, a drug deal, a gang-related incident, even a mugging or a fight. But this case didn't slot nicely into any of those categories and it bothered her. There appeared to be no motive for killing Deanna Brightman at all. She shook her head as she remembered Kev's relevant quip – 'and yet she was dead'. The fact was inescapable. Somewhere there was a reason.

She sighed and walked around the bed sheet that was protecting the exhaust assembly from the concrete floor. She wanted to sink to her knees and lose herself amongst the uncomplicated chrome. But her gaze kept lifting to the wall that separated the garage from the kitchen and the drawer that still held the letter. For some inexplicable reason she had been unable to throw it away.

Part of her couldn't help being curious about what was contained within the incendiary envelope, but her encounter with Alex had been placed into a box and stored in the recesses of her mind. Maybe the occasional question leaked out wondering just how close she'd come to losing her grip on sanity. And when it did she simply chased it away.

Opening that letter was more than opening a letter. It opened a gateway. Alexandra Thorne was safely in prison serving her time for the deaths she had engineered. And that was all Kim needed to know.

Feeling resolute she headed back to the kitchen and leafed through the post she'd picked up on her way in.

Nothing unusual – until she got to the last one. It was a plain brown window envelope with her name typewritten on it. But it was the postmark that held her attention. The envelope had travelled from Chester.

The only thing she had a connection to in Chester was the Grantley Care facility. A lovely name for the psychiatric unit that had held her bitch of a mother for the last twenty-eight years.

They had never written to her before.

A slight tremble entered her fingers as she turned the envelope around. There was a written instruction on her mother's file that she was only to be contacted in the event of one thing – her mother's death.

For some reason she had expected a phone call. She'd expected to hear from Lily – the woman she had spoken to for almost twenty years.

She paused for a moment before ripping open the envelope. She unfolded the single sheet of paper and took a deep breath before starting to read.

She tried to ready herself for what she was about to read. A rush of emotion was surging around her body but it had no name. It was not grief, nor loss, nor regret or even a hint of sadness. Neither was it relief or cheer. It was intense, expectant.

Her eyes scanned for key words like death, funeral and condolences.

She frowned as her gaze caught none of them but stumbled over 'parole' and 'hearing'.

She turned the page over as though there would be a painting of a clown face or an explanation of this cruel joke. She turned the page back. It was the brown embossed logo of Grantley which told her it was a genuine communication.

She could feel her head moving from side to side as though her physical denial would erase the letter.

How the hell was this happening, she wondered and immediately took out her phone.

'Damn it,' she growled as her thumb refused to stay on the button long enough to register her print. She needed to stop this. Right now. That woman could not be allowed to leave that facility under any circumstances.

Kim held the phone as she paced the room. What the hell had changed? Her mother had never sought release from Grantley. In fact, she'd had a violent episode right before every other hearing, ensuring her continued incarceration.

Kim had not known that her mother was deliberately keeping herself locked away until the sociopath that was Alexandra Thorne had told her.

'Oh shit,' she said as her legs came to a standstill and her eyes glanced towards the kitchen drawer.

She experienced a sudden sinking sensation as she recalled the letter from the previous day. There was no way in hell that these two intrusions into her life were coincidental.

She took two deep breaths before placing her thumb on the button again. This time the screen flickered into life. Perfect.

She turned her back on the kitchen drawer. She could only deal with one evil bitch at a time.

She scrolled to the number for Grantley Care and pressed.

The facility would now be on night mode but that still meant the phone got answered. And it did on the third ring.

'Kim Stone,' she said. 'Relative of Patty Stone.' The word daughter could not make it out of her mouth. 'Is Lily there?'

'I'm sorry but Lily rarely works the night shift anymore. Is there anything I can help with?'

Kim wanted to reach in and throttle the perfectly modulated and pleasantly trained voice. It was not that kind of conversation.

'I've received a letter,' Kim stated, waving the piece of paper in the air.

The female hesitated for a second, and then caught up.

'About the parole hearing? We always inform family when—'

'Is she aware of it? I mean, does… Patty know about it? She's never allowed one to go ahead before.'

'I know,' she said with a smile in her voice. 'We were surprised too. Both the medical and psychological assessments presented to the parole board have been positive for the last seven years. The overall improvement in your mother's mental health has been substantial during her incarceration. It was only the occasional outbursts that—'

'And there has been no sudden violence at all?' Kim asked. Her stomach churned more with every response.

'None at all,' she said. 'Your mother has been the perfect patient. She's been well-behaved, pleasant, helpful. A true delight.'

Kim could feel the nausea building in her stomach. The world was tipping and there was nothing she could do to stop it.

This woman was evil to the core, and Kim would never believe otherwise. She didn't care who had assessed and monitored her or for how long. Only she had endured the cruelty and abuse that flowed from her mother so easily. And she had been living with the consequences of her mother's actions all her life.

'You should be very proud,' the voice said cheerfully. 'We all know the change in her behaviour is down to you.'

'Excuse me?' Kim asked. She hadn't changed a thing since she'd found out where her mother was. A monthly phone call to check she was still there was the extent of her involvement in the murdering bitch's life.

'Oh yes, it's all down to you. It all began to change when she started to receive your letters.'

Kim heard no more as both the letter and the phone fell to the ground.

CHAPTER TWENTY-ONE

15 December 2007

Dear Diary,

Today I touched her. I had to.

The pleasure was both painful and exquisite at the same time. My fingers touched the back of her head as I undid the gag that had kept her quiet through the night.

I had instructed her beforehand. Make a sound and die.

She had listened.

Her hair wound itself around my hand, silky and soft with a smell of Jasmine. I know the smell of Jasmine. It is a favourite of my mother's. It felt as soft as the hair on a new-born baby. I stroked it in wonder. I sniffed it and rubbed it against my cheek.

So cool.

I felt my arousal grow as I tugged on it, hard, and felt her sharp intake of breath, a tiny groan of pain and an instant look of apology.

She had made a sound.

I let it go. Just this once.

I tipped the juice into her mouth. It dribbled deliciously over the side of her lips and down onto her chin. It was both disgusting and erotic at the same time. I wiped it away and felt the warm velvet of her lower lip. It trembled beneath my touch. It was not with desire but with fear. Good. I prefer fear.

I squeezed her lip between my thumb and forefinger as though trying to burst a zit. I increased the pressure until the soft, pliant flesh flooded with colour and turned crimson beneath my touch.

She writhed, trying not to cry out. She was learning how to play the game.

Good.

I told her about the search. I sat beside her and whispered tenderly into her ear. I told her that her parents no longer thought she was with a friend. They were worried, scared. I told her she hadn't made the national press. After all, she'd only been missing a day. She wasn't important enough for that. I told her that her photo had been on the local news and on the front of the Dudley Star. I saw the hope enter her eyes but I chased it away. Silly girl. No one was going to find her. She didn't need to worry. We had lots of time together.

As I whispered into her ear my lips brushed the fair downy hair on her lobe. It sent a surge of ecstasy around my body.

But it wasn't enough. The experience has only made me hungry, desperate for more. I want to touch, squeeze, torture, own every single inch of her.

And tomorrow I will.

I must.

CHAPTER TWENTY-TWO

'Righty folks, what do we have?'

'A growing list of patrons with no memory,' Dawson said, morosely. The accompanying smile was just a second too late.

'Have you got them all?' Kim asked.

He shrugged. 'Gotta be close. The same names are now coming up for the fourth, fifth time.'

'Any joy with the Chinese takeaway?' Kim asked.

'Much harder, boss.'

Kim understood. The pub was a point for people to gather socially. It was the local. There was an element of memory by association. As people searched their recollections they were able to pinpoint who was sitting where, who was playing pool or darts. Who was standing at the fruit machine. Who'd had enough to drink, got belligerent. They might not be able to supply full names but maybe a surname, a nickname that would prompt the memory of someone else. Eventually the net closed.

Not the same situation with the takeaway. You walk in, order, collect, leave. Few people would notice Elton John playing his piano in the corner.

'Good work, Kev. Keep at it.'

From all the people who had been around that night it only took one to recall a face, a shape, anything.

'Stace, phones?'

'Yep, must have bin a slow day yesterday as two of the networks have confirmed that folks were where they said they were. Phone records for Anna and Sylvie should be with me later today, but still waiting on the permission from Rebecca and Mitchell.'

Kim frowned. That should have been through yesterday. Bryant had requested they all inform their providers to save them gaining warrants.

Bryant shrugged, indicating he had no idea why Mitchell and Rebecca would not have done so.

'Okay, we'll look into that. Stace, while you're waiting for the phone records I want you to dig a bit into the Brightmans' financial situation. That house did not come from the salaries of two civil servants.'

'On it, boss.'

'Okay, guys, keep at it,' she said, heading towards The Bowl.

She stepped inside and closed the door. She took out her phone and turned her back on the curious glances. Her call was answered on the second ring.

'Lily… please,' Kim said.

The fingers of her left hand were already drumming against the desk.

'Kim, how lovely to hear from you,' said the warm voice that had not changed in years.

'What the hell is going on?' Kim exploded.

The frustration of the situation had intensified throughout the hours of darkness when she had been able to do nothing except for pace, sit, make coffee and pace some more. And now she was pacing again.

She had convinced herself that one call to Lily, her only contact at Grantley, would straighten out this whole mess. Lily would assure her the letter had been sent out in error. That it was nothing more than an administrative hiccup. And then she'd be able to breathe again.

'I'm sorry, Kim, please be more—'

'The letter. The parole hearing letter. It's just a mistake, isn't it?'

The silence at the other end ignited the anxiety in her stomach. Where was the reassuring chuckle, the warm placations that it was an error that would never happen again?

She waited.

'Lily… ?'

'It's not a mistake, Kim.'

Kim fell into the chair as a mini quake shifted the ground beneath her feet.

'But how… I mean… why… ?'

'Your letters have had a profound effect on your mother, Kim. I'm so pleased you finally—'

'I didn't,' Kim growled, trying to understand.

'Didn't what?'

'I didn't write any letters, Lily. They didn't come from me.'

The silence between them was now filled with confusion.

'But I read them. You talked about forgiveness, second chances, starting again.'

The nausea rose inside her stomach at the very thought. They would be wearing winter woollies in hell before those words came out of her mouth.

'It wasn't me,' Kim repeated.

'They were all signed "your loving daughter". Are you sure you didn't—?'

'No,' Kim said again.

'Not any of them?' Lily asked, doubtfully.

She could tell that Lily was struggling to digest this information.

'No,' Kim snapped.

'But who… ?'

'I have a pretty good idea,' Kim said, glancing at the envelope she'd brought into work.

Silence fell between them.

'Lily?' Kim said, wondering if she was still there.

'I just… don't know what to say.'

Kim could hear the doubt in the woman's voice. She shook her head at the notion of having to convince this woman that the letters had not come from her.

'Lily, we have spoken many times over the years. Have I once uttered anything resembling the words forgiveness or new starts?'

'Well, no, but I thought perhaps you'd come to a point in your life where—'

'I haven't,' Kim said sharply. Okay, she told herself. It wasn't a mistake that her mother had a parole hearing. Plan A was a fail. Now to Plan B. How to get it stopped. 'How did you allow this to happen, Lily?' she said, accusingly. 'Why were you not consulted?'

There was a silence that was leading towards something Kim did not want to hear.

'I was consulted, Kim. And I heartily recommend her release.'

Kim looked around for the hand that had just slapped her.

'You did what?'

'She's ready, Kim. I've been one of her primary carers for more than two decades. She deserves her last few years—'

'She deserves to have been boiled until the flesh fell from her bones for what she did, but then I suppose we have differing views on justice,' Kim said, hearing the bitterness in her voice.

For some reason she was stung by Lily's approval. Although they'd never met, Kim had felt that, in some small way, Lily was an ally and understood her mother like she did. That Lily was on her side.

'Why the hell wasn't I informed?' Kim asked.

'There is a note on her file that you are to be informed only of her death. You specifically requested—'

'I know what I requested,' Kim said, shortly. 'But surely the fact that you were going to recommend her release warranted a phone call?'

Kim couldn't work out which one of them was being unreasonable.

'Kim, if you would just come and see—'

'I have to go,' she said, ending the call.

The contact was already longer than the usual call to make sure her evil bitch mother was safely incarcerated. She shook her head. Her mother out of custody was not something her mind could control.

Suddenly the world around her looked different. It was no longer a place that she understood. A foreign country had risen up around her and changed the landscape completely.

And she knew it was all down to one woman.

She reached into the backpack and removed the envelope.

She turned it around in her hands, hating the intelligence behind the woman who had written it. Alex knew that she had now made it impossible to ignore.

She raised her foot and rested it on the wastepaper bin as she tore open the envelope.

As she removed the single sheet her foot tapped the top of the bin, reflecting her trepidation at contact with a woman who had taken her so close to the edge.

She took a deep breath and began to read. Her own thoughts interrupting the words in black and white.

Dear Kimmy,

The bitch knew the only person to call her that was her mother.

I hope this letter finds you well.

Liar.

I have missed you and find myself disappointed that you have not yet been to visit. Especially after our last encounter on the canal side where we talked at length about your mother. I was sure we had made progress and elevated our relationship to another level.

Do you remember that moment when I almost brought you to your knees?

I know how important your mother's well-being is to you and I have been keeping an eye on her as you have been a bit busy.

You were stupid to take your eye off that ball.

I'm sure you've heard by now that she feels well enough to attend her next parole hearing. I'm sure the idea of your mother being a free woman has made you very emotional indeed.

I hope this news has fucked with your head.

It has been gratifying to share correspondence with your dear mother. It has helped fill my days although as you know I have always been able to find a way to amuse myself.

And it was all because of me.

There are many souls within these walls who can benefit from my expertise.

Surely you remember exactly what I can do.

But acquaintances and letters can only fill so much of the day.
Personal visits from my closest friends would mean so much
more.

Come and see me or people will suffer.

If you do get a spare moment I would love the opportunity
to share some of your mother's thoughts, probably sooner
rather than later.

And do it now.

Love as always

Alex

Kim slammed the sheet onto her desk and tried to count the number
of veiled messages in that one short letter, but the one that screamed
loudest was the one the sender had intended her to hear.

I have the knowledge you need to keep her locked away.

Kim felt herself being backed into a corner.

Her last encounter with Alex had been instigated following
the murder of a known rapist. Only Kim had felt the woman's
involvement in the crime and had eventually been proven right.
Months of manipulation and a visualisation exercise had propelled
the rapist's victim to stab him four times.

Alex had used the occupants of a halfway house to perfect her
manipulation techniques. One young man had almost beaten
a fellow to death after a few hours with Alex and another had
attempted to murder his wife and her new husband. But the
final, most despicable, act had included a mother suffering from
post-natal psychosis and her young son.

Kim shuddered. She could remember blowing air into the body of that lifeless child.

And all in the name of experimentation.

Oh yes, Kim knew full well what Alexandra Thorne was capable of, and she had vowed never to go anywhere near her again.

She swore as her foot launched the bin across the room.

CHAPTER TWENTY-THREE

Alex sat on the metal chair to the immediate right of the door to the warden's office. She could understand why she'd heard it said that the feeling was not unlike waiting to be scolded by the headmaster. But Alex didn't feel that way. She had engineered the meeting and she would control it.

Her dossier contained a sizeable section on Mr Roger Edwards. The man's career progression had been less than stellar. His work history read like a dance. One step forward, two steps backwards and many steps to the side.

Although she hadn't met the warden of the prison her information indicated that he was ineffectual, and after several failed attempts at promotion he had settled like dust at Drake Hall Prison and was going to spend the next two years treading water until his pension kicked in.

The door opened. 'Please come in, Alexandra.'

Alex bristled as she passed by him. Although it was only just after 9 a.m. she detected the faint smell of body odour.

She took the seat on the nearside of the desk. There were two framed photographs: one of a plain blonde woman with an unfortunate-looking daughter; the other picture, which was double the size, was of himself and a German Shepherd. She supposed that said it all.

He squeezed around the desk and sat down. The material of his navy jacket strained around his shoulders. She wondered if he was also trying to stretch his current wardrobe to the end of his career.

'I'm sorry I wasn't able to see you yesterday, Alexandra, but I was at an all-day meeting with the Chief Inspectorate.'

Alex inwardly groaned. There had been no requirement for any kind of explanation but his ego demanded it. She was unimpressed and irritated.

'Mr Edwards, I do not believe that we are acquainted in any way, and I would be appreciative if you would refrain from using my first name.'

Alex held his gaze. He coloured but said nothing.

Good, she was pleased that they had that straight.

She would not be reduced to being treated as though she bore any resemblance to the rest of the pitiful idiots inside these walls. He may be the big dog in this pen, but she ate big dogs for breakfast.

He opened his hands and smiled insincerely. 'So, would you like to tell me exactly what happened?'

'Yes, I was savagely attacked by one of your inmates, and I am deeply perturbed that I was placed in a position of grave danger.'

Alex touched her swollen eye for effect.

'Yes, very strange business.' He looked at the file on his desk, searching for a name. 'Cassie Yates has been a model prisoner. You understand that we could not have foreseen such a brutal attack?'

Alex narrowed her eyes. 'I'm not so sure my lawyer would agree with you there, Mr Edwards. If you had no suspicion of one of your charges acting in such an aggressive manner, then obviously you had not delved deeply enough into her psyche because clearly it happened.'

He could not dispute the condition of her face. It was staring right at him.

'Well, yes, I see that but are you sure that there was nothing you did… ?'

'Really, Mr Edwards,' Alex exploded. 'Are you really going to try and blame me for this attack?'

His face reddened even more and he held up his hands. 'No, no… '

'It certainly sounds as though you are trying to apportion blame to me, Mr Edwards, which will be stated very clearly in the letters I intend to write to the Chief Inspectorate about the safety of this facility.'

As Alex began to wonder who had been called in to see whom, she saw panic leap into his eyes. Yes, it was time he realised that he wasn't dealing with one of the many gimps that lined this place wall to wall. Under his supervision the prison had leapt from seventh to second place for incidents of assault between prisoners. She knew full well that his career could not take another scandal; it was an integral part of her plan.

'Slow down, Ms Thorne, I think this incident warrants further discussion.'

'There is nothing further to discuss. You have failed to protect me from a dangerous criminal, and I intend to ensure that I am not placed in a vulnerable position again.'

Realisation began to dawn on his face. He picked up a pencil and began shaking it between his fingers.

'Aah, I understand, Ms Thorne. You'd like to be placed in a single cell so that nothing like this happens again?'

His smug smile was amusing to her. *Did he really think she was that simple to understand?*

She shook her head. 'No, Mr Edwards, that's not what I want at all.' For the first time she smiled. 'Both Tanya Neale and I have spare beds. I would like her to be moved in with me.'

She was rewarded when he dropped the pencil onto the desk and his mouth hung open. She waited a full thirty seconds for him to speak.

'Who on earth do you think you are coming in here to make demands? May I remind you that you are a prisoner in this facility and—'

'And I have not been protected,' Alex said, sitting forward. 'Which both the newspapers and the Chief Inspectorate will be hearing about if I don't get what I want.' She took a moment to smile. 'And while I'm writing the letters I may inadvertently refer to an incident whereby a formal complaint was hushed up after you had inappropriately touched the breasts of a young prisoner.'

Alex sat back again and crossed her legs, enjoying the colour that flooded his face. His tongue made a slight darting movement out of his mouth even though he managed to maintain eye contact.

'How dare you try and threaten me into—'

'It's no threat, Mr Edwards. My solicitors have a written statement from the prisoner concerned and will be instructed to use it.'

Oh thank you, Cassie, Alex thought. She was certainly the gift that kept on giving.

Like a drowning man she saw his lifestyle, pension and a whole lot of explanations pass before his eyes.

He pulled himself up straight before he spoke.

'Let me understand this; you have been subjected to a brutal attack by one of our mild-mannered prisoners and you are now making a request to share a cell with the single most dangerous female in the whole prison?'

Alex nodded slowly, enjoying his confusion. That he thought he could keep up with her was reward enough for the injuries she'd sustained.

'Yes, Mr Edwards, that's exactly what I want and your swift arrangement would be greatly appreciated.'

CHAPTER TWENTY-FOUR

'You all right, guv?' Bryant asked.

'Why wouldn't I be?' she asked.

'Aah, answering a question with a question is your number one deflection – which tells me I'm right. Normally you would say "mind your own business, Bryant".'

'Mind your own business, Bryant,' she said.

'Yeah two sentences too late and I fed you the line. Oh, and your left foot hasn't stopped tapping yet.'

She instantly stilled it in the footwell.

'Is the prince okay?' he asked, referring to Barney and the way she treated him.

'Of course, why?'

'Because the last time I saw you this distracted was when he had to go to the vets for a filling.'

'Extraction,' she clarified.

'Yeah, but—'

'Talk to me about the case, Bryant,' she said. Thoughts of her mother and Alex were tumbling around her head.

He offered her a look before taking her advice.

'What are your thoughts on the money?'

Kim shrugged. 'Possibly an inheritance from either of the families or some kind of windfall but there's definitely been an injection of cash from somewhere.'

'Got no kids, though. So, disposable income is quite high.'

'They've lived in that house for fifteen years. Deanna's job probably paid more than Mitchell's forty-two grand, but she only got that promotion four years ago so back when they bought it…'

'Zoopla says they paid almost a million for it,' Bryant said.

'Who the hell is Zoopla?' she asked and then changed her mind. She didn't want to know. 'No way would their combined salaries have been enough to get a mortgage for anywhere near that.'

'She held quite a responsible position, though,' Bryant queried.

'Still a civil servant, and we both know how that works,' Kim answered. To her knowledge it would have been no more than seventy thousand a year and still not enough for that house.

'What about the phone records?' Bryant asked. 'Any reason why the husband has delayed the permission?'

'Absent-mindedness on his part, I'd say. There's no doubt he loved her very much. He's distraught.'

'We're ruling him out already?' Bryant asked, surprised.

'We're ruling out no one. Grief can be feigned.'

'What about—?'

'Okay, Bryant, enough,' Kim said, cutting off his next question. 'I said talk to me about the case not conduct a second briefing.'

'Jesus, this car trip reminds me of taking a stroppy teenager to school a few years back. Talk to me, Dad. Don't talk to me, Dad.'

A chuckle escaped from between her lips as they pulled up outside the Brightman residence.

Kim was not surprised to see Sylvie's sporty Mazda parked in the exact same spot as the previous day.

Anna's Corsa was parked up too which gave Kim an idea.

'You talk to Mitchell and Rebecca, and I'll talk to Anna,' Kim instructed.

Bryant looked puzzled. They didn't need her permission. They'd got it and her alibi had checked out. Her phone had dinged a tower just two miles away from the Wolverhampton Grand, so he didn't understand why his boss wanted to question her again.

Especially as it was the other three that possibly had something to hide.

CHAPTER TWENTY-FIVE

Bryant stepped into the same room they'd spoken in the previous day and, other than a change of clothes, time could have stood still.

Today the curtains were open, revealing a wall of glass that stretched the entire room. The view comprised Halesowen town centre to the stunning Clent Hills on the other side. Bryant would have happily taken the oversized television down from the wall if he had that to look at every evening.

Mitchell Brightman was now dressed in light jeans and an open-necked rugby shirt. Short, wiry, black hairs peeped out of the top. His chin was covered with a dark stubble. Bryant guessed that a shave was just a step too far. A quick shower and getting dressed was probably as much as he could manage at this point. If he'd just lost his wife, Bryant wasn't sure he'd have been able to manage even that. Not that he'd ever tell her.

Bryant was secure enough to acknowledge that, for a man in his early fifties, Mitchell Brightman was very attractive. He could imagine that women of all ages might be drawn to such a man, although there was no evidence to suggest that he had encouraged any such attention.

'It's helpful that you're back here so early,' Bryant offered pleasantly to Sylvie and Rebecca. 'Makes my job easier.'

Rebecca sat on the same chair with her legs draped over the arm, swinging them to and fro. There was no acknowledgement from her, and her eyes didn't lift from the phone.

'No, no, we stayed over,' Sylvie offered. 'There are spare rooms, and I just threw on something of Deanna's. We were a similar size.'

Mitchell turned to look at Sylvie as though he hadn't even noticed. And the fleeting anger told Bryant that he certainly hadn't been asked for permission.

Fresh sadness swept through Mitchell's eyes as he saw the light blue quarter length trousers and flowered blouse that she wore.

Bryant couldn't help the faint distaste he felt in his mouth. Yes, they were sisters and, it appeared, quite close but still…

'I just needed to check with you about the permission to the phone companies so that we can—'

'Oh my God, I'm so sorry,' Mitchell said, shaking his head. 'It clean went out of my mind once you left.'

'It's fine, Mr Brightman,' he said, holding up his hand to stop the explanation, which looked genuine to him. It was perfectly understandable.

'I gave mine,' Sylvie said, twirling the stone encrusted bangle on her left wrist.

Bryant nodded but found himself wondering if she was wearing the jewellery of her dead sister too.

'Rebecca?' Bryant said, as Sylvie's gaze followed his.

'What?' she said, without looking up.

'Rebecca,' Sylvie snapped, and he was grateful.

His own teenager's tantrums had lasted all of one day. He remembered a particularly awful show of bad manners one day when Laura was fourteen years old. Laura had returned home from school to find her mother out and a note on the kitchen table. He remembered it word for word.

Dear Laura,

As you see fit to speak to me as though I am your servant and employee, I have decided that I no longer want this job and have quit.

Your gym kit is scrunched in the corner of your room where you left it, your bed is unmade and your dinner is whatever you choose to cook from the freezer.

It had taken only two hours for Laura to call and apologise.

Neither he nor his wife could stomach bad manners, he thought, as all eyes turned to Rebecca.

'I don't see why I have to—'

'We can get a warrant, Rebecca, but it would just be easier if you gave your permission,' he said, demonstrating more patience than he felt.

'Okay, then,' she said, nonchalantly, although her feet were no longer swinging.

Bryant bit back the words that were trying to burst out of his mouth. She wasn't his daughter to chastise.

He stood. 'That's all for now. Thank you both.'

Mitchell stood. 'I'll walk you out,' he said.

'It's fine, I know the way.'

'It's no trouble, officer,' Mitchell insisted.

Bryant shrugged and turned towards the hallway, from where he could see the front door.

Yet, Mitchell Brightman was two steps behind him.

Bryant opened the front door and stepped outside.

'Well, thank you for your assistance, Mr Brightman.'

Mitchell Brightman put his hands deep into his pockets and rocked forward on the balls of his feet.

Bryant wondered at the purpose of this escort to the doorway.

Mitchell Brightman opened his mouth and asked him a very strange question.

CHAPTER TWENTY-SIX

'So, how's he doing?' Kim asked Anna once they were in the kitchen.

'Much as you'd expect,' she said, wearily. 'A great deal of time spent staring out of windows. Walking from room to room, hoping his grief won't follow him. Hiding the fact he's been crying,' she said, lowering cups into the soapy water. 'Why do men do that?' she asked.

Kim shrugged and took a step closer. 'I need to ask you something.'

'Of course you do,' Anna said, placing a soapy cup onto the drainer.

'Was Deanna seeing someone?'

The question had been nudging forward in her mind since they'd learned of Deanna's absence at the Italian restaurant.

Anna's hands stilled in the sink.

'Why would you ask me that?'

Because she wasn't where she was supposed to be, Kim thought. And lying about your activities to your husband normally only meant one thing.

'I have my reasons,' Kim said.

Anna resumed washing up but said nothing.

'You haven't said no.'

'Inspector, I'm here as a part-time housekeeper not a CCTV camera. I don't watch their every move. Deanna was a very kind and charitable woman who cared deeply for her husband.'

Kim noted the tears that filled her eyes.

'But you still haven't said no.'

Silence.

Kim continued. 'It's not disloyal to her memory to tell us anything that might help us catch the person who killed her, especially if it was someone that she knew,' Kim offered.

Anna's head snapped around. 'You're not saying—'

'I'm saying we have to rule out the involvement of anyone that knew her but we need to know where to look.'

Anna dried her hands on the tea towel.

'I don't know anything,' she said, reaching up to open a cupboard door. The door was heavy and appeared to sag on its hinges.

'Bloody snagging works,' Anna growled. 'Kitchen fitter was here for weeks and the job still isn't finished. Nice looking bloke but completely unreliable,' she said looking at Kim directly.

'What's his name?' Kim asked, playing along. 'Just so I know not to use him, of course.'

'Jason Cross. I'm sure you'll find him in the yellow pages.'

'Thank you, Anna. Thank you very much.'

CHAPTER TWENTY-SEVEN

Kim found Bryant standing against the car.

'Get it?' she asked about the permission.

'And more,' he answered.

She held up her hand and took out her phone. Stacey answered on the second ring.

'Stace, get me details for a kitchen fitter named Jason Cross when you can.'

Stacey acknowledged the request, and Kim ended the call.

Bryant frowned.

'He may be able to tell us where she was the night she died,' Kim said, meaningfully.

'She was seeing the kitchen guy?'

Kim shrugged. 'That's what we're going to find out.' She nodded back towards the house. 'The hair certainly didn't come from any of them.'

'Interesting,' he said. 'Just like the question Mitchell Brightman asked me away from the others.'

'Which was?'

'If he would have to explain everything we found on his mobile phone.'

Kim's hand paused on the door handle, and she looked back at the house.

'Bryant, what the hell have we opened up here?'

'Your guess is as good… '

His words trailed away as her phone rang.

She frowned when she saw it was Keats. They had nothing outstanding.

'Stone,' she answered.

'Inspector, I hope you're not too busy… '

'Oh, just chilling with Bryant, as normal. You know how it is.'

'As I thought. Well, you might want to happen along to my location, if you have a minute.'

'You're inviting me over to your place, Keats?' she asked. He very rarely volunteered to see her by choice.

'I am inviting you, Inspector, to a crime scene because I think this is something you need to see.'

CHAPTER TWENTY-EIGHT

Alex sat on the bed and waited patiently. The bed opposite had been stripped and all Cassie's possessions had been removed. The woman had been gone for less than twenty-four hours, and Alex could barely remember what she looked like. She had no idea where Cassie was now or what would happen to her, and the beauty of it was, she didn't care.

The only thing she cared about was the fact her plan was now coming to fruition.

Mistakes could definitely occur when trying to orchestrate what she was attempting to do, but the key lay in bite-sized portions. Nibbling away at small chunks of the problem.

And patience.

There were many things she had wanted to do from the moment she'd been incarcerated but that would have been foolish: actions based on anger for some small satisfaction but no eventual gain. So, she had sat on her hands and planned. And it was working out swimmingly.

A noise sounded from the hallway and Tanya appeared in the doorway: a bin liner trailing behind her and a murderous look on her face.

Oh dear, it appeared her request had made the toughest, most feared inmate of the prison angry.

Too bad.

'You is one dead bitch, ho,' she growled.

Alex remained sitting against the wall but she allowed a smile to form on her face.

'Hello, Tanya. Welcome to your new home.'

'Fuck that,' Tanya said, dropping the bag and advancing on her. 'What you think you playin' at, bitch?'

Alex felt a second of anxiety. This woman was capable of murder with her bare hands. She forced herself to remain calm.

'Step away and I'll tell you,' she said coolly.

'Step away you say?' Tanya screamed, as the rage hit a whole new level. 'You lucky I don't shank you right now you fucking slag, whore, bitch. I'll step away when it suits me to step the fuck away and that—'

'Tanya, calm down,' Alex urged, not enjoying the positioning of Tanya towering over her. The aroma of milky Weetabix was wafting down towards her.

Tanya snarled. 'Don't tell me to calm down, slut. No one tells me what the fuck to do.'

Alex really wanted the woman to step back and let her talk.

'Tanya, it is in both of our interests for you to stop drawing attention to us.'

The last thing Alex wanted was for the officers to sense trouble between them. They would move Tanya back in a heartbeat.

The word 'interests' seemed to get her attention. She unbent her upper half and returned to a standing position.

'Talk fast, or you get it right now,' she said.

Alex knew she had gained control and laughed out loud. 'Oh, Tanya, please do me the courtesy of a real threat.'

It was daytime and the place was buzzing with guards. Not Tanya's style.

'Your first opportunity will be tonight, once that door is locked, so hold your breath until then.'

Tanya glared at her. 'You telling me when to shank you, slag?' Tanya asked, disbelievingly.

'If we're going to have pet names for each other so soon, I prefer bitch, and all I'm doing is detailing your best opportunity to shank me if you still want to, but I don't think you will.'

'What game you playin', bitch?' she repeated.

One that you can't even begin to imagine, Alex thought. She shrugged. 'What were you told?'

'Reallocation,' she spat.

'Looks like you're stuck here, then,' she said, looking towards the spare bed. 'May as well get comfy.'

Tanya's light jeans dragged on the floor as she took a step back. Her plain black T-shirt stretched across her ample bosom.

Alex didn't flinch as Tanya leaned forward again but not as close. The woman wrinkled her nose in disgust as she peered closer at Alex's face. 'That little snip of a thing do that to you?' she asked, sarcastically.

'No, I did it to myself,' Alex said, meeting her gaze.

'You kidding, bitch,' Tanya said, looking unsure.

'Actually, Tanya, I'm not,' Alex said, seriously.

Tanya searched her face for some hint at humour.

Alex locked on to her gaze and didn't let go.

'You one weird fucking bitch,' Tanya said, throwing her bin bag onto the bed.

You'd better believe it, Alex thought.

'And I don't fucking like yer one little bit.'

Alex said nothing but just watched as her new cellmate began slamming her possessions onto the table.

'And don't think we are gonna stay up late chatting and swapping stories.'

Alex didn't need to swap stories. There was little about Tanya that she didn't already know.

'And by this time tomorrow, you'll be dead,' Tanya said, without turning.

Alex smiled at the back of the figure that had just threatened her life.

Somehow she didn't think so.

CHAPTER TWENTY-NINE

Kim turned right into the road that led to the Saltwells Nature Reserve. Known as one of the largest urban nature reserves in the country, it covered an area of 247 acres.

At the heart lay forty hectares of Saltwells Wood. The area had been a popular choice for school trips. She still remembered that the area west of the Black Brook was called Lady Dudley's Plantation, thought to be in honour of Lady Dudley.

They were heading for Birch Wood which spread east.

Kim parked the car a hundred feet away from the Saltwells Inn which was busy with disgruntled lunchtime trade being ushered out the doors by four or five uniforms. People were heading towards cars.

'Bryant,' Kim said.

'On it, guv,' he said, getting out of the car.

She backed up the car and placed it right in the middle of the exit driveway. No one was leaving until they had witness statements.

She locked the car and shouted to her colleague. She tossed the keys towards him mid-trot, which he caught with one hand. He could move the car once potential witnesses had been documented and accounted for.

She neared the perimeter as a second constable arrived to assist the WPC at the cordon entry.

'Druggie in the bushes,' she heard the WPC explain.

Kim shook her head and passed without speaking.

As she entered the woods she could hear voices in the distance. She traversed what were known to be some of the finest bluebell woods in the country. There was little evidence now of their spring flowering.

She caught the movement of either a crime tech suit or a yeti through the trees. She betted on tech and headed towards it.

'Bloody hell,' Kim said as she reached the inner cordon tape. There was no shortage of trees around which to loop it. She ducked under it and entered a canopy of branches that belied the autumn sun that had just warmed her.

Gathering forensic evidence from a scene like this was a techie's worst nightmare. Open to the elements, animals, insects. Even a gentle breeze could destroy something that could potentially lead to the crime being solved.

It was universally known that not every piece of evidence could be found at a crime scene but it was good if the guys had a fighting chance. They would be here for days and might still find nothing.

She took a moment to look around. There were officially marked pathways and also trodden-down routes and short cuts everywhere as people made their own way through bramble and shrubbery. Establishing the access and egress points would be near impossible.

'Hello again, Detective Inspector,' Jonathan Bullock said from beside her.

'Inspector will do,' she answered.

'Thank you,' he said as though she had given him permission to use her first name. He nodded towards the location of the body. 'Do you know what I think?' he asked.

She raised an eyebrow.

'Absolutely nothing,' he said with a shy smile.

She smiled in return. She liked fast learners.

'Aah, Inspector, lovely to see you again,' Keats said.

'What do you have?' Kim asked, stepping further into the tape circle.

'A better attitude than you,' Keats retorted.

'No great feat,' Kim said, approaching the body.

She looked down into what should have been a pretty face amongst a mop of tight blonde curls. Kim guessed her to be late teens/early twenties but her face was ravaged by cold sore scars. Her cheeks were gaunt and her eyes more sunken than they should be. There was an air of sadness to the face that Kim could not fathom.

'Drug addict?' she asked, quietly, as she swatted away a fly from her ear.

Keats nodded. 'Fresh needle marks between the toes.'

Often the sign of a long-term user. Heroin addicts chose to move sites for various reasons. Sometimes it was due to collapsed veins at other injection sites and other times it was to hide the fact they were still injecting. Whatever the reason it was a painful way to get the drugs into the body.

'Are you aware of what you do, Inspector?' Keats asked with a puzzled expression.

She narrowed her eyes. 'What are you talking about?'

Once the words left her mouth she realised she had just opened herself up for a whole barrage of one-liners.

'Touch the victim,' he said, glancing down at her blue gloved right hand which was resting on the woman's shoulder. His voice was quieter than usual. 'You've done it at every one of my crime scenes. Just saying.'

Kim hadn't been aware. She felt real sympathy for this poor kid but she suspected this young girl would not be one of hers.

'What are you showing me?' she asked. 'This girl is nothing like my victim. There is no similarity—'

She stopped speaking as he slowly lifted the black T-shirt.

Her emaciated body, ravaged by the effects of heroin, had one single stab wound that looked as though it had been lifted from the body of Deanna Brightman.

Two stabbing victims in as many days with the exact same wound.

She looked to Keats.

'No hesitation marks and the measurements are exactly the same.'

Kim sighed deeply. Only two days into the week and she was already just one body short of a serial killer.

CHAPTER THIRTY

Kim felt the sadness of the girl's death surround her as she headed out of the woods. As though sensing her mood the autumn sun had disappeared behind a dense grey cloud.

Just like the crime scene of Deanna Brightman, no effort appeared to have been made to disrupt the investigation. The victim had already been identified and there was someone that needed to know.

She stopped at the cordon tape. The male and female constables smiled at her questioningly, wondering why she'd paused.

She did not smile in return as she fixed her gaze on the WPC.

'The "druggie in the woods" is named Maxine Wakeman and is twenty-two years of age. She has blonde hair, brown eyes and a small birthmark on her shoulder. She has a stab wound in her abdomen that bled out until she died. She has a handmade bracelet on her wrist and her toes are painted baby pink.' Kim stared into the woman's eyes and enjoyed the shame that she found there. 'I just thought you should know.'

Kim offered no opportunity for a response before she turned and walked away. She arrived back at the car just as Bryant was moving it to the side.

Bryant shoved his head out of the window. 'Did you know that Saltwells takes its name from brine spas which used to be right next to the Saltwells Inn? Apparently saline water welled up on the mine workings and people came to bathe thinking it had healing properties.'

'I didn't know that but I can see how it's imperative to the case,' she offered, drily.

'No one saw a thing,' Bryant said as he got out of the car. 'But we have the details of everyone.' He turned towards the bench. 'That woman with the poodle found her. Still pretty shook up.'

Kim would have imagined so.

'WPC Perks is going to stay with her until Dawson gets here.'

Sometimes it was good that Bryant knew her so well. They had other leads to follow, but this witness needed deep and gentle questioning. Calling Dawson is what she would have done.

'So, our guy or not?' Bryant asked.

'Difficult to say for certain but the wound is exactly the same as Deanna's. It's the victims that don't match.'

'Copycat?' Bryant asked, leaning against the car door.

'The detail was withheld from the press,' Kim said, 'making a copycat unlikely. Also, Deanna's murder only made the papers last night and the approximate time of death for our new victim was ten thirty last night. Not a lot of time to plan a copycat killing.'

'But our victims have nothing in common?' Bryant said.

'Except the wound,' Kim said, taking out her phone.

'Yeah, there is that,' Bryant said.

'I was just gonna ring you,' Stacey said, answering the phone.

'Go on,' she said.

'Got an address for Jason Cross but cor find out where he's working today.'

'Give me the office number,' Kim instructed. She then read it out to Bryant, who keyed it into his phone.

'Thanks, Stace, now I need an address for a Maxine Wakeman.'

'Who is… ?'

'Probably a second victim,' Kim said.

'You're joking?'

'See what you can find out,' Kim said and ended the call.

'Pass me your phone,' she said to Bryant.

'Why, what has your own done to offend you?'

She ignored him and hit the key to call the number read out from Stacey.

It was answered on the second ring.

'Jay's kitchen fitting services.'

'Hi there,' Kim said, cheerfully. 'It's Amelia from the plumbers' merchants. Jason called through an urgent order for a mixer tap and I'm trying to get it to him, but I took down the wrong post-code, I think, because I seem to be heading right out of the area.'

There was a hesitation.

'Never mind,' Kim said. 'I'll head back to the office and wait for him to call if you can't—'

'Wait a minute. He's working in Wombourne,' she said and read off the postcode.

Kim thanked her and ended the call as Dawson pulled up beside them.

Time to find out if Deanna had been doing something she shouldn't have been.

CHAPTER THIRTY-ONE

Alex walked around the library studiously but it was not a book she sought. It was a location. She went back to the doorway and glanced in again.

Her eye went straight to the four chairs around a small square dining table.

She placed herself in the chair that meant her back was to the door. Other than her the library was empty. The council-run facility was open every day. They offered a poetry reading group, storybooks for mums and a Sunday reading group. Luckily for her the dinner gong was imminent, which meant the hordes were already gravitating towards the dinner hall as though meal times were events to be relished.

She arched her back and positioned her head in her hands, her fingers in her hair.

Within minutes she heard the unmistakeable sound of cheap shoes squeaking along the polished floor. Not hurried or focussed, just regular and relaxed. On patrol.

She leaned forward and began to tremble her back ever so slightly. She dug her fingernails into her scalp.

The footsteps stopped twenty feet behind her.

'Alex, are you okay?'

Alex smiled behind the tears that were slowly building in her eyes. It was Katie – perfect.

She dug her nails in harder but offered no reply.

'Alex, what's wrong?'

Alex shook her head slightly and continued to dig away until a tear rolled down her cheek.

'Alex, what's happened?' Katie asked, taking a chair beside her.

'It's nothing,' Alex spluttered, raising her head.

She watched as the concern filled Katie's face. Oh, there was nothing like exploiting the maternal concern and hormonal circus of a brand new mother.

'Doesn't look like nothing,' she said, gently, touching her on the forearm.

Alex took a dramatic deep breath. 'It's my sister. She's recently had a little girl but when I called yesterday they were just considering calling an ambulance. A rash and a fever, they said. And now I can't get them at all.'

'I'm sure everything will be okay,' Katie said, reassuringly.

'My little niece,' she sobbed, shaking her head. 'I keep imagining her crying with the pain. That rosy little face scrunched up in agony. Her little fists clenched and her cries… '

'Now, now, try not to think about it,' Katie said. 'I'm sure it will all be fine.'

'How can I not think about it, Katie?' she asked, slipping in the first name reference. 'How would you feel?' Alex asked. 'If you had to come to work and your poor baby was poorly and you couldn't carry your phone so you wouldn't know. That's how I feel.'

She dug her nails in deeper.

'She could be dead by now for all I know,' Alex said, allowing the volume of her voice to rise to a stage of near-hysterics.

'Calm down, Alex,' Katie said, looking around.

'But you know how it feels, don't you?' Alex asked, cementing their common problem. It was almost in the bag. 'Once you're inside these walls you don't have a clue what's happening with your baby—'

'Lewis,' she supplied helpfully.

'It's the same for me with baby Kirsty. I don't know anything. Anything could happen and we wouldn't know,' she said, beseechingly.

'I'd know,' Katie said, seriously.

'Of course,' Alex nodded and offered a wry smile. 'Your sitter would call the office and they'd put out a call… '

'No,' she said, tapping her pocket. 'I'd know straightaway.'

Of course she would, Alex thought, as the mouse headed towards the cat exactly as she had suspected. No new mother would be incommunicado while leaving their newborn in the care of someone else, regardless of what the rules said.

Katie was clearly someone who could choose which rules could and could not be broken. Perfect.

There were real rules like don't give your access card to an inmate. Don't smuggle in drugs or alcohol. Everyone knew those were rules not to be broken. But carrying a mobile phone while on duty. Well, what harm could that do?

A different class of rule, surely? And she'd just given that information away for free.

Alex allowed gradual understanding to dawn in her yes. She nodded slowly, in a 'good for you' kind of way. A tremulous smile communicated that it would remain their secret.

'I'm so pleased you're able to stay in touch. I just feel so sorry for my sister. She's alone, you see. No husband to help. Our parents died years ago.' Alex summoned more tears. 'We only have each other and I can't even be there to help her.'

Alex saw Katie glance to the door. Not one person had passed by during their conversation.

Drive it home, Alex, she thought to herself.

'What I wouldn't give just to know my sister and her poor baby are okay.'

Katie reached into her pocket and produced an older model iPhone.

'Here,' she whispered, pushing the phone towards her beneath her hand. 'Quick, go behind that bookshelf and make the call. One minute.'

'Are you—?'

'Just do it,' Katie said, pressing the phone into her hand.

Alex grabbed the phone and headed to the area suggested as Katie stood and moved towards the door.

Alex smiled as she keyed in the number that she had memorised, followed by the two words that were expected at the other end.

The recipient already knew what the words 'do it' meant.

CHAPTER THIRTY-TWO

The postcode they'd obtained for Jason Cross's whereabouts was enough to take them to the twelve properties it covered; spotting his liveried van on the drive had not posed much of a challenge.

'Not a bad working environment,' Bryant observed, and Kim had to agree.

The house, like the Brightman residence, was large and in an affluent area.

'He gets very good clients,' Bryant said, parking right behind the van.

'He must be very good at what he does,' Kim answered, getting out of the car.

'Must be,' Bryant agreed.

The front door to the property was wide open in line with the rear of the van for easy access. They walked straight in.

This hallway was even more spacious than the one at the Brightman home. And much more opulent. A theme of gold swathed the entire space. The ornate bannister of the sweeping staircase was gold encrusted. Vases set in recessed wall spaces were decorated with gold. An imposing glass table was edged with gold. The photo frames that lined the wall were formed of gold.

Kim had the feeling of having entered an undiscovered Egyptian tomb.

Bryant's wrinkled nose said it all. The Brightman residence was tasteful. This one was not.

The sound of the radio drew them towards the back of the house. They arrived at the doorway to a large kitchen area in disarray. Every available space was filled with shiny white cabinets like the ones she'd seen before. A six ring stainless steel oven unit was an abandoned island in the middle of the room.

Kim was about to call out when a soft curse sounded from beneath the double sink unit in the corner.

'Jason Cross,' Kim said.

'Yep, that's me. Give me a minute.'

The absence of surprise told her he'd known they were coming.

Bryant took a step closer and then realised it was not an easy trip to make and stepped back.

'Gotcha,' they heard before the sound of rustling came from the sink.

Jason Cross emerged and smiled in her direction.

Kim was immediately struck by his obvious good looks. His T-shirt was black and bore the company logo. His trousers were also black and appeared to have pockets at every angle. He was an inch short of six feet tall and built like a working man. She could see the muscles of his upper arms stretching the cuff of his short sleeve.

The prettiness of his face was emphasised by the light, bright blue irises that appeared translucent from across the room. His hair was a dirty blonde with natural highlights left over from the summer.

If every person had one imperfection, then Kim surmised that his was hiding somewhere beneath his clothes.

'Have you brought the mixer tap I didn't order?' he asked with a lopsided smile that seemed a natural expression on his face. Kim could understand how that smile would be appealing.

She held up her identification.

'We'd like to ask a couple of questions about Deanna Bright-man.'

His face closed down slightly as he took a cloth from his back pocket and wiped his hands.

'Of course.'

He leaned back against the sink unit and crossed his arms over his chest.

'You recently worked at Deanna's home?' Kim asked.

'Yes, I've been there on and off for the last couple of months. Deanna didn't want too much disruption at any one time and had the kitchen done in stages.'

'Like this one?' Kim asked, deliberately, as something in his answer struck her.

He shook his head. 'No. Mrs Richmond has taken herself off to Kenya for a two-week safari and wants it done by the time she returns.'

Aha, as she had thought. She tipped her head, questioningly. 'Sorry, but I couldn't help notice the first name reference for Deanna, but a more formal address for this customer. Any particular reason why?'

He shrugged before reaching for the cloth to wipe his hands again. They appeared to be clean.

'Some clients prefer a more informal approach. And I was there for quite some time.'

'The two of you became familiar?'

'We talked,' he admitted. 'She was a very sociable lady.'

And from Deanna's point of view there were worse people to pass the time of day with, Kim suspected.

'About what?' she pushed.

Again, the arms folded across the chest. Jason Cross was developing quite a telling pattern.

'Many things, officer.'

'So the two of you became quite friendly, Mr Cross?'

He coloured. 'Is there something you'd like to ask me, Inspector?' he said, meeting her gaze.

She didn't hesitate. She didn't pass up such attractive invitations. 'Were you sleeping with Deanna Brightman?'

'Absolutely not,' he replied, swiftly. There was no shock at the question. No defensiveness at being asked such a thing. No anger at questioning his professionalism. Just a flat out denial that he had been waiting to offer.

'Have you ever been in Deanna Brightman's car?' she asked.

'Absolutely not, never,' he answered, shaking his head. 'I would have no reason to.' Again, with the 'absolutely' not. And the additional 'never'.

'Would you be prepared to give us a DNA sample?' she asked.

'As soon as I see the warrant, Inspector,' he answered shortly. His initial open smile appeared to have deserted him.

'It would be helpful to us if we didn't have to,' she said, watching, as he reached again for the cloth, realised what he was doing, and thrust his hands into two of his many front pockets.

'It would be helpful if you could nail someone for her murder within forty-eight hours too, but it's not going to be me.'

Kim knew the issue of a warrant on what she had was a shot in the dark. If Woody wasn't on holiday, perhaps, but without him she didn't have a chance.

'Mr Cross, are you married?'

He nodded. 'Happily,' he qualified, unnecessarily.

'Children?'

'Yes. A boy, he's seven.'

Kim nodded. 'That's a lot to lose.'

He reached for the cloth for the third time.

'I have no intention of losing them, Inspector, so if there's nothing further—'

'Where were you on Sunday night, Mr Cross?' she asked, pointedly.

'At home, watching television.'

'And your wife can verify that?'

'I was alone. She and Donnie were at her mother's.'

'Hmmm… ' Kim said.

He threw the cloth on the side. 'Inspector, I don't like the direction of this conversation, and I think you should leave.'

'Do you know anyone by the name of Maxine Wakeman?'

His eyebrows drew together and he began to shake his head before he realised he was answering the question.

'Please leave,' he repeated.

'I'm finished, Mr Cross, for now, but please don't go too far away. I have the feeling we may need to talk again.'

'I won't be going anywhere,' he said, turning away from her.

Bryant sighed heavily as they stepped back into the watery afternoon sun.

'Bloody hell, guv. That got wintry pretty quick. Do you think you could have gone a bit—'

'He's lying,' she said, flatly. 'About how much I'm not sure but I'm willing to bet your pension that the hair found in the car belongs to him.'

'Doesn't exactly look like the murdering type, guv.'

'Who the hell does?' she asked, seriously.

CHAPTER THIRTY-THREE

'Seeing as you asked pretty boy about Maxine, I'm assuming we are treating it as one case?' Bryant asked when they were back in the car.

Kim thought for a moment. This was a first for her. Every other multiple murder case she'd worked had shared a commonality amongst the victims. At the minute she had only the manner of death to link them together.

Deanna Brightman was a wealthy middle-aged woman with a responsible job and a loving family. Maxine Wakeman was twenty-two years old, a drug addict, who was known to the neighbourhood team for prolific shoplifting to feed her habit.

'Bryant, I'm honestly not sure.'

She allowed the question to circulate in her subconscious as a vision of Alex came into her mind. Or rather became clearer in her mind. The woman had been lurking in there all day.

The contents of the letter were still running around causing havoc in her memory. She had tried to find a box to put them in but it wasn't working yet. Too many emotions were being prodded by the woman's intrusion. Normally she was able to keep everything packaged away until she decided to think about it. Where Alex was concerned there appeared to be a bleed. A blurring of the edges.

'What're you thinking?' Bryant asked to fill the silence.

She offered no response. He really wouldn't like her response. The course of action that she knew she had to take would prompt him to fill out the forms to have her sectioned. No, the less Bryant knew at the moment the better it was for her.

The rest of the journey passed in easy silence until Bryant brought the car to a stop in front of an end terrace in a street that was bursting with cars.

'Are you sure this is the right address?'

She wasn't sure what prompted the question. Perhaps it was the fact that every property they'd visited so far had been affluent.

Plant Street lay behind Cradley Heath Library that was situated on the Reddal Hill Road. At the top of the street was a small park and an open field used often as a shortcut for the many estates that had a primary school close by.

'This is the place,' Bryant confirmed.

The door was opened by a woman in her mid-forties. Her hair was dark and showed tell-tale evidence around the temples of being recently dyed.

Her green uniform was that of a hospital auxiliary.

'Mrs Wakeman?' Kim asked.

The smile was open and unsuspecting. She nodded cheerfully. Kim hated that she was about to wipe that smile from the woman's pleasant face.

'We're here about Maxine… '

'My daughter?' she asked.

Kim nodded as the woman stood back.

'Please, come in.'

Kim stepped into a small room that held two armchairs, a gas fire and a sideboard covered in Capo di Monte. Mrs Wakeman continued past a poky passageway that led up a narrow flight of stairs.

Quickly they had reached a small, brightly decorated kitchen at the end of the house. Kim realised if she were to measure it in steps it would have been no more than thirteen paces long.

'How is she?' the woman asked, eagerly.

Kim looked to Bryant for a clue. Who the hell did this woman think they were?

She slowly took out her identification and introduced them both.

The woman looked confused. 'I'm sorry; I thought you were from the clinic.'

Kim was unsure why she'd thought that but alarm bells were going off in her head.

'Mrs Wakeman, may I ask when you last saw your daughter?'

'Well, it's been a while but she's still my child. Well… my daughter… you know what I mean.'

Kim had no idea what she meant and was beginning to doubt the woman's ability to answer questions.

'Mrs Wakeman, I think you should sit down and tell us when you last saw Maxine.'

The woman did as she was told as she looked from one to the other. Her expression was still open and obliging.

'It's been a few months since I've actually seen her. She used to phone a lot, even wrote to me a few times when she was in the clinic, but I've not heard anything for a while now.' Finally, doubt and concern rested on her face. 'She's still off the drugs, isn't she?'

'Mrs Wakeman, can you tell me why you haven't seen your daughter in so long?' Kim asked, gently. She knew she needed a better understanding before she ruined this poor woman's life.

'Well the grass is always greener, isn't it?' she answered.

'What grass?' Kim asked, feeling bewildered by the riddles this woman seemed to be using to communicate.

'I told her the truth years ago, you see. As soon as she was old enough to understand. Completely uninterested she was. Didn't care. Not until she turned sixteen and we started having all sorts of problems. By then she thought the world had been invented just for her. Her mouth had the answer to every question and we were arguing like cat and dog,' she said, as though that answered everything.

'Please, go on,' Kim encouraged, realising it was the best course of action. She could allow Mrs Wakeman a few more moments of normality before her world crashed down around her.

'She'd already dabbled in drugs by then. Not the hard stuff, I don't think, but enough to change her from the Maxine I knew. Well, the more I tried to keep her away from the bad stuff the more she rebelled against me and the more we fought. That's when she began to show an interest in what I'd told her.'

'Which was?' Kim said, patiently. They still had the terrible news to break to the woman.

'The identity of her real mother. We adopted Maxine when she was seven months old.'

'And Maxine left to be with her?' Kim asked.

Mrs Wakeman nodded. 'I didn't really mind at the time. I thought a rest would do us both good. Since her father died when she was eight it had always been just the two of us. Just trying to muddle through.

'And I hoped her real mother would be able to help with the drug problem. She could afford to send her to a private rehab and get her cured once and for all.'

Kim did not comment on the naiveté of that statement. If only that was all it took.

'Of course, I never thought for a minute she'd be gone this long. I thought she'd be back within a few weeks and we could just start again.' The sadness in her expression was unmistakeable, and Kim's stomach dropped another couple of inches as the news she was here to share stayed inside her for a few minutes longer.

Mrs Wakeman continued. 'I called her birth mother a couple of times but just got bog standard responses and a promise that she'd call soon.'

'So you know the birth mother?' Kim asked, nonplussed.

Mrs Wakeman rolled her eyes. 'Oh yeah, I know her and you probably know of her too. She's on the television almost every day.'

Kim was satisfied that they would be able to take the next step in talking to Maxine's birth mother but, before they did, Kim had no choice but to break this woman's heart.

She looked to Bryant seeing her own regret mirrored in his eyes.

She reached for the woman's hand. 'Mrs Wakeman, I'm afraid we're here to bring you some very bad news…'

CHAPTER THIRTY-FOUR

Kim kicked the speed of the Kawasaki Ninja up to 65 mph and gunned the middle lane to overtake two tankers and a motorhome. She slipped back into the slow lane a hundred metres before she took the slip road and left the M6.

The ride had helped blow away some of the cobwebs spun by the outpouring of grief both she and Bryant had witnessed from Mrs Wakeman, who had blamed every bad thing on herself. Surprisingly, there was no rage towards the birth mother. That may come later, Kim reasoned.

Kim couldn't help but feel sad that Maxine Wakeman had seen fit to go searching for something more than she already had. What did an adoption certificate really mean? In an ideal world it should have meant that the mother and daughter bond was forged for ever. But it didn't. It had turned Mrs Wakeman into a caretaker until a better option had come along.

And what of the birth mother? Did she deserve a second chance with the child she had given away? Kim was not blinkered enough to think that there were not genuine reasons for surrendering a child to the state. Hell, she wished her own mother had done it – but surely there had to be a finality. Once it was done it was done. No going back.

These thoughts had been buzzing around her mind since she and Bryant had driven away from the residence, solemn, still under the cloud of the woman's grief. She had called an end to the day; they would pick up with the Maxine Wakeman case in the morning.

Her evening walk with Barney had been interrupted by other thoughts. She had felt as though her brain was being divided in half. One side was as clear as a summer day. It was focussed and driven and determined to put together the pieces of the puzzle to find out who had killed Deanna Brightman and possibly Maxine Wakeman. The other side was grey and dark and crowded with thoughts and feelings that she didn't want.

And those thoughts had brought her here, she thought, as she parked the bike outside Drake Hall Prison.

She had felt the decision brewing inside her during the car ride with Bryant earlier, which was why she hadn't dared reveal to him what she'd been thinking, but the journey had been fraught with indecision; each motorway exit had beckoned her back to the safety of home and ignorance.

To enter the arena with Alex again was risking much more than she was willing to lose. But she knew Alex was behind this sudden change in her mother, and the thought that her mother could ever be free again was beyond her tolerance.

She was not as surprised as she should have been that Alex had come crashing back into her life. A small part of her had always known that she had not seen the last of the devious, emotionless woman. During their last encounter Kim had known that Alex was obsessed with her. She had found out everything about her. Perversely, Alex probably knew more than anyone about the horror, terror and pain that had been her childhood: she had researched every incident of cruelty, abuse and neglect, and she had tried to use every single fact she'd learned to drive her towards insanity.

Alex had said she felt there was some kind of bond between them and that Kim's own unwillingness to get close to anyone further linked them somehow. But Kim saw no similarities between the two of them, saw no twisted bond. None at all.

She could have turned back, ignored the taunts from Alex and trusted in the system, trusted that the parole board would see the truth and refuse the woman's freedom. *But then there's Lily*, said a small voice inside her head. The one woman Kim saw as an ally had been fooled and deceived. She couldn't take the chance that the parole board would feel the same way.

What if all they saw was a pleasant woman in her early sixties – contrite and remorseful for what she'd done to Mikey and her? What if her demonstration of sanity earned her a place back in the free world? In her world. Could she learn to live with the thought that the bitch was free?

No, she couldn't take that chance. If Alex had something that would help keep her mother safely locked away, then she had no choice but to find out what it was. And of course there would be a price to pay.

She just hoped it was a price she could afford.

CHAPTER THIRTY-FIVE

Alex enjoyed the frisson of excitement that passed through her whole body. She followed Katie to the visitors' room, forcing the smile away from her mouth. Triumph so early was not graceful.

She had known the detective inspector would come. Kim Stone had very few weaknesses, but her mother was the biggest and the most easily exploited. A little more challenge in getting her to come would have entertained her briefly, but they were not yet into the game.

Alex paused in the doorway and quickly assessed the figure that stood at the window. Her black canvas jeans were snug against her bottom and legs without being tight. The biker boots lifted her five feet nine height by an inch. The black leather jacket hugged her upper body.

As though sensing her presence, Kim turned, and Alex felt a slight jump in her stomach as their eyes met and locked for the first time since they had fought violently on the canal side. Alex offered a conciliatory smile that hit the brick wall of Kim's impenetrable expression. It was a look she remembered well. And how she had missed it.

Rarely did anyone get to see the emotion behind the mask, but Alex had been lucky enough to glimpse it once or twice. And she hoped to see it again.

They headed for the same table in the middle of the room.

'You're looking well, Kimmy,' Alex said and meant it. Her short, black hair was thick and glossy. Her skin was clear and healthy and still bore some summer colour.

'Don't call me that,' Kim growled, sitting forward in the chair.

Alex sat forward and smiled. It was a cheap shot, using her mother's name for her, but it was a shot all the same.

'What the hell have you been doing?'

Alex shrugged. 'A bit of reading, a bit of cooking. You know, anything to fill the time.'

'You know what I mean,' Kim snapped, tucking a piece of hair behind her ear.

Alex did the same.

'Why are you copying everything I do?' Kim asked.

Oh, how I've missed you, Alex thought. Not many people were a match for her intelligence, but Kim Stone was definitely one of the few. Which was why their time together had been so entertaining. And much too short.

But as with everything about Kim Stone, every action gave her some kind of information. Yes, she was using the mirroring and matching technique to establish rapport. People were instantly drawn to familiar things, like breathing patterns, matched speech patterns, body posture and language; it was a technique that appealed to the subconscious.

And the fact that Kim had spotted it so quickly was a testament to just how closely the woman was watching Alex's every move. This told her she was cautious, guarded, anxious.

Alex smiled. 'I'm sorry. I thought you were being polite and well-mannered; enquiring about my health and well-being before you got down to business.'

'Like I give a shit about that. What have you been doing with my... mother?'

Alex could hardly fail to notice that Kim could barely force the word past her lips. Oh yes, she'd chosen the correct weakness to exploit. The woman had not moved on at all.

'I missed you, Kim. After all that quality time we spent together bonding, I was hurt when you didn't come to visit and—'

'Alex, cut the bullshit. I honestly cannot stomach it. I can't even imagine how you've managed to do it and I don't care. I do care about why you've been writing to her.'

The how had been easy. The return address was a PO box, and the letters brought in by one of her trusted visitors. The mail was barely glanced at. Staff offered cursory glances for key words and then passed them on. Another remnant of the facility's days as an open prison. Little had changed except the classification.

'We got on famously when we met,' Alex said, choosing to forget the moment the woman had launched an attack and pulled out a chunk of her hair.

'If I remember correctly, the scratch on your face said otherwise,' Kim stated. 'So, try again to convince me.'

'For amusement?' Alex said.

Kim rolled her eyes. 'More accurate, but still not truthful as that would not include involvement from me at all. So, what the hell were you hoping to achieve by writing to her and pretending to be me?'

'I wanted to offer her some comfort. She hasn't heard from you, and I felt a connection—'

'Oh, Alex, try again,' Kim said, yawning.

'I care about you, Kim. We learned a lot about each other last year. I think it's time you forgave her.'

Kim pushed back the chair and stood.

'I've heard enough. How dare you presume to know—'

'I know more than anyone, Kim, and you're well aware of it. That's why you're here. You know I understand the dynamic between the two of you. We should really talk about it some time.'

'Of course we should. Over coffee and cake. Oh, hang on, I forgot: you're a despicable sociopath who is locked up for causing countless deaths and misery. So, I'll pass. Maybe another time.'

'I think you should at least go and see her.'

'I don't give a fuck what you think; now, tell me why you wanted me to come. Where are the letters she sent you?'

'Safe,' Alex answered. 'And I'll give them to you... once you've been to see her.'

Alex enjoyed the horror that crept over Kim's face.

'Obviously the experts were wrong about sociopathy not being a form of mental illness because you've clearly lost your mind.'

Alex ignored the insult. They had reached the business end of the meeting. 'I mean it, Kim. Go and see her and I'll hand them over.'

'Keep them,' Kim said as she began to walk away.

'She has something that you want,' Alex called.

Kim turned. Alex was pleased to see that her eyes were dark with hatred. Good.

'That woman has nothing that I want.'

Alex stood. 'Oh yes she does. She has something you will want very much.'

Kim's eyes narrowed. 'How do you know?'

'Because I'm the one who told her how to get it.'

Kim offered a look of unadulterated loathing. It seeped from every pore.

'Fuck you, Alex,' she shouted as she marched from the room.

Alex laughed out loud. There was a warmth spreading inside her. It was as close to affection as a person without empathy could achieve. Kim Stone was back in her life and it felt good.

In their first meeting, Kim had already allowed her back in. Had she been able to maintain the cool, unruffled exterior with which she'd entered then Alex would have been concerned. The anger and hatred was just simmering below the surface and had already made an appearance.

Alex had spent many hours planning how this game of theirs would play out. There would be serves and deuces and an occasional ace for good measure.

This time she would not make the same mistakes. She would not underestimate the woman's strength or resolve and certainly not her intelligence.

But this time she would win.

Detective Inspector Kim Stone made few mistakes, but she had made a big one. She had not listened when Alex had told her it wasn't over.

CHAPTER THIRTY-SIX

Dawson watched as the last car drove away from Saltwells Pub.

Right now the car park should have been filling up with the evening trade. The place was best known for reasonably priced meals. It was a pleasant evening and popping out for a quick bite and a cold pint would be an easy choice to make. But not tonight. The pub would remain closed until the techies confirmed they were done. The owners had accepted the news without argument. No one liked to lose a night's trade but Dawson got the impression they needed time to process the events of the day anyway.

The nature reserve was not an easy place to keep sterile but officers were stationed at the main entrances and trails.

He sat on the bench and loosened his tie. He looked at his watch. It was almost seven. He whipped it off completely.

He wished he had left it to the uniforms to carry on collating the information after he'd questioned the witness, like the boss had told him. But he'd hoped someone here had seen something, and it wasn't like he was getting anywhere with the patrons of the pub and the takeaway.

He glanced at the closed doors of the pub regretfully. A couple of pints would have really sweetened his mood right now.

For some reason he felt on the outside of this investigation. There was a voice that said he was being given busy work and yet he knew that wasn't the case. Things within the team were how they always were. Stacey stayed home and looked after the house. Mum and Dad were out doing all the interesting work, and he was told to go out and amuse himself.

He sighed and shook his head. Realistically, he knew this wasn't the case, but it just felt that way sometimes.

Deep down he knew what he wanted and his irritation and restlessness were stemming from that. He wanted to make decisions. He wanted the thrill of a good call or even the blame of a bad one. He had no problem with accountability. He would take it any day instead of what was now beginning to feel like mindless drudgery.

There were times when he disagreed with the boss but he always trusted her instinct and her experience. Sometimes he tried to argue his point – it rarely got him anywhere.

He sighed and stood. Time to go home, take a hot shower and nurse a couple of cold beers in the garden. Tomorrow was another day.

A rustle sounded to the right of him. He stilled and listened. There was nothing. He shook his head and took a step towards his car. Again he heard a rustle parallel with his own steps.

He shook his head and cursed himself. It was broad daylight and he was in a nature reserve. In his experience that meant he probably wasn't the only living thing in the area.

Two more steps. He heard a sharp intake of breath.

He stopped walking. He wasn't sure what insects, rodents or small animals cursed under their breath.

He took a leaf from the boss's playbook.

'All right, you may as well come out now. I know you're there,' he called, confidently.

The worst that could happen was he was chatting to the wildlife.

A figure appeared from the bushes wearing combat style shorts, a Hawaiian shirt and a stupid grin.

'What the hell are you doing here?' Dawson asked, as his eyes fell on the young reporter. The name Bubba just would not pass his lips.

The lad leaned down and scratched furiously at a red mark on his calf that was spreading by the second. Dawson could see white lumps already sprouting up from the skin.

'Just seeing what's going on,' he answered.

Dawson folded his arms. 'You know the entire area is out of bounds. It's a bloody crime scene.'

'All of it?' he asked, feigning innocence.

Dawson offered him a look. Some people may believe the kid's naiveté. He did not. The kid was clearly a trainee reporter but he was a clever little shit who was obviously learning well from his mentor, Tracy Frost.

'How did you get in?' he asked. Any weaknesses in the perimeter would need to be communicated and efforts made to tighten the boundary.

'A short cut my nan told me about just off Coppice Lane,' he said, having another scratch.

Dawson found himself amazed at the colourful motifs on the kid's shirt. He had to admit that wearing a shirt like that outside the house took some courage.

'Well, it's time to get off home,' Dawson said, turning towards the dirt path that led back to the road.

'Same killer as the Brightman woman?' he asked.

Dawson shook his head with wonder. That the kid thought he was going to actually answer these questions was nothing short of ridiculous.

'Mate, get on your—'

'What I don't understand is why there hasn't been an appeal for witnesses to come forward,' he said, licking his fingers and scratching again.

Dawson was struggling to hold a conversation with a guy who looked like he was drowning in parrots. He reached over and ripped a leaf from a tree. 'Rub that against the nettle sting,' he said.

Bubba looked at it. 'It's not a dock leaf.'

'Doesn't need to be. It's the motion of rubbing vigorously that releases the moist sap from the leaves which soothes the skin.'

The kid frowned. 'They teach you that at police school?'

Dawson couldn't help but smile. 'No, I have a nan too.'

Bubba's smirk turned to a genuine smile.

'Okay, off the record,' he paused. 'Do people actually say "off the record"?'

Dawson nodded.

'Why hasn't there been an appeal for witnesses on the Brightman case? The car was parked on a main road in front of a row of shops.'

'There are reasons, which are none of your business,' Dawson said, stiffening.

'I hope they're good ones,' Bubba said, shrugging.

'Why do you say that?'

He inclined his head towards the woods. 'Because if the same guy killed her in there then he's not stopping, is he?'

'It's not as simple as that,' Dawson bristled.

'Probably not, and you're right, it's none of my business. But it's yours.'

Dawson hoped his expression didn't reflect the fact he agreed with every word the kid was saying. Or that he had tried to argue this point with his boss.

'The thing is,' Bubba said, throwing the wrinkled, spent leaf to the side. 'It's the one time the press can actually help an investigation. We can reach more people with a single article than you spending the next two years trawling pubs for witnesses.'

'Yeah, well, thanks for the advice,' Dawson said, as Bubba stepped past him.

'You're welcome, and here's a bit more. Another couple of days and folks are going to have forgotten where they even were on Sunday night.'

Bubba shrugged and began walking down the dirt road.

Dawson hesitated and then took a deep breath.

'Hey, kid, wait up. Jump in and I'll give you a lift.'

CHAPTER THIRTY-SEVEN

Kim had barely removed her helmet when she heard a knock at the door.

She shook her head and smiled at the same time.

'It's open,' she called, as she unzipped her boots and kicked them off. Barney was still jumping excitedly around her feet.

'What have you bought me?' she asked Bryant as he stepped into her living room.

'Nothing,' he said, handing Barney a juicy green apple.

Kim sighed as he took it to his favourite spot on the rug, turned three times and lay down.

'I remember the days you brought me food, coffee… '

'Hey, you chose to have kids,' he said, nodding towards the dog. 'And that's what happens. Everyone buys for the kids and forget the parents.'

'Well, if you're gonna stay long enough to ask me what's wrong and for me to tell you to piss off, you can pour the coffee.'

'Any point, seeing as you've just conducted our entire conversation on your own?'

'Please yourself,' she said, heading upstairs.

Once in the house, her work clothes had to be discarded. It was ritualistic and symbolic for throwing off the day. Well, most of it, she admitted to herself. She was unsure a fresh pair of jeans and a T-shirt would erase her trip to Stafford.

A quick wash of her face would do until a shower before bedtime.

She found her colleague and friend outside, staring down in amazement.

'You bought a patio set?'

'It's hardly that,' she said. 'It's a bistro table with two chairs. If they'd sold it with just the one chair I'd have bought that,' she said, honestly.

'But it's garden furniture,' he said, putting the drinks down.

She looked at the table and chairs aghast. 'Damn it, they never told me that in the shop,' she said, sarcastically.

Her garden reflected her interest in the outside space she owned. It was half slabbed and half turfed, with a big green storage box, left by the last owners, at the end.

Bryant knew her well enough to know that if she was home she was most likely to be found in the garage.

But throughout the summer she had found Barney lying on the slabs close to the house, peacefully sniffing the air for just a few minutes at a time before coming back inside to find her. She had grown concerned about his intake of fresh air, but he wouldn't stay outside without her. She wasn't going to admit that to Bryant; he teased her enough about the dog as it was.

Bryant sat and crossed one ankle over the other. Barney settled to his right and nuzzled his hand. He automatically raised it and started stroking the dog's head.

Yep, that's my boy, Kim thought. Loyal to the person who last gave him food.

'So, are you gonna tell me what's wrong?'

'Probably not,' she said, sitting in the other chair.

She didn't even bother to ask how he knew there was something on her mind. It could have been one of a hundred small things that no one but Bryant would have picked up on.

'Was it me using my own office?' she asked.

'Nope.'

'The fact that I sent everyone home early?'

'A good pointer, but no, and it wasn't all that early: it was four o'clock, and we started at seven.'

'Oh, what then?'

'That,' he said, nodding towards her foot that was knocking against her left ankle. 'Your conscious mind isn't a foot tapper but your subconscious mind is.'

She instantly stopped tapping.

Bryant laughed. 'And there you go: thinking you can control it when you don't even know you're doing it. It'll be off again in a minute.'

'Bugger off,' she said.

'You could always do that thing where you talk to yourself and I pretend I'm not here?' he offered.

'So, why wouldn't I just wait until you've gone?'

'Good point,' he said, staring forward.

Silence fell between them as Bryant continued to stroke Barney's head.

'It's nothing you can help with,' she said.

'Probably not.'

'So, there's not really any point going on about it,' she said.

'Not really,' he said.

'For God's sake, stop interrogating me. My mother is up for parole, okay?'

'Shit, Kim.' His hand paused above Barney's head.

'And I've had a letter from Alexandra Thorne.'

His head snapped around. 'You're joking?'

She shook her head.

'Jesus, I'm surprised it's only your foot that's been tapping. Okay, start from the beginning and go slowly. I'm old and I need time to process all of this.'

Kim took a deep breath.

'My mother has a parole hearing at the end of the week. As her only relative I have been informed.'

He frowned. 'But she's been there a very long time, surely—'

'Bryant, don't even think she's done enough,' Kim snapped. That was one betrayal too far.

'After what she did, three lifetimes wouldn't be enough. What I was going to say was, she's been there a long time so surely this has come up before.'

Kim shook her head. 'My mother has always managed to engineer some kind of violent episode right before a parole hearing is due.'

He looked at her questioningly. 'Intentionally?'

'Yeah, believe it or not, it was Alex who put all the dates together and surmised that she keeps herself locked away as a present to me, because she knows that's what I want.'

'How the hell would Alex know that?' he exploded.

'She worked it out when she visited Grantley last year.'

'Alex the sociopath visited your mother the paranoid schizophrenic in a facility that houses the criminally insane?'

'Bryant, do try and keep up.'

He shook his head with bewilderment.

'Only, this time, there have been no violent episodes and my mother is going ahead with the hearing,' Kim explained.

She had thought that saying all these things out loud might bring some semblance of order to the thoughts in her head. So far that was a big fat no.

'What changed her mind?' Bryant asked.

Kim smiled. 'My letters. Apparently my forgiveness has given her a whole new outlook and the second chance—'

'Whoa there. Back up. I'm trying to keep up but… hold on. You're not going to tell me that our crazy doctor has been writing to your mother as you?'

She shrugged. 'Okay, I won't tell you that but, in a nutshell, yes.'

'Shiiiit,' he said, and sat back.

Kim rose and went to the kitchen. She snatched both letters from the drawer and took them outside. She held them aloft. Bryant took them and continued to look at her.

'This is not like your recent project in the garage is missing a handlebar and you can't get it for a few months kind of problem, is it?' he asked.

'Not quite,' she said, retaking her seat.

As Bryant's hands were now occupied holding the letters Barney moved to her side of the table.

He read the one from Grantley and placed it face down on the table, while quietly shaking his head. As he read the letter from Alex his jaw dropped lower and lower.

'Bloody hell, Kim,' he said, when he'd finished. 'I can hear the menace in every single sentence.'

He caught her eye and forced her to meet his gaze.

'You do know that you can't go and see her, right?'

Kim said nothing. That was clearly a conversation for another day.

'Damn it, Kim. You've already been, haven't you?'

Or maybe not. Sometimes she wished he didn't know her quite so well.

He dropped his head into his hands and swore.

'I had to, Bryant. I had to know what she's up to.'

'And do you?' he asked, forcefully. 'Did she melt under your fear-inducing gaze and tell you everything?' he asked, nonplussed.

'Well… n—'

'Of course she didn't. Because whatever she's up to has been planned for months so she was never going to tell you, but now you've done the worst possible thing.'

'What?' she asked.

'You've entertained her. Whatever plan she had for you would have been difficult to execute with absolutely no involvement on your part.'

'But I wanted to know… '

'What?' he asked, waving the page at her. 'You already knew. You knew that she'd been communicating with your mother as you. Whatever comes next was reliant on you taking the bait.'

Kim said nothing. He was right. It was a nightmarish round-about ride and she had voluntarily climbed aboard.

When he eventually spoke, his voice was quiet, reflective. 'You know, when I was a kid we lived by playing fields and there was a small building which served as the changing rooms for the footballers. The pavilion we called it.

'The walls were awash with graffiti and insults. This was years before Mark Zuckerberg was even born. People would write "Paula is a slag", or "Karen is a bitch", or tallies of how many boys a girl had slept with. There was nothing good daubed on that pavilion yet every girl I knew went and checked it every night. My sister included.

'One night she ran into the house in floods of tears, and I asked her why she had to go and read it every night, and it was simply because she had to know. And sometimes knowing isn't all that.'

Kim had listened to and understood his words. 'But how can I prepare myself for what's coming?'

'You can't, because she's never going to tell you what she wants.'

'She wants me to go and see my mother,' Kim blurted out. Damn it, he might as well know it all.

Bryant shook his head. 'Don't do it, Kim.'

'She says my mother has something I want.'

'Can you not see that she is already playing you? She is manipulating your need to know, to get you to do what she wants.'

'But I want those letters she has from my mother,' she said. 'There may be something I can use to keep her inside.'

'She'll never give you anything you can use. How would that benefit her in any way, and what could your mother have that you'd want? If you haven't needed it in twenty-eight years, do you really need it now?'

Kim heard the words. They were going into her ear. She just wasn't sure they were reaching her brain.

Bryant let out a long sigh. His voice turned quiet, serious.

'You can't have forgotten how close you came? How she almost destroyed you the last time?'

'Of course I remember, Bryant. I was there. But doesn't that make me better armed this time?'

'And therein lies your problem. That you are under the impression you have any armour at all.'

Kim knew what he was saying. The fact that she had still not addressed or dealt with her issues ensured that she was still vulnerable to their manipulation.

'And having given you plenty of advice that you didn't ask for and that you'll refuse to follow, I shall say good night.'

Kim followed him to the door. He stepped out and turned.

'Is there anything I can say that will persuade you not to go and see your mother?'

Kim stared at the ground. 'I thought you'd appreciate that I'm addressing some of my demons?'

Bryant put his hands into his front pockets. 'But you're not, are you? This isn't a decision you've come to of your own free will. This is not you choosing to address your feelings of hate and anger. You're being goaded into it and that in itself means it's not the right time.'

Kim accepted his words. They were true enough. But the decision had been made.

He waited for an answer to his original question.

She shook her head. 'The answer is no.'

He sighed and gave a backwards wave when he reached the top of the drive.

Every single word Bryant had said made sense. Anyone who knew Alex would advise her to stay away. Anyone who knew her would try to insist.

And yes, she had to admit that the woman knew her every weakness.

But Kim had to believe she knew Alex's too.

CHAPTER THIRTY-EIGHT

He melded back into the shadows as he watched her colleague leave. What was he doing here so late at night?

It would not be long now until he got the answer to his question.

This one woman had saved people from the devil that talked inside his head.

I can make you clean.
I can make you forget.
I can make you whole.
I can give you back your life.

He knew he would never escape Alexandra Thorne. Maybe once he could have. Maybe if the bitch across the road had tried to save him he'd have had a chance.

But the devil picked him up and threw him aside when it suited Alexandra Thorne, and he allowed it. Would always allow it. Had always allowed it: from the moment she had taken his hand and smiled into his soul and promised him she could take away his pain.

Of course, she'd never had any intention of doing that. He had only ever been her plaything: an experiment, a test to see how far she could go. He had been nothing but a test of her own manipulations.

But for a while he had believed.

He had beaten a man half to death before he'd realised the man was not his uncle; that he was no longer in that tiny bedroom.

The man had only shaken him awake in the darkness to disrupt him from the torture of his nightmares. But so strong were the words of the devil he had seen only one face. And it was a face he had already destroyed.

And then he had known that he would never be clean. He would never be whole. He could never be saved.

There had been other potential victims of the devil and the bitch across the road had saved them.

So why the fuck hadn't she saved him?

CHAPTER THIRTY-NINE

Kim tore her gaze away from the curious round object on her desk and headed into the main office.

From her spot on the edge of the spare desk she could still see it from the corner of her eye.

Who had placed it by her front door? Was it some kind of taunt? Was it Alex playing mind games with her? No one left gifts on her doorstep.

'Okay, folks,' she said, turning away, 'as you all know we have a potential second victim.'

Kim moved towards the board that she had updated first thing: for her, this morning, it had been a few minutes after six. She had desperately chased sleep but that place of limbo between awake and asleep had been filled with visions of both Alex and her mother. She had been unable to find her way past and had taken Barney for his morning run just after four o'clock.

'Her name is Maxine Wakeman, and she is a confirmed drug addict who has been in and out of rehab,' Bryant said, bringing her back to the room. She wasn't aware that she had stopped talking.

'She is twenty-two years old and adopted,' Kim added. 'Bryant and I have spoken to her adoptive mother, who hasn't seen her in a while. We'll be speaking to her birth mother this morning.'

'Nice area,' Stacey said, wheeling towards Bryant and handing him a piece of paper with the address.

'Maxine's mother is a television personality... apparently,' Kim said. The name had not been familiar to her. 'She appears on a morning show as the resident psychiatrist.'

'Geraldine Hall?' Dawson asked.

Kim nodded, surprised.

'Missus watches her every day. Well most days. Really knows her stuff, so she says.'

'Thanks for that, Kev,' Kim said.

'No similarity between the victims,' Stacey said, frowning.

Kim shook her head. She felt like she'd already had this conversation fifteen times, although the fact of the matter was still troubling her.

One of the most crucial aspects of an investigation was finding the thread, the commonality between victims. The denominator that linked seemingly random victims back to a motive. The link could be an area, a certain type or physical description, age bracket, income bracket, workplace – any one of a hundred things – and yet Kim could not think of even one that would link Deanna Brightman to Maxine Wakeman.

'Stace, what do we have on the Brightmans?' Kim asked.

'Yer were right about the financials,' Stacey said. 'A deposit in the six figures was put down on that house twenty-one years ago. A year earlier Deanna went into hospital seven months pregnant and came out not.'

'A medical malpractice settlement?' Kim asked.

Stacey nodded. 'That's wor I'm thinking. I'm still trying to gather more—'

'No. That's enough,' Kim said. It was enough detail. Especially if the negligence also explained why the couple had no children of their own. 'Carry on trying to get the number for that old phone of Deanna's.'

No one had it: her family had updated their phones in the six years since it had been her only phone. The fact that it was the only thing missing told Kim it had to mean something.

'And I want you to focus on Jason Cross. I want to know more about him. He's a liar and got very defensive when pushed too far.'

Stacey made a note.

'Kev?' Kim asked.

'Nothing to report, boss,' he said. 'Interviewed everyone at the Saltwells yesterday. None of them were in the pub the night before when Maxine Wakeman was murdered, and I also got a pretty long list of the patrons who were in the pub that night.'

'So?' Kim asked, struggling to define the young detective's mood.

'I'll be making a start on some of those names, and I'll take photos of Maxine, Deanna and the car with me just in case anyone recognises anything.'

Kim nodded her agreement.

'Okay, well, as we know that Maxine Wakeman was adopted, it's about time we found out what her real mother has to say.'

CHAPTER FORTY

Alex woke and glanced at the bed opposite.

Tanya sat with her back against the wall, her dirty trainers dangling over the edge of the bed. Her feet tapped together, and the comb in her right hand was being slapped against the palm of her left as she stared intently at her.

'Morning,' Alex said, with a pleasant smile.

Other people might have chosen to stay awake, fearing for their life in the company of the most feared woman in the place.

Tanya continued to stare as though Alex had not spoken.

'Good morning, Tanya,' Alex repeated.

'You know I am gonna hurt you, yeah?' Tanya said, definitely.

Alex sat up. 'No, you're not,' she said, calmly.

Alex was rewarded with the snarl she had come to know so well in such a short time.

'You just wait… '

'For what, Tanya?' Alex asked. 'I've just been sound asleep for seven hours, two feet away from you. If you wanted to kill me I'd already be dead,' she said, looking at the comb in Tanya's hand.

Alex had spent many hours deciding which methods or techniques she might use on Tanya once she had her in the cell. Conversational hypnosis had been her manipulation of choice. She preferred the term 'covert hypnosis': it was basically the art of causing people to change their minds or see things your way without them even knowing you were influencing them.

She had begun the process last night. She had continually told Tanya that she wasn't going to hurt her while she slept. Despite it being exactly what Tanya had wanted to do she had chosen not to. Her subconscious had taken over. The expressions and terminology she had used were all alluding to something, and Tanya now wanted to know what it was. It differed from regular hypnosis, which was a direct suggestion, whereas covert worked indirectly.

It was the difference between 'have a piece of cake' and 'this cake is delicious'. It was about planting the seed of suggestion so the decision to reach for a piece of cake was made by the person themselves.

'I chose you for many reasons, not least of which was your intelligence. You are not a stupid woman. You're curious about what I'm up to. As you should be.'

'What game you playing, bitch?' Tanya asked, narrowing her eyes.

'Oh, it's no game, Tanya, I can assure you of that,' Alex said, combing her hair. 'I know all about you.'

'You know fuck all about… '

'I know everything, Tanya. I know that your mother died when you were twelve years old. I know that you fought tooth and nail to stay with your ten-year-old sister, even staying in the system with no hope of foster care or adoption for you both. I know you protected Tina from everything you could. And when you were old enough you left the care system and still protected her. But you couldn't protect her from everything, could you?'

The comb was no longer tapping against the palm. Her left hand had closed around the teeth, the knuckles whitening.

'How many men raped her that night, Tanya?'

Tanya said nothing.

'Of course, it was three, wasn't it? And you and your sister killed them all, didn't you?'

Tanya continued to stare as the hate filled her eyes.

Alex tipped her head. 'And which one of you cut off their penises before you killed them?'

There was no answer, and Alex didn't really need one. The fact that both Tanya and her sister, Tina, were equally vicious was good enough for her.

'Did you ever find out which one of them was the father of your nephew, Kai?'

And there was the next bombshell. Just dropping his name between them changed everything. The most precious things to Tanya, her sister and her nephew, were now here in the room with them. It was no longer just about her.

Alex waited for an answer. The air was charged between them. If ever Tanya was going to launch across the room and grab her by the throat it was now.

The rage of everything that had happened to the two of them danced in her eyes. Her hand was still gripped around the comb.

Alex smiled.

'So I do know everything, Tanya, but the most important thing is that I know that you and your sister had to be separated. But you're still in contact with her.'

And that was a vital part of the plan.

CHAPTER FORTY-ONE

'So, what's with the desk furniture?' Bryant asked, as they passed the turning to the Clent Hills.

She should have known he'd seen the cactus plant in her office.

Other people had chosen to dress their desks up to make their workplace more homely. Photographs, ornaments, plastic motivational cards with clichéd messages. She saw all kinds of personal objects that she simply didn't understand. It was as though people needed to remember who they were to get them through the working day. If she were to bring reminders from home there would be a socket wrench, a dog chew and… she really couldn't think of anything else. And that was fine with her.

'It was left on my doorstep,' she said by way of explanation. It had been quicker to bring it with her than reopen her house.

'I mean it kind of fits, if you know what I mean. You're a bit—'

'Bryant, do not finish that sentence in work time,' she warned, as realisation dawned.

'It's from Gemma,' she said.

'Who on earth is Gemma?'

Kim offered him a brief rundown of the events when she'd returned home from Deanna Brightman's crime scene.

'You don't half attract them,' he said, slowing down the car as they approached the address in Middlefield Lane, Hagley.

Being back in Alex's old stomping ground was unnerving, and she couldn't help feeling uncomfortable that the woman's home and office was only a mile west of where they were now.

Kim pushed the thought away and focussed on the property. It was by far the largest and most luxurious-looking house they had visited so far.

'Another visit to the poor and impoverished folks of the Black Country,' Bryant said.

A high wall surrounding the house rose gradually towards – and ended at – seven-feet brick pillars and a double gate.

Bryant approached the gate and spoke into an intercom fixed to the wall. The family had been informed of the death of Maxine Wakeman, and the gates began to swing back promptly.

The house was white in colour, and Kim counted eleven windows on the upper level. A sizeable garage was fixed to the left-hand side.

The doorbell chimed throughout the house.

It was a good minute and a half before they heard heels on a tiled floor. Kim guessed that if you were at the other end of the house it could take a while to reach the front door.

Eventually the door swung back and revealed a woman in her early sixties despite efforts to appear to the contrary. The lips had been plumped and the face had been lifted. Kim was reminded of the autumn flowers she'd seen in the woods the night before. Almost done but just trying to reach towards that last bit of sunlight.

But her age showed in the neck skin like the rings inside a tree.

The woman's face was attractive but a little too made up. The lipstick a shade too red. Navy trousers and a floral blouse clothed the petite body.

Three thin gold bangles clanged together on the left wrist.

Kim noticed a proprietary air surrounding the woman as Bryant introduced them both.

This was not Maxine's mother, but she was Maxine's something. She held out her hand. 'Amelia Trent. Geraldine's mother.'

Kim noted the attachment to the name of her daughter, not granddaughter.

Bryant offered their condolences as they stepped into the hall.

The woman barely nodded before pointing to the floor.

'Oh, be careful of that tile there, it's just been replaced. Had to be flown all the way from Milan.'

The hallway would have eaten Kim's entire lower floor for breakfast and still had room for dessert.

The staircase spiralled out of the space and led to a viewing balcony.

'It came from Marseilles,' she said, following Kim's gaze up to the chandelier.

'Mrs Trent, may we speak with your daughter?' Kim said. They were not here for a guided tour of the property.

'Of course,' she said, coolly, as she headed to the left of the staircase.

'Didn't realise being a TV shrink paid this well,' Bryant mumbled as they passed through a formal, fully laid dining area beneath a glass apex that seemed to mark the centre of the house.

Kim could see what he meant.

'Neeta, where are you?' Amelia called. There was no reply. She turned and rolled her eyes. 'She's new and still gets lost around the house.'

Amelia guided them into a drawing room that was pleasant but comfortable. A warm cream rug contrasted with the solid oak wood flooring beneath her feet. Two caramel leather sofas were at a right angle before a marble fireplace. It was a room to crawl into on a dark, cold night.

Geraldine Hall stood at the window, leaning against the wall. A second female was propped up by pillows on the sofa nearest to the wall. Her left leg was encased in a plaster cast from thigh to ankle.

Geraldine Hall was thinner than she had appeared on the catch-up show Kim had watched the night before. Much thinner.

Her limbs were long and spindly. Her face was attractive but gaunt and appeared to be the wrong size for her body.

Her eyes were red, and she clutched a handkerchief.

'My daughter, Geraldine Hill,' said Amelia, as though she was introducing an after-dinner speaker. 'And her friend, Belinda Hughes.'

Geraldine moved to the sofa and placed a hand on the woman's shoulder.

'This is Belinda, my partner.'

Kim nodded in response to the woman who offered a smile in her direction.

A faint look of irritation on Amelia's face was hidden beneath a tolerant smile.

'Soon to be wife,' Belinda added, reaching over and covering her partner's hand.

Kim couldn't help noticing how Amelia's gaze followed the hand on the shoulder and stayed there.

'We're here about Maxine,' Kim said, sitting down.

Geraldine's eyes reddened immediately as she removed her hand from Belinda's to retrieve the handkerchief from her pocket. She sat down on the edge of the sofa.

'I should think so,' Amelia said, as a woman in her early twenties appeared in the doorway. 'Neeta, where have you been?' Amelia asked coldly.

'In the guest wing… '

'Never mind. Please offer our guests some refreshments.'

Kim held up her hand to refuse.

'Coffee – white, with two sugars, please,' Bryant said, offering the girl a smile.

'Same for me,' Geraldine said, while Belinda shook her head.

'Tch, green tea for my daughter,' Amelia corrected, using her right hand to shoo the woman away.

Geraldine opened her mouth to protest and then closed it again.

'How long had you been in contact with Maxine?' Kim asked.

'Four years now,' Geraldine answered. 'She was eighteen years old and full of angst.'

'And drugs,' Amelia interjected.

Kim ignored her.

'And how had that been going?' she asked.

Geraldine's smile was sad. 'Not well, to be honest. It was a bit of a surprise when she just appeared on the doorstep. I was less than gracious… '

'Understandably,' Amelia said, frowning. 'Adoption is supposed to mean—'

'Ooooh, sorry to interrupt,' Belinda said, moving her good leg to the side. 'I need the loo, and my crutches… Amelia, would you mind… ?'

Amelia shot her future daughter-in-law a withering glance before stepping forward and offering her arm.

Belinda shot her partner a knowing look before hobbling away clutching the older woman's hand.

'Please continue,' Kim said.

'It took a while,' Geraldine said, 'for us to recover from that initial meeting,' she said, honestly. 'Neither of us seemed to know what to do or how to act, but eventually we found a way to communicate. If I'm honest, it wasn't as mother and daughter. Maxine had a mother but we were growing close.'

'Despite the drugs?' Kim asked.

'Maybe because of it,' Geraldine answered.

Kim waited for her to explain.

'I developed a drink problem in my early teens, officer. I understand addiction.'

'You tried to help her?' Bryant asked.

'Of course. I may not have had the history and relationship of a mother with her but I certainly had the instincts.'

Kim couldn't help but marvel at the complexity of human relationships. Especially the mother and daughter bond. Geraldine's own relationship with her mother appeared no less complicated.

Her own was the exception. There was nothing complicated there.

'Did Maxine seem troubled at all?' Kim asked.

'Officer, she was always troubled. It was only a question of degrees. In some ways she was very young for her age.'

'Did she ever talk about having trouble with anyone, feeling threatened?' Kim asked.

Geraldine thought for a moment before nodding. 'She was a drug addict, Inspector. Most of the time she thought the whole world was out to get her.'

'Anything in particular?' Kim pushed. 'Anyone that might want to hurt her, any enemies?'

Geraldine shook her head. 'She didn't mention anything specific to me. I don't know if she mentioned anything at home.'

'Her mother hadn't seen her for quite some time,' Bryant interjected.

Geraldine didn't flinch at the term being used in relation to someone else. Kim couldn't help the grudging admiration she felt for the woman's complete acceptance of the fact it was a title she had not earned.

There was no bitterness that another woman had taken that role.

'She wasn't with me, unfortunately. Or I would have urged her to make contact. Maxine did that, you see. Initially she would play us off against each other, you know, come to me when she having trouble at home and then back home if there was a problem here.'

'How many times did she try to get clean?' Kim asked.

Geraldine wiped at her eyes. 'Too many to count. Sometimes she would stay one or two days. Other times she would stay a couple of weeks, and once or twice she almost completed the programme.'

'And you kept trying?' Bryant asked, disbelievingly.

'Of course. It only has to work once.'

Kim thought that view was a little simplistic, as Neeta brought in a tray and placed it on the wooden coffee table.

Geraldine thanked her.

'So, how long had it been since you'd last seen her?'

'Seven weeks,' she said, as her gaze fell to the ground.

Kim sensed the added sadness immediately. And the woman knew exactly how many weeks, probably days and possibly even hours.

'We had a fight,' Geraldine whispered, without looking up.

'About what?'

Geraldine began to shake her head as colour flooded her cheeks.

'Please, we need to know,' Kim urged, gently.

Geraldine reached and took a mug from the tray. If Bryant noted that she'd taken his drink, and her original choice, he chose not to mention it.

'Maxine asked me if I was ashamed of her.'

'And were you?' Kim asked, not unkindly.

Geraldine shook her head. 'Absolutely not. But she wanted to know why she hadn't yet met any of my friends. She wanted to visit me at the studio.'

Understandable, Kim thought.

'I said no, and we had this huge argument. I thought it was just a culmination of us venting but then I didn't hear from her for weeks.'

'Why did you say no?' Kim asked.

'It's difficult to explain, officer, but it has nothing to do with being ashamed.'

'Damage to your public persona?' Kim asked.

Geraldine smiled wryly. 'No, that bothers other people far more than it bothers me. It's about deceit. It's about working backwards and explaining to your friends, colleagues why you said you have no children. As far as I knew she was lost to me for ever, and I lived my life accordingly. She was here,' she said, pointing at her chest, 'but I never dreamed that we would meet. I had a child in my heart but not in my head. I gave up that right when I signed those papers and gave her away.'

There was an integrity about this woman that Kim respected.

Geraldine swallowed. 'I'm just glad that we made our peace before... before... '

'You saw her again?'

Geraldine shook her head. 'No, I didn't see her but eventually she answered my calls. I finally managed to explain and tell her the decision I'd made. The timing of her... '

'Decision?' Kim asked.

Geraldine took another sip of the coffee and placed it back on the tray as they all heard Belinda cough from the hallway.

'Yes, officer, I was about to publicly acknowledge my daughter.'

CHAPTER FORTY-TWO

'Well, that was interesting,' Bryant said, as they headed towards the car. 'Geraldine is a young forty-four, don't you think?'

'Some weird dynamics going on in there,' she agreed. 'Talk about controlling.'

'You're not that bad, guv,' he said, with a smirk.

She raised one eyebrow.

He continued. 'Not even allowing her a coffee so she stole mine,' he observed.

'Hardly stole and to be fair, Bryant, she's a grown woman in her own home. It's a situation she's allowed.'

'Oh come on, guv. Family undercurrents are a bit more complicated than that.'

'And she's a psychiatrist. I'm pretty sure that would have come up in her training. Just like the quickest, cleanest, most efficient way to stab someone.'

'You can't think… ?'

'Look, psychiatrists are real doctors too. They all do the same medical training before deciding which area to specialise in.'

'But she's the girl's mother.'

Kim snapped the seat belt into place. 'And mothers can kill their children.'

Bryant opened his mouth and then closed it again wisely. He turned to her. 'Yeah, but she hardly—'

'Don't you dare say again that she doesn't look like a murderer. Look at Ted Bundy. Half the prison guards and police officers were in love with that guy.'

He nodded, conceding her point.

'The mother's a bit mutton dressed… '

Kim agreed. She was definitely trying to outrun the ageing process and appeared to be using her daughter's money to do it.

Again, it was no concern of hers. She took out her phone and dialled Stacey.

'Boss?' she answered.

'Let Dawson know that Maxine has been missing in action for a few weeks. We need to try and find out where she's been and who with. Neither mother has seen her for weeks.' She hesitated. 'And see what you can find out about Geraldine's contract. I want to know if there's any scandal clause.'

'On it, boss,' Stacey said, before Kim hung up.

'Where to, guv?' Bryant asked, as the wooden gates closed behind them.

'Head towards Wombourne,' she said.

She wanted to see Jason Cross again. He was lying about something. That much she knew. About what she couldn't be sure.

His defensiveness when she'd pushed him had set her instincts on fire.

It was time to see what happened if she pushed him too far.

CHAPTER FORTY-THREE

Alex moved along the dinner line silently. The offering consisted of cottage pie. The fact that the tasteless mashed potato and overcooked mince had any name at all was purely aspirational. The peas were like tiny bullets, and the gravy was a thick greasy pool. As usual, she would eat what she needed to survive.

She had initially tried to trick her taste buds by picturing the oysters and lobster she had enjoyed on a regular basis. Even the delicious tortillas from the Mexican just along the road from her Victorian home in Hagley.

Unfortunately, her taste buds were not so easily fooled, and her enjoyment of food had been temporarily suspended.

She walked from the dinner line and looked for a single seat away from the groups.

A few heads turned her way as they had done every meal time. Some were just curious glances. She knew she was different to the people in here, and they knew it too.

Others tried to catch her eye to offer an incline of the head towards a spare seat.

She wasn't interested.

The human condition had a propensity to belong. Groups formed and people felt more comfortable being part of a collective. Individuals were drawn to like-minded people to gain from strength in numbers.

She did not.

It wasn't the only reason she was different. She was superior and she knew it. Her intelligence outweighed that of all of the cliques combined.

Of course they all wanted her to join their little friendship circles. She was an asset to any group. She could do many things for them, but they could do nothing for her.

She had identified the people that could be of use to her. No one else mattered. They were extras in a film. Paid to represent an anonymous body as part of a crowd.

And once she had identified the people who were useful she had taken the time to understand their weaknesses, exploit their vulnerabilities.

Of course, being imprisoned curtailed her imagination somewhat but it simply called for a higher level of creativity, although the plan itself had started forming in her mind the moment she'd been led away from the canal side in handcuffs.

And she had always known that the plan would include Detective Inspector Kim Stone.

Alex had known from their very first meeting that their futures were intertwined.

She had seen the darkness and the hate that lived inside. She had seen the rage that danced permanently behind the eyes. The impenetrable expression that welcomed no one.

Her sharp intelligence had shone like a beacon, and Alex had relished the challenge of matching her. Beating her.

They had played with each other, mauled and danced and eventually physically fought. And Kim may have won the first battle but the war had only just begun.

Just as Alex understood the woman's strengths she also knew her weaknesses, and for Kim Stone those weaknesses would never go away. Her pain was so deep-rooted in the past that it was what lay at the very core of her. It held her together.

Her refusal to address the issues ensured they weren't going anywhere, which suited Alex just fine. She needed that poison that lived inside her: she needed to tap into it, break the seal and let the venom free, to corrode the person that she was.

Alex had dreamed many times of their first meeting, and Kim had not disappointed her. Alex allowed herself a genuine smile. And she never had.

The few extra pounds agreed with her and that was the only difference. Her raven black hair was still short and untidy, framing a face that was more attractive than the owner would ever know. The woman's refusal to enhance any feature with make-up made her all the more attractive. The strong square jaw that could have been masculine but was not. It simply added further intrigue to an intense, complicated face.

Her manner was unchanged but for one small but vital thing: she had been guarded, which warmed Alex right through to the place her heart should have been. It meant that she knew there was something to fear, that her vulnerabilities had been exposed. Had Kim been confident of her own defences, she would not have been wearing her guard.

For the hundredth time Alex had to wonder just how close she'd come that day on the canal bank to breaking the woman's tenuous grip on her sanity.

But like any scab, if you picked at it enough it would bleed.

Alex left her delicious thoughts of Kim in the favourite part of her mind as she saw Tanya near the end of the dinner line.

Her cronies were in the usual place, occupying an entire table to the far left. A seat had been saved in the middle for their leader.

Alex had seated herself at the furthest point to the right surrounded by empty seats.

As Tanya reached the end of the line she would have to choose to turn left or turn right.

Alex looked back down at her plate. She didn't need to watch. Tanya would turn right.

Another mouthful of food, and her cellmate lowered herself onto the seat opposite.

'What you doing snooping around on my sister?' she asked, setting free the question that had burned in her brain all morning.

Find the weakness, control the puppet, Alex thought to herself. For her plan to succeed she was relying on her knowledge of human behaviour, although, now and again, she liked to be surprised.

What if Tanya had chosen to turn left and sit with her friends? Alex would have been forced to find another way, would have faced a challenge.

Unfortunately and fortunately there was not one person here who presented a challenge.

One night in Tanya's company was not long enough to perfect any of her manipulation techniques. She had always known that. For this pawn in her game she could only use the direct threat approach.

'There's something I want your sister to do for me,' Alex said.

Tanya shook her head. 'You talking to me, bitch. You leave her out of it.'

Alex shook her head. 'I can't. You're not in the right place. It has to be your sister.'

'Nah, my sister ain't doing nothing for no one, bitch. She's keeping her head down, do her time, get out,'

Of course she was, Alex thought. All twenty-three years of it.

'She will,' Alex said, calmly. 'She will do exactly what I want her to do and, what's more, the instruction will come from you.'

Nothing like a guiding hand of encouragement from the older sister that you love and trust. An extra touch, yet vital to her plan.

Tanya took hold of her tray and moved herself backwards.

'You ain't listening, bitch. My sister gonna stay out of trouble, get out and be with her son.'

Alex smiled. 'And where is your nephew supposed to be right now, Tanya? I wonder if he's safe and sound.'

Tanya's eyes lit with fire as Alex's meaning became clear.

'Go, on, Tanya,' she goaded. 'Make the call and find out.'

CHAPTER FORTY-FOUR

Kim noted the absence of the liveried van as they approached the house in Wombourne.

In its place was a brand new Golf GTI. The personalised number plate of JAC 247 told her it was Jason Cross's personal vehicle. Kim couldn't help feeling it was a touch indulgent for such a happy family man.

This time the front door was closed, denying them immediate access, but the faint sound of the radio was travelling from the back of the house.

Kim headed around the side and paused to look into the kitchen window.

As though sensing her presence he looked up from the instruction diagram he was studying. Displeasure shaped his features. He glanced at the door and moved towards it.

Not quickly enough, Kim thought, as she stepped into the chaos that appeared unchanged from the previous day.

'Good morning, Mr Cross,' Kim said pleasantly. 'It's nice to see you again too.'

He glared at her. 'I think I made my position clear yesterday,' he said, taking out his phone.

'Feel free to call your lawyer, Mr Cross. You are incredibly defensive for a man who has done nothing wrong or has nothing to hide.

'We came here yesterday for a simple discussion that could have ended there. You got quite hostile and even had the audacity to lie to us.' She glanced to her left. 'And Bryant here doesn't like to have his intelligence insulted. It makes him even keener, if you know what I mean.'

'I didn't lie to you,' he said, still holding the phone.

'Yes you did,' she said, confidently. 'And that's my worry.'

'So what did I lie about?' he asked, placing the phone on top of an unopened box.

'You slept with Deanna, Mr Cross, which doesn't bother me in the slightest, but your reason for lying does.' She paused. 'It makes Bryant wonder what else you're hiding and when he starts digging...'

'Okay, it was just the once,' he said, grudgingly.

And score for her gut, Kim thought, now that he had finally admitted it.

She offered no response, and he allowed the silence to stretch for just a few seconds.

'I swear. It was only once,' he said again.

Kim still said nothing. Silence demanded speech and it wasn't going to come from her. As if he was going to get away with that level of detail after such an admission.

He sighed heavily. 'It was while I was ripping out the old kitchen. There was a leak from the drain. I got covered in dirty water and sink waste. Deanna insisted I go upstairs and take off my clothes while she found something of her husband's for me to wear.

'I was getting undressed when she came in and we just stared at each other.' He shook his head. 'I don't even remember how it happened but there was just a moment and the next thing I knew we were...'

Still Kim said nothing. She wanted it all.

'We both knew afterwards it had been a mistake. She didn't want her husband to know. She told me twenty times how much she loved him. I took a shower and when I'd finished my clothes were washed and dried. I didn't see Deanna again. She avoided me until I finished the job and then her husband sorted out the final invoice.'

Kim wondered if he saw the seediness in what he'd just said. Mitchell Brightman had the task of paying the man that had slept with his wife.

'I'm not convinced it was only once,' Kim said, finally speaking. 'I know that's going to be your hair found in her car.'

He shrugged his shoulders. 'I can't answer that. It must have been on her clothes or something but it was only the one time, I swear.'

She gazed at him for a long minute before turning to Bryant. 'Satisfied now?'

Her colleague raised one eyebrow. 'For now,' he said.

The relief on the face of Jason Cross had Kim thinking he was going to launch across and hug Bryant for saying those two words.

'Okay, Mr Cross, thank you for your time, and don't go too far in case we need to speak to you again.'

The relief drained from his face.

Kim headed out of the kitchen and towards the car.

'You do know he's not telling us the whole truth, don't you?' Bryant offered.

'Of course,' Kim spat, insulted. 'But pushing him too hard is going to get us a solicitor who won't let us near him until we have a DNA match.'

'Jeez, this is a bit softly, softly for you after your conversation with him yesterday, guv.'

There was nothing soft about her approach to Jason Cross. He was hiding much more than he was sharing. During their meeting yesterday she had observed his mannerisms. His tell was a neck stretch. When uncomfortable he would push his chin slightly higher every few seconds, as though trying to clear his throat.

Admitting the truth should have cleared the head bob. If he had nothing more to hide. But it hadn't. His chin had continued to raise every few seconds.

No, there was nothing softly, softly about her approach

It was more about getting all her little ducks in a row, Kim thought as her phone began to ring.

'Stace?' Kim said, answering the call.

There was a hesitation on the other end that led all the way to her stomach.

'Stace?' she repeated.

'Boss, you might wanna pop back to the station.'

'Why?' she asked, looking to Bryant. There was an element of dread in the constable's voice that she didn't like.

'The afternoon edition of the *Dudley Star* has just come out. And I don't think you're gonna like it one little bit.'

Kim closed her eyes as she sensed the shit storm that was building around her.

And she had a good idea where it had started.

CHAPTER FORTY-FIVE

Alex was standing just inside the door when she heard the footsteps along the hall. She counted backwards on her fingers.

Three, two, one.

'Bitch, you better tell me where the fuck—' Tanya stormed, as her hand grabbed Alex around the throat and pushed her backwards.

Alex groaned as her back hit the wardrobe door. Damn it, she thought, as her eyes began to water. She'd thought they were beyond this by now.

The anger she had seen in Tanya before paled beside the pulsating rage she could feel as the hand tightened around her throat.

'Loose me or he dies,' Alex spluttered.

The hand loosened but did not drop.

'If you hurt one fucking hair on his head, I swear I will… '

'Let me go and we can talk,' Alex said. 'And I'll tell you where he is.'

The hand unclasped her throat.

'Calm down, Tanya,' Alex instructed, rubbing her throat. 'He will not be harmed as long as you do as I say. Now sit down and we can talk about this calmly.'

Tanya took two steps back.

'Calm down you fucking psycho. You've kidnapped my nephew and you want me to calm down. My aunt is going mental.'

'Has she called the police?'

'Of course she's called the fuck—'

'And have you told her to cancel them like I told you?'

The woman hesitated. 'Yes, but you'd better—'

'Tanya, sit down,' Alex instructed as she sat herself. She wasn't going to talk to the woman while she was on her feet. Seated on the bed gave Alex some warning of any intent to strike her again.

Tanya sat.

'There is no reason for your nephew to be harmed. He will be taken care of and will be home in an hour. This is a demonstration, Tanya. I need you to understand what I can and will do.'

'You're sending him back?'

Alex nodded. She was not in the business of kidnapping children. This was simply a lesson in power and validation that she was the one who had it.

Alex felt the point had been proved and now it was down to business.

'Who do you use to communicate with your sister?' she asked.

'I'm telling you, bitch. You hurt one hair on his head.'

Could this woman not move on? Alex thought, wondering why she was still desperately trying to get the upper hand.

'Look, Tanya. You have to understand that my intelligence ensures that I will get what I want. I have shown you that, even from in here, I can engineer the abduction of your nephew. The quicker you accept that I am in control of this situation the better for you and your nephew. He may be having a nice time today, but the next time will not be… '

'My cousin, Jenson, visits both of us,' she said, quietly.

Good, Alex thought. The woman was talking to her in a conspiratorial manner so the guards wouldn't overhear.

'You need to get your cousin to come and see you, and he has to take a message to your sister. It's a name,' Alex said.

'Of what?' Tanya asked.

Alex allowed the smile to form on her face.

'It's the name of the person your sister is going to kill.'

CHAPTER FORTY-SIX

'What the fuck were you thinking, Kev?' Kim screamed at the young detective.

Dawson had pulled up in the car park at the same time as she and Bryant, after she'd instructed Stacey to call him in. Stacey had then called her back and read the piece to her word for word.

The article was not an appeal for witnesses, although the sentence was in there, buried amongst the attempt to link both Deanna and Maxine to a drugs deal gone bad. The piece referred to the place where Deanna's car was found as a known 'drug den'. The full-page spread rehashed the accurate record of Deanna's murder printed earlier in the week with headlines that screamed prostitution and drug use. And who the hell was Bubba something or other?

By the time Stacey had finished reading, Kim's anger had reduced to red hot, but the sight of Dawson had turned her rage straight back up to boiling.

Bryant had headed upstairs, and she had brought Dawson to the far edge of the car park.

Her hands were on her hips as she waited for an answer.

'You asked me if we should appeal for witnesses and I said no. You do remember that part, don't you? The bit where I said no?' she raged.

Dawson was busy staring at the ground while chewing the inside of his lip.

'Do you think either family is going to gain anything from that tripe that's been written? The connotations attached to the names of both women will stick… '

'It was supposed to be an appeal for witnesses,' he offered, lamely.

'Oh, it'll be that all right,' she raged. 'Do you have any idea what we're going to have now?'

He moved from one foot to the other. Kim found herself wishing there was a naughty step because Dawson would be sitting on it for the rest of the damn month.

'How the hell did this happen, Kev?'

'It was that kid,' he said, miserably. 'The one from the paper. He kept—'

'Hang on, you're really going to try and blame some kid that doesn't know better? That is beneath you,' she said with disgust. He had fucked up and now she expected him to own it.

He shook his head and looked back down to his shoes. 'No, boss, it was my fault.'

'Anyway, I don't care about him. I'm not responsible for his actions, but I am responsible for yours. Help me out here, Kev. What did you think you were doing?'

'I just thought it would be a good idea to appeal for anyone that might have seen… '

'We'll see just how good that idea was later but I'm not talking about that. We've disagreed many times before but you've always respected the decisions I've made.'

His hands were burrowed deeply into his pocket as he kicked at a loose stone.

He remained silent.

She let out a long sigh and tried to expel the balance of her anger. It was melting into a pool of disappointment.

Silence stood between them for a minute and a half. There was a problem here and it needed to be sorted.

'Okay, call me Kim,' she instructed.

His head snapped up.

'Go on. Do it. Call me Kim and then let's get it out, right here, right now.'

He shook his head. 'I can't call you… '

'Yes you can,' she insisted. 'This conversation is so far away from the disciplinary guidelines and professionalism that we might as well make the most of it. Now call me by my first name.'

She said it as though she'd offered him the first free punch.

He looked from side to side. 'Okay, Kim… ' He frowned. 'I can't… '

'Keep going,' she urged. 'I'm not your boss right now so get it off your chest. Let me have it.'

A squad car turned into the station. The officers glanced in their direction, their faces filled with curiosity.

'Ignore them and just tell me,' she said.

'You never work with me. It's always with Bryant,' he blurted out. His face registered surprise as though that wasn't what he'd been expecting to emerge.

Kim was less surprised than he was. 'Go on.'

'It's like a foregone conclusion. You're with Bryant all the time so you get to see how he works. He gets to impress you. Stacey always manages to produce a data miracle, and I'm just out doing the drudgery of… '

'Is that really what you think?' Kim asked. She suddenly felt like a mother being accused of having favourites.

'I feel like you don't trust me to make decisions, to run any part of the investigation. I feel like you just push me out of the way to keep busy.'

Kim shook her head in wonder.

'Just for a minute, before it hits 5 p.m. and I turn into boss again, I'll tell you the truth. That is not because of you it's because of me. Woody likes me to pair up with Bryant. He possesses skills that I do not. People like him far more than they like me. He provides damage limitation. He reduces the complaints that land on Woody's desk about my behaviour, my attitude, my actions. Not only that, Kev, it works for what we're trying to achieve.'

His eyebrows drew together. 'How so?'

'You have a quality that I've not seen very often, and it reminds me of myself. You have the ability to analyse quickly, on your feet. You can swiftly work out what to follow up and what to discard. It makes you invaluable out in the field when questioning witnesses and following potential leads. It's a sense and it can't be taught. Do you know what I mean?'

Dawson nodded slowly.

'You're out on your own because I trust… trusted you… '

He looked at her earnestly. 'I fucked up, boss,' he said.

She nodded and sighed. 'Yeah, Kev, you really, really, did.'

CHAPTER FORTY-SEVEN

Kim knew that Dawson wanted to say more but she shook her head as they walked across the car park. Now was not the time. Now they had to face the consequences of his actions.

He held the door open for a woman to exit the building. Kim glanced her way and then took a better look. The shoulders were hunched and the pale blonde head was focussed on the floor.

'Carry on up,' she said to Dawson, who glanced at the figure and nodded.

'Kerry,' she called, striding to catch up with the figure heading towards a parked car.

Kerry Hinton turned, and Kim saw that her face held no colour except for the red ring around her eyes. Exactly how she'd looked on the night of the interview.

Kerry was a thirty-one-year-old wife, mother and teacher and had been the final victim of Martin Copson.

There was no smile but a nod of recognition.

'How are you doing?' Kim asked before she could stop herself. It was such an automatic question even when you knew the answer.

Kerry simply shook her head and Kim understood.

'Identity parade?' she asked.

'Yes,' Kerry breathed.

Kim already knew they had the right man in custody; identification was a necessary evil.

'That must have been hard for you to—'

'Hard was enduring his penis inside me. Hard was not being able to make him stop. Hard was trying to stay conscious as my head bounced off the ground.'

Kim swallowed. She knew. She had sat with Kerry for three and a half hours immediately after the physical examination.

'Hard was lying awake every night knowing he was still out there.'

'I know.'

Kerry frowned. 'Was it you that caught him?'

Kim nodded.

Kerry clutched her hand. 'Thank you. I knew it would have been you. That must have taken… '

'We only got him because of what you went through, Kerry,' Kim said, honestly. 'It was his attack on you that gave us the DNA. You caught him, not me.'

Kim would take little credit in the face of what this woman had endured in both the attack itself, the events that had followed and, moreover, what was yet to come in court.

'It's little consolation for what you suffered but, because of you, it will not happen again.'

Kerry opened her mouth to argue but Kim shook her head. 'Your bravery caught him, Kerry,' Kim said, squeezing her hand in return. 'Now leave him here with us. Get your life back. As best you can.'

With one final squeeze Kerry turned and headed towards her husband, waiting in the car.

Kim waited and watched the car disappear from view. There was a part of her that wished she could have done more. She wished she could have erased the whole experience that Kerry had suffered. Put her back to normal. Mend her. But she couldn't and she had to accept that.

She headed up the stairs and through the squad room without speaking.

Kim was not surprised to see the red light on her phone flashing furiously as she stepped into The Bowl. And she had a pretty good idea who it was.

She ignored it for a minute. He wasn't going anywhere.

She closed the door behind her and sat down. The red light stopped for two seconds and then started again.

She sat down and turned her back on the squad room. This conversation would be better if she wasn't looking directly at Dawson.

She picked up the phone. 'Stone,' she answered.

'Inspector, it's Martha. I have Detective Superintendent Baldwin for you.'

Of course you have, Kim thought as she murmured her understanding.

She closed her eyes in readiness.

'What the devil is going on over there, Stone?' his voice boomed into her ear.

She moved the phone slightly away.

'Sir, would you care to be a bit more… ?'

'Do not play games with me. I am not DCI Woodward.'

No you certainly ain't, she thought, opening her eyes.

'I assume you're talking about the piece in the *Dudley Star*?' she asked.

'Unless there are some other major fu… mistakes you've been making over there.'

Kim wondered why Halesowen had suddenly become 'over there'.

'Not that I'm aware of,' she answered and was tempted to add 'but give me time'.

'You know full well that appeals to the public have to follow protocols.'

'I do,' she said.

'You know we have to liaise with the press office about what we can and can't mention.'

'I do,' she repeated.

'You also know… '

'Yes, sir. I know it's a huge mistake,' she finished for him.

Her total agreement was very slowly defusing the rage coursing along the phone line. It was difficult to maintain that level of anger when no one was fighting you back.

'So, who was responsible for this, Stone?'

'It's my team,' she answered, grateful she couldn't see Dawson's face right now.

'And the individual within your team?' he pushed.

'It's my team, sir,' she repeated.

'I want a name, Stone.'

'Then take mine, sir. It's… '

'Your team. Yes, I get it.' He paused for a moment and when he spoke his voice was much calmer. 'Then just explain to me how it happened, Stone.'

'It was a miscommunication, sir,' she offered.

'Tends to happen around you a lot, Stone,' he said, tersely.

She didn't answer. The storm had passed.

'From this point on I want a progress briefing, daily, at 5 p.m. Do you understand?'

She rolled her eyes as he tied her arms and legs firmly behind her back.

'Do you understand?' he repeated.

'Yes, sir,' she answered before he ended the call.

Kim continued to hold the phone to her ear. She had no doubt that Dawson would be watching her every move from the squad room and would want to read the expression on her face the second she turned around.

She wasn't ready for him to see her face quite yet. It still bore the marks of having been verbally spanked by her temporary boss, who just happened to be her boss's boss.

But it was more than that. Like Baldwin, her anger had faded, even the pool of disappointment had dried but there was a residue that felt like hurt. There was a part of her that had taken Dawson's actions personally, as a direct betrayal, and she needed a moment to put that out of her mind. That was her problem not his.

She took a few deep breaths and replaced the receiver. She immediately stood and headed into the squad room.

'Okay, what have we got?' she asked, standing next to the coffee machine.

'Seventeen walk-in leads and one hundred and twenty-six phone calls,' Dawson said, regretfully.

Kim folded her arms and counted down in her head. Three… two… one…

'Pass some here,' Bryant said.

Stacey's hand shot across the desk clicking her fingers. 'And here.'

Finally, Kim took a step forward. 'Yeah, and I'll take a few as well.'

CHAPTER FORTY-EIGHT

Ruth chuckled as Elenya read the sentence for the second time.

'No, that says rhubarb not rahubarb,' she explained, pronouncing it as Elenya kept saying it.

'But that makes nonsense,' Elenya said, making Ruth laugh more. Elenya threw the book down in frustration.

Ruth checked the clock on the wall. It was seven thirty. 'We have fifteen more minutes before lock-up. We can finish this page.'

Elenya sighed dramatically and reached for the book.

The feeling of unease had still not left her but spending time with Elenya had distracted her. She had looked for clues everywhere, but had found nothing.

As Elenya continued to read, Ruth glanced around the room.

'The princess did not know that the frog... '

A few groups chatted on the periphery and a couple of singles were reading or just staring at the soundless television on a bracket in the corner. The volume remote had disappeared weeks ago and the guards wouldn't allow anyone to try and reach it to turn it up manually. Health and Safety risk.

'She leaned down and kissed the frog... ugh,' Elenya said.

Few of them watched the television when there was the opportunity for socialising. Most prisoners had a television in their cell which they rented for a nominal fee each week so as not to cost the taxpayer.

'The frog hoped—'

'Hopped,' Ruth corrected, as she watched a group of women gather around a short Asian female who looked petrified, while pushing herself back against the wall. No one touched her but Ruth watched as she slid to the ground.

'Guard,' Manny called. 'Kid's passed out.'

Manny was one of the toughest females in the prison. Her name was Amanda but she preferred Manny. At five feet eleven no one argued with her. She ran the kitchen with an iron fist.

Ruth was no longer listening to her companion reading as the guard ran towards the young girl who was flat out on the ground.

'What's this word?' Elenya asked, reclaiming her attention.

Ruth looked to where her finger was pointing but a whoosh of air startled her.

Dark shadows had appeared to the left, right and behind them. Ruth immediately checked herself for pain and realised it wasn't her.

Manny's hand was wrapped tightly in Elenya's hair.

'Give it back, bitch,' Manny said, turning her hand another ninety degrees.

'I don't have—'

'You took something; now give it the fuck back and no one will get hurt.'

Elenya looked to her imploringly. 'B... but... I don't...'

Manny pulled at the hair again. Elenya let out a small cry. Ruth looked to the guard who was tending to the girl on the floor.

Ruth made to stand up. She could try and get the guard's attention. A firm hand on her shoulder pushed her back down.

'You're not involved yet, love, but you could be,' Manny said, menacingly.

Ruth looked to her friend. Tears were seeping out of the corner of her eyes, even though she had them scrunched shut in pain.

'Elenya,' Ruth said.

Elenya shook her head. 'I swear I didn't take… '

Ruth believed her. Elenya had been waiting months to get a spot in the kitchen. She wouldn't risk it by doing something so blatantly stupid.

'Linda saw you slip something into your pocket, so don't lie,' Manny said with another little tug. 'Just give back whatever it was and we'll leave you alone.'

Ruth couldn't help but note how the atmosphere could change. One minute she and Elenya had been minding their own business, chuckling away on the periphery, and now they were the star attraction. The terror around them was palpable. You could never forget where you were. Not even for a minute.

'I swear, I didn't,' Elenya cried, desperately. She tried to shake her head but Manny's grip was tight.

'Ladies, is everything okay over there?' the guard asked. Her voice grew louder, which told Ruth she was heading towards them despite the fact she couldn't see the woman beyond the wall of heavies. The one closest to her looked to Manny for instruction.

'I will find out, bitch,' Manny whispered, before loosening the hair and smacking Elenya hard on the back of the head.

'Everything's okay, officer,' Manny said, pleasantly, as the wall dispersed.

The guard looked to Elenya whose eyes were still red and watery. Elenya nodded quickly. The guard looked to her again. She hesitated before nodding her agreement.

Somehow acquiescence seemed like the wrong thing to do. And yet she wasn't sure what choice she had.

The guard gave them one more look. She wasn't stupid. She was aware that something had occurred but, without anyone willing to speak up, there was little she could do.

As the guard walked away Ruth wondered if she'd had some kind of sixth sense this was going to happen. That this had been the reason for her growing unease during the week. And now the anxiety would fade.

She hoped so.

CHAPTER FORTY-NINE

Barney finished his evening meal and then looked to her for guidance. Most nights she was already changed and on her way into the garage, but tonight she wasn't so sure.

Normally the assortment of bike parts would ease her brain away from the case she was working. The puzzle of the parts would replace the puzzle in her mind.

She was still bothered by two key things: the complete disparity in her victims and what appeared to be the complete absence of emotion in the attack.

She had been called to murder scenes where the rage had been palpable. The number of wounds, different depths and lengths signalling a frenzy. Others where the wounds inflicted had been slow and deliberate, precise, to prolong the enjoyment. Other times there had been clues in the wound site, around the genital area. But this killer was giving her nothing. One single stab wound to each of the victims. It was characterless, almost banal. The killer was not trying to tell her anything. There were no messages in the attack for her to find.

Her thoughts drifted back to Dawson, who was probably still at his desk wading through the numerous leads that would now haunt them to the end of the case. The volume would slow but they would continue to dribble in until an arrest was made. With what they had now Kim couldn't even imagine when that might be.

Her earlier feelings towards her colleague had dulled but not disappeared. They had all hit the phones to help him, but when he had asked for them to leave him to it she had given the nod to both Bryant and Stacey. She hoped the lesson had been learned.

And then there was Alex.

No matter how much she wished otherwise her meeting with Alex, and the woman's involvement with her mother, just would not go away. Bryant's words of warning still sprung up like signposts in her mind.

Since their episode on the canal side Kim had convinced herself that Alex did not know her as well as she'd thought. A twenty-minute meeting had already shaken the foundations of that belief.

She should not have been surprised at the audacity of the woman presuming to be her and communicating with her mother. Their last encounter had taught her there were no boundaries with Alex. The only thing that consumed the woman were her own wants and needs. And that raised another question: what more did Alex want with her? She had tried to break Kim once and had failed. So what now? And what did her mother have that Kim would want?

'Damn it,' Kim said aloud. Because, despite Bryant's countless warnings, she now had no choice but to find out.

CHAPTER FIFTY

He stepped back as the garage door opened.

She wheeled out the bike that he had watched her wheel in only an hour before. The helmet dangled from the handlebar. This time her face was exposed. For a moment he was transfixed by her expression. He tried to look away but couldn't. There was a beauty in her that he hadn't expected.

She paused and took a breath before reaching for the helmet.

There was indecision in her movement. He sensed that there was a force driving her forward and yet something holding her back too.

But there was something else. Something that travelled the distance between them.

It was not visible: he could not hear it, touch it or smell it but it was there all the same.

He could not tear away his gaze as she threw her leg over the bike and kick-started it into life.

She rolled forward to the bottom of the drive and paused.

She looked both ways, and his heart almost stopped when her eyes glazed over him.

For a second he thought their eyes might meet.

But they didn't. She looked beyond him as though he didn't exist. And in some ways he didn't, and he never had.

* * *

His uncle had first entered his room when he was five years old. It was his first real memory. Everything before had been obliterated by the terror and confusion of that one night. And everything since had been coloured by it.

He couldn't remember marking his childhood in the same way as other kids. He didn't navigate that landscape with peaks of birthday parties or holidays and troughs of football game losses and Christmas disappointments.

From five years of age his uncle came into his room and raped him. The years after that were a blur.

Only the abuse was clear. It became everything. Childhood passed in a litany of the first time it happened; the first time he'd cried so hard he'd vomited. The first time he'd considered trying to die somehow. The first time he'd realised that his prayers were not going to be answered. And finally, the first time he'd realised that he could end the torture himself.

His twelfth birthday marked the change. It marked the moment he knew what he had to do. It was the day he had seen himself in the mirror and realised he no longer had the physical characteristics of the little boy that was still curled up inside him. Almost without him realising he had reached a height of five feet four inches and his skin was filling out.

The plan had begun to form and was astounding in its simplicity. He could make it stop. He had the power. The consequences did not matter to him. Nothing could be worse. He cherished this new knowledge to himself until the next time came.

And when it did he was ready.

He grabbed the kitchen knife from beneath his pillow.

'You're not going to stab me,' his uncle mocked him with a smirk.

And he had known his uncle was right. He dropped the knife beside the bed that had been his prison for seven years. The first punch had landed to the right of the man's temple and had knocked his uncle sideways.

He didn't want the speed of the knife. He wanted to feel every punch and kick. He wanted to feel the man's death beneath his fingertips because then he would know. He would know for sure it was over.

Afterwards, he had sat downstairs and waited. His parents returned from the theatre excited and flushed as they walked in the door. The mood surrounding them disappeared when they saw him sitting forward on the sofa, dried blood covering his hands.

He had explained everything. They had been shocked, horrified, and eventually disbelieving. Even the invasive medical assessments had failed to convince them. They maintained he had been 'experimenting' with other boys at school.

He continued to die inside as he was tried as an adult and sentenced to twelve years in a young offenders' institute.

He'd only wanted the abuse to stop but, of course, it hadn't. He had lost everything and it still didn't end.

Until he went to Hardwick House. The only place where he had slept without the fear of the night time terror.

And then he had met Doctor Thorne. The devil inside his head.

Of course the detective inspector hadn't seen him. He was a non-person. He was nothing more than a sum of all the bad things that had happened to him over the years. There was no personality, no likes or dislikes. Only a deep hatred for everything.

And that included Kim Stone.

CHAPTER FIFTY-ONE

Dawson crossed out another name on the list. Four more to go and he was done. He had politely asked the others to leave an hour ago. He had been thankful for their help but as the clock had continued towards and beyond finishing time his discomfort at their inconvenience had grown exponentially. It was his mistake and it was up to him to fix it.

He was in no doubt that new leads would continue to come in and they would be as much use as the ones that had already been actioned and dismissed.

His gaze drifted to The Bowl and his shame burned once more. He knew his boss had taken a kicking from the Super and yet she hadn't chosen to pass it along. Knowing his boss, she wouldn't have revealed who had messed up. He really wished she had done. Perversely, he was not concerned about the Super's opinion of him. The opinion of his immediate boss was far more of a priority. And he didn't know if the injury there was irrevocable.

On the face of it she had been her normal self. She had made the calls along with the rest of them, but there was something missing, something fractured. A reason why she had looked at him less while doing it. There was something in her face she did not want him to see.

He thought he knew what it was and it made him sick to the stomach.

He sighed heavily and reached for the phone just as it started to ring.

'Dawson,' he answered.

'Got a woman down here who saw the *Dudley Star* article online. Wants a word,' Jack on the front desk said.

Great, another walk in, he thought. He was never getting home tonight.

'I'll be down in a minute,' he said.

He took a swig of cold coffee and headed out the door. As he took the stairs he wondered which pile he'd file this one on once he'd finished.

Perhaps it would be the 'oh, I'm sorry, I've got the wrong night' pile. Or the 'it was a Mazda, Audi, MR2 car in the lay-by' pile. He'd even had one witness insisting it was a Bentley.

To say he'd learned his lesson was an understatement. It was exactly as the boss had said. The appeal for information had brought forward witnesses with bad memories instead of sticking to the people who were known to have been in the area.

He keyed himself through to the reception and nodded in Jack's direction.

The woman was early to mid-fifties with a full head of tidy grey hair. She wore a dark blue uniform and a pair of grey crocs.

'Detective Sergeant Dawson. Can I help you?'

She held out her hand. 'Mrs Lawson, I'm a nurse at the private hospital on Colman Hill. I'm here about the incident on Sunday night.'

Dawson returned the firm, dry handshake.

'Did you see the car?' he asked, hopefully.

'No, I didn't see anything Sunday night,' she explained.

Dawson immediately knew what pile this lead was landing on.

'But I didn't need to,' she said. 'As soon as I read the article I knew exactly which car it was.'

'How?' he asked, frowning.

'It's my dream car, officer. I have that very car on my aspiration board at home. I look at it every day before I go to work.'

Dawson still wasn't sure where this was heading.

'So you knew it was a Vauxhall—'

'Well it's not just a Vauxhall, is it, officer?' she asked. 'It's a brand new Cascada Elite Convertible with heated front seats, eighteen inch alloys and the OnStar programme costing around thirty grand.'

Dawson couldn't help the tired smile that lifted his mouth.

'I told you, it's my dream car,' she repeated. 'And you don't see that many of them in Colley Gate.'

'So what exactly can you tell me, Mrs Lawson,' he asked, politely.

'I can tell you it was normally driven by an attractive woman in her late forties or early fifties but, more importantly, I can confirm that the car has been parked there many times before.'

Dawson hid his surprise. This was not a fact that had come up before. His night at the station continued to stretch out in front of him but right now he didn't care.

New information was like an injection of pure adrenaline. This was a woman who remembered detail.

He smiled as he opened the inner door.

'Mrs Lawson, would you like to follow me?'

CHAPTER FIFTY-TWO

The building was not what Kim had been expecting, or hoping for, if she was honest.

The gravel drive had guided her from the main road and wound through two rows of gnarly oak trees for a quarter of a mile before spitting her out at the edge of perfectly manicured lawns. Benches were dotted around an area being used as a bowling green. The star of the show was an imposing red-brick structure that had retained its seventeenth-century appearance with tall, narrow windows formed of smaller glass panes.

Bardsley House was a wing within the Grantley Care facility. Situated four miles east of Chester town centre it housed the criminally insane. Externally it bore no sign of the madness within.

Small groups were dotted around the lawns, but it was the house that took her breath away and brought the bile to the back of her throat.

She eased the bike to a stop in front of the visitor parking sign and removed her helmet.

She took a good, long look at the care facility that had housed her mother for the last twenty-eight years. Betrayal of her brother's memory burned inside her at the surroundings where her mother lived.

She suddenly remembered the day that Mikey's dead body had been ripped from her arms.

She had held on tightly until her fingers were gently prised away from his arms. Even though he'd been gone for two days the child inside her had still hoped the big people could save him.

She had screamed as they removed him from her side. Although his body had no longer been warm from life, only from the radiator, her flesh had felt bereft when his presence was removed. Her six-year-old screams had pierced her own ears as she'd desperately begged for them not to take him away. Eventually her tortured cries had turned to uncontrollable sobs as she suffered that final goodbye.

At that moment she had wanted to die. She had wanted to be carried out with her twin, so they would be together for ever.

And then she had been swallowed by the blackness.

It had taken two weeks in hospital to restore her health. The job of the medical staff made harder as they battled to save a life that had not wanted to be saved.

She remembered being so close to Mikey that she could almost touch him. His pale, frightened face had loomed in the distance and she had ached to reach it, to be reunited with the tender, loving, sweet other half of herself.

And yet the anger, the white hot rage that ran through her, would not let her rest. It nudged her back from the peace that beckoned like a recurring nightmare.

It had always been the anger that had kept her alive.

When she'd been strong enough a faceless stranger with blonde curly hair and a tired smile collected her from the hospital.

A short, impersonal car ride deposited her at Fairview Hall on the outskirts of Tividale.

The children's home was new and ugly. It was a functional grey concrete slab that rose out of the ground. Tiny windows deeply recessed into the fabric of the building like cushion buttons.

To the left was a foundry billowing out grey smoke day and night. To the right was a smelly recycling plant.

The inside had been no warmer, despite the June sunshine.

A brief conversation and the handover was complete.

She was home.

She was guided through corridors not unlike the ones she'd left in the hospital and deposited in a room on the second floor that had a window that was too high to reach.

Two of the beds were personalised, their bedside cabinets awash with photos, costume jewellery, a notepad, a pair of glasses. The third one was stark.

The woman placed a carrier bag on the bed. Kim knew it contained clothes. She didn't know where they had come from but they were not hers. She had no items of her own.

She shrunk away from the hand that touched her shoulder.

'I'll leave you to settle in,' she said.

Kim had known right away that she was never going to settle in. And she never had.

And now she was observing these tranquil surroundings, the sign that pointed towards a 'Deer Park'. She struggled to swallow the irony that she had been taken and deposited at the stark functionality of Fairview while her mother had been brought here and cared for in the tranquillity and grandeur of Bardsley House.

She was about to enter the door marked reception when a voice sounded behind her.

'Hello, may I help you?'

Kim didn't need to look around to know she was being addressed by Lily, the woman to whom she had spoken on the telephone for sixteen years.

Despite the betrayal she couldn't help the smile that formed on her face as she turned towards the familiar voice.

The woman wore a colourful smock top that was loose over her generous proportions and a pair of plain black trousers. Her hair was dyed auburn and cut short. An owl motif dangled from each earlobe.

This was a woman that was made for grandchildren, Kim couldn't help thinking.

It was easy to picture her cooking up a storm each Sunday lunchtime ready for a horde of children and toddlers.

'Kim Stone,' she said, extending her hand.

A slow smile began to spread across the woman's face. She ignored the outstretched hand and stepped forward, encasing Kim in a big warm hug.

'Kim, I'm so pleased you've come,' she said, finally stepping back. 'After all these years…'

Kim knew the words were not a reproach. Lily had been asking her to visit for a long time and she had steadfastly refused.

Kim didn't like to admit that she was only here now because she wanted to know what her mother had that she would want.

'I just—'

'It doesn't matter. You're here now,' she said, warmly.

And now that she was here she had no idea how she'd thought this would play out. Her plan had consisted of getting here, taking whatever it was, and going home. The details had been sketchy.

How did she get something from a woman whose very existence was like a constant kick to the stomach?

Just knowing she was even in the area was bringing an ache to her jaw. But maybe she wouldn't have to. Perhaps Lily would do it for her.

'Follow me and we can have a chat,' Lily said, stepping into the building.

The reception area was unlike a hospital foyer. Comfortable wing-backed chairs littered the area, with occasional tables scattered throughout. Gentle watercolour paintings of local landscapes dotted the walls and pan pipes sounded gently from a speaker that rested above a CCTV camera.

Kim slowed to a halt and looked around. 'Nice place,' she said, quietly.

Lily halted alongside her and followed her gaze around the hallway. 'It was, many years ago. Do you know the story?'

Kim shook her head.

'Bardsley House was built and then owned by the Bardsley family for two hundred years. In that time, it saw seven murders, a suicide and a curse that no female ensconced within would live beyond her fortieth birthday.

'The seventh and last generation Bardsley pooh poohed the curse until his wife was taken ill at the tender age of thirty-seven. In 1887 he moved to one of the farmer's cottages and gifted the house to the local council, believing that his charitable act would lift the curse for ever.'

Kim didn't believe in curses but that was one hell of a history.

Lily continued. 'We use only one quarter of the building now. We get no more money than any other state facility and it works on a headcount. We stretch it as far as we can but the 'no sale' clause in the gift prevents the local council from profiting from the building or land. Mr Bardsley did not want any other families suffering the same fate as his own.'

Kim hoped her expression reflected her feelings. She wasn't here for a tour.

'Come on, let's go and have a chat,' Lily said.

Kim followed her through a deserted hallway and stopped short of a key coded door.

A quick left and they were in a small office with a single desk wedged against the wall. There were no filing cabinets but two shelves on the longest wall crammed with text books and medical journals. Some variations of a rota covered in red pen were scattered over the desk.

'Bloody admin,' she said, pushing them aside. Kim sat on the chair to the left of the desk. It felt like a doctor's visit.

'So, what brings you here, Kim?' Lily asked, facing her.

Despite her warm greeting, Kim understood that Lily's priority was her charges, her patients. After years of trying to persuade her to visit her mother she would be naturally suspicious of her sudden appearance.

'The letters,' Kim said.

Lily frowned. 'Ah, yes we've been trying to get to the back of that. Are you quite sure they didn't come from you?'

Kim raised one eyebrow. Yes, she was sure.

'We no longer have the envelopes to check the postmark but neither myself nor the staff recall anything suspicious. Do you have any idea who would have done this?'

'No,' Kim said, quickly.

She had spent too many hours of her life trying to explain the evil that was Alexandra Thorne. She could not cope with that look of disbelief again.

'What I don't understand is that clearly the letters were designed for a positive effect,' Lily said.

Oh, you can't even begin to understand how wrong you are, Kim thought. Alex knew that it was imperative to Kim's own well-being that her mother remain in this place, although she now knew it wasn't the kind of place that had lived in her mind all those years.

Okay, maybe she hadn't pictured her mother in a damp, dark, smelly windowless basement chained to the wall, with a metal tray skidded in her direction a couple of times a day. But neither had she imagined the grandeur of a stately home surrounded by people who were genuinely caring and compassionate.

Kim could sense there was an element of doubt that remained in the woman's eyes.

'I will never forgive her for what she did, Lily,' Kim said, quietly. She stopped herself asking why the woman thought she would lie. 'But would I be able to see them?' she asked.

Lily shook her head. 'If you didn't write them then they have nothing to do with you. They are your mother's private property.'

Kim wondered at the Human Rights Act that had given a schizophrenic murdering bitch such power.

Lily turned towards her. 'I think you'd be surprised if you met her. She is greatly changed and since your… the letters started coming there is a new peace within her.'

'I don't want her to have peace,' Kim exploded. The hatred and anger was no less now than it had been back then for one simple reason: Mikey was still dead.

'You can't mean that, Kim,' Lily said, quietly, obviously hoping Kim would follow suit and lower her voice.

She did not.

'Her state of mind means nothing to me. I don't care how she feels or thinks. My only wish for that woman is that she stays here until the day she dies, so she can cause no more harm to anyone.'

'But this might not be the right place for her anymore,' Lily said, gently.

'It will always be the right place for her. I just don't understand how there is a possibility that she will leave,' Kim said, honestly, still rooted in disbelief that the whole world didn't agree with her. 'You've read her file; you know what she did.'

Kim saw the sympathy in her expression. 'Of course I know what she did but I can't allow that knowledge to colour the level of care she receives. Other people made the decisions about her crime and punishment. And then they sent her here. It's not for me to judge the fairness of the system. It's my job to try and rehabilitate her ready for re-entry into the—'

'But she's assaulted people here,' Kim raged. 'How can you feel she's fit to live in society?'

'Kim, calm down. There's been no violence for months now; she has been a model patient.'

Kim would have preferred the term inmate.

Lily continued. 'We do believe in rehabilitation, Kim. We don't lock people up and throw away the key. We hope to help them get better. If not, seventy per cent of what we do would be a complete waste of time. Otherwise we should kill them on sentencing.'

Kim chose not to answer. That idea sounded fine to her.

Lily leaned forward. 'Maybe if you meet with her, see for yourself?'

Kim said nothing.

She had dreamed many times of coming face to face with her mother but the scenario always ended with her hands around the woman's throat, squeezing every last breath from her body.

'Could you ever give her a chance?' Lily asked, tipping her head.

Kim simply shook her head. Mikey had been everything to her. No day went by without her imagining her life with him still in it. To forgive the woman who killed him diminished the enormity of his suffering and his eventual death.

Lily opened her mouth to say more, but seeing Kim's expression kept the words on the right side of her tongue.

Lily placed her hands on her knees.

'How about I show you where she is and we can take it from there. You don't need to speak to her if you don't want to.'

Kim hesitated and then nodded.

She followed Lily back through the corridor and out the front door instead of heading back towards the gravel car park.

She turned left and walked along the front terrace to the corner of the house.

Four ladies were busy on a small putting green. A cursory glance told her that none of these ladies was her mother.

She turned to Lily for clarification when she heard a sound that reached inside and wrapped an icy fist around her heart.

The laugh was softer than she recalled, less manic than the one that had played in her head for the last twenty-eight years. But she remembered it well. She'd heard it every time the bitch had managed to outsmart her and get to Mikey. It was a laugh that she had learned to fear. It was a laugh that meant she was winning.

'Your mother is the one… '

'I know which one she is,' Kim said, without emotion.

Her eyes had followed the sound that still haunted her to a slight woman wearing pale blue cotton trousers and a cerise T-shirt.

The black hair, gifted to Kim herself, no longer hung down to the middle of the shoulder blades. It was completely white and ended at the nape of her neck.

Kim felt the bile rise to the back of her throat as she watched her mother do a little victory dance.

A low chuckle escaped from the woman beside her and Kim realised they were watching two completely different pictures: Lily wanted to see the woman happy and relaxed, but Kim hated every second of it. Every laugh, smile, peaceful moment was an insult to her dead brother.

The thoughts were turning so quickly in her mind she wondered if her head was going to begin rotating and then fly off into the distance.

She forced herself to continue watching as the woman approached her nearest companion and demonstrated the exact movement she'd used to pot the ball. She stood by her side adjusting her hand on the golf club.

Kim could not reconcile this figure with the one who had handcuffed her and her twin to a heated radiator in the middle of a sweltering summer. This could not be the woman who had put her own medication in Kim's drinks to tranquilise her so she could get her hands on her brother.

The drugs had sedated her but not knocked her out. She had lain against the bathroom door while her mother tried to shake the devil from her brother.

Eventually she had crawled up the porcelain pedestal of the sink and put in the plug. She had turned on both taps full and waited for the sink to overflow. She had cried with frustration for the ten minutes it had taken Mr Randall from downstairs to come knocking about the leak.

Mikey had stumbled towards her, drunkenly, his brain still reverberating in his head. That was the night she had discovered she could stay awake with the help of a pin.

She had lain beside her brother with the pin pointing towards her arm. If her arm began to relax the sharp prick into her flesh helped to keep her awake. It was also the day she learned to count her mother's tranquilisers morning and night.

And here she was staring at a stranger cheerfully playing golf.

Could she really do this? Kim wondered to herself. Could she really be this close to that woman without causing her physical harm? Could she swallow her hatred and bitterness to find out what it was that her mother had that she would want?

This surreal picture of her mother playing golf and laughing with her friends in the grounds of a grand estate was almost too much to bear. And yet, for a moment, she could see the picture before them through Lily's eyes. That very same description was what gave Lily the opinion that the woman could live a productive life on the outside. But Lily had not seen her mother before. The darkness in the eyes, the hatred on the cruel face and the spittle that had erupted from her mouth when she had called Mikey terrible, cruel, horrific names.

Kim stared hard at the back of the head, willing her to feel the hatred that was burning inside her.

Her breath caught in her throat as the figure began to turn. She felt her heartbeat increase as her eyes rested on the face she knew so well.

Her mother's gaze rested on Lily. She raised her hand but it stilled mid-wave as the golf club fell from her other hand.

Kim saw the recognition in her mother's eyes, followed by shock.

For a moment they were locked in the exact same battle they'd always been locked in. Kim felt the years slip away as their eyes remained fixed on each other.

Her mother's eyes softened with hope, tenderness, love.

As her mother took a tentative step forward Kim knew one thing beyond a shadow of a doubt.

Whatever her mother had, it wasn't worth this.

She allowed every bit of repulsion to show on her face before she turned and walked away.

CHAPTER FIFTY-THREE

The ride back from Grantley was a blur. Kim was surprised to find herself in Halesowen.

Her mother's new face was everywhere. And that smile, that fucking smile. How dare she smile. How dare she even be able to smile.

Her mind had held the same last memory of the woman since she was six years old.

She had stood at the front door of the high-rise flat, triumph shining from her eyes, as she had left them chained to the radiator. Her final words to them both had been, 'If I have to kill you to kill him, that's what I'll do.'

As the hours had stretched into days the few dry crackers and half bottle of Coke had dwindled until she had offered everything to Mikey. Slowly she had felt his life fading away, and she had known.

Their last few hours were spent with Kim telling Mikey of all the things they would do when they were rescued. She talked to him of juicy pizza and strawberry ice cream and of a park where the rides took you high into the sky.

She had saved her tears for when he fell asleep. She refused to share her despair. During the fourth night, as she stroked his hair, she felt the last frail breath leave his body.

It was two days until they finally found her.

Today she had not seen the woman who had left them that day. And yet she had. Her mind could not compute the two expressions. She'd had only one picture in her mind, another one was too much. She couldn't cope with another vision in her mind.

She passed the station and debated popping in but her mind turned instead to Barney, who would be now anticipating his late-night walk.

She turned onto Whistler Road. The quarter-mile road had wasteland on one side and a recently built trading park on the other. It wasn't barrier controlled and acted as a magnet for illicit activity in the dark corners behind the units.

The car in front slowed down causing her to brake sharply. A figure stepped out of the shadows and approached the passenger window. Kim saw a shock of green hair, and she got the picture.

She hit her horn, twice. The car began to pull away, and the face beneath the green hair looked murderous.

'What the… ?' she exploded as Kim brought the bike to rest beside her. She wasn't wearing the usual suggestive clothes of the night workers but she was in the right place.

'What are you doing?' Kim asked.

'Waiting for my chauffeur to pick me up, bitch. What the fuck's it look like?'

'Thanks for the plant,' Kim said, ignoring the attitude.

Gemma stared at her dolefully.

'Spikey, cactus – clever,' Kim said.

Gemma shrugged. 'I nicked it.'

Kim had guessed as much. 'Still a nice gesture,' she said.

'Yeah well. I got manners, yer know.'

Amongst the bad language, dramatic attitude, and shop theft, the girl had manners, Kim thought.

'Did you report the mugging?' Kim asked.

She snorted. 'Yeah, CID, MI5, CIA, they're all over it.'

Kim laughed out loud, surprising them both. An ounce of tension fell from her body.

'Seriously, what are you doing?' Kim repeated.

'Seriously, I'm seeing if any of the nice men who drive down here want to contribute to my lunch fund. It was a no-go on crowd funder.'

'No job?' Kim asked.

'You new to the area?' Gemma retorted.

'There are—'

'I ain't debating this, bitch. Now fuck off and let me get some food money.'

Kim dug in her pocket and held out a tenner.

Gemma looked at it suspiciously.

'What I gotta do?'

'Nothing, except get off this street, at least for tonight.'

Her expression softened, just for a second, before rearming itself. She took the note and stuffed it in her pocket. 'Okay, I'll leave it tonight.'

Kim reached for her helmet. 'And tomorrow night there'll be something potentially edible on my table around seven.'

Gemma opened her mouth to speak.

'Come, don't come,' Kim shrugged. 'You know where I live.'

She put on the helmet, revved the bike and pulled away.

She drove to the end of the street and turned left. She travelled a hundred metres and turned left again. She continued going left until she was back on Whistler Road.

She eased the bike along slowly. A few shapes were visible in the darkness but as she neared the telephone box she breathed a sigh of relief.

The green-haired girl was gone.

CHAPTER FIFTY-FOUR

16 December 2007

Dear Diary,

Her eyes were alight with fear as I opened the door. Her hair did not smell as good as yesterday but I did not want to repeat myself anyway. There were too many other parts to explore. She reminds me of a computer game. Who wants to stay on level one?

There are many differences to the girl I saw on Monday. Her big-girl mascara that looked so assured and fitting has now bled from her lashes in rivulets down her cheeks. The lipstick applied secretly after leaving the house is now gone without a trace.

A stain beneath each armpit is growing and appears the colour of teak wood on the cotton shirt. How is that possible? I wondered. Sweat is not brown.

And although she has not left the place where I've stored her there is a grubbiness that is inevitably attracted to the white fabric of her shirt.

And today her shirt was the focus of my attention. I could not tear my eyes away from the fullness of her breasts straining against the cloth, their outline deliciously clear. The cloth stretching as her laboured breathing intensified beneath my stare.

I swallowed deeply as I reached out and felt the roundness beneath my palm. A jolt of electricity shot through me. Instantly I wanted to know what lay beneath. Would her bra be pink, lacy, white, virginal, smooth?

That instant electricity gave way to hunger for more. I tore open her shirt and ignored the pleading in her eyes. This wasn't about her. It was about me.

I told her to shut her eyes. I didn't want the interaction right then. She was not a person but an inanimate object solely for my exploration.

The bra was white, bright against the grubby shirt. Fresh, untouched. The fabric was smooth, uncluttered by lace or useless, decorative bows. No flesh swelled above the curve of the fabric as it reached down to her breastbone.

I swallowed hard to stop the saliva from spilling out of my mouth.

I cupped the breast and squeezed, the jolt that coursed through me was stronger. I squeezed harder and ignored the cry that died in her throat.

It was too much. My body lit up as the fire throbbed through my veins. My hand dived inside the bra and felt the supple skin against my fingers, a nipple against my palm.

The ecstasy that overwhelmed me subsided quickly, like a minor explosion and left a trail of hunger for that deeper satisfaction, the satiation that could only be gained one way.

I placed the nipple between my thumb and forefinger and squeezed.

Hard.

CHAPTER FIFTY-FIVE

'Come on, folks, enthusiasm please,' Kim said, clapping her hands.

Her whole team seemed to have walked in dragging a lead weight this morning. Even Bryant.

Every case they worked was different. They were dealing with killers that had different motivations, different priorities, methods but some cases seemed to falter to a definite stop part way. Sometimes a different perspective was needed.

She stood at the top of the office. This was going to be a briefing with a difference.

No hand feeding. More active thinking.

'Everyone, move round a seat. Stace to Kev's chair, Kev to Bryant's, and Bryant take Stacey's seat.'

They all looked at her before getting up and moving around the room.

They sat down and glanced across at each other and then at their surroundings. Stacey was now looking at the back of her own computer, Bryant was looking at a very tidy desk, and Dawson was staring at the photograph board. They were all looking around as though she had dropped them onto an alien planet.

'Okay, let's recap. Yesterday we learned that Geraldine was going to publicly acknowledge Maxine as her daughter.

'We found out that her mother is a controlling "pageant mom" who barely gives her daughter permission to breathe. We learned that Jason Cross did indeed sleep with Deanna Brightman, he says once, I'm not so sure. And we now have the phone records of the whole Brightman family.'

'Except Deanna's old phone,' Stacey interjected. 'Still, ay got the bloody number.'

Kim frowned. It really shouldn't have been that difficult.

She continued, 'We're still waiting on the confirmation of the DNA match for the hair, and we now know from Kev that Deanna's car had been parked in that lay-by before.'

'At least three times,' Dawson confirmed.

'So, given what we have and, more pertinent, what we don't have, where to now, folks?'

She looked at her team, who all looked a little uncomfortable in their new surroundings.

'Go,' she prompted.

'Need to compare phone records to see if any strange numbers turn up,' Stacey said.

'Yep,' Kim said.

Dawson leaned forward. 'Need to get back to tracing Maxine's whereabouts in recent weeks. Get to know her larger circle of acquaintances and see if there's any crossover.'

Kim nodded. He was now free to resume that line of enquiry. Any further witnesses would be dealt with as and when they were back in the office.

Stacey twirled Dawson's pen between her fingers. 'It might be an idea to see if we've got anything else on Jason Cross – do some digging.'

'Sounds good, Stace,' Kim agreed.

'Need to have another chat with Geraldine without the mother present,' Bryant said.

'Absolutely,' she said.

'Need to find out if any other forces have had anything similar,' Dawson offered.

'Good one, Kev,' Kim said as Stacey tipped her head.

'Hey, guys, why are most of these suggestions adding work for me?'

Kim smiled as both Bryant and Dawson shrugged.

She reassessed her team. They were all sitting forward: alert, keen and eager to get started.

'Okay then, seems we all know what we're doing,' Kim said, heading out the door in front of Bryant.

Kim felt that today was make or break for this case. If something didn't crack open today, she was beginning to wonder if it ever would.

CHAPTER FIFTY-SIX

Alex stood against the vending machine and watched.

Tanya spoke earnestly to her cousin, who glanced over at Alex a couple of times.

At first he shook his head definitely but Tanya grabbed at his forearm. He still shook his head, but with less conviction and then he stopped shaking it at all. And just listened.

The glances towards her were murderous. She didn't flinch.

There was little point in Tanya trying to adopt the moral high ground. She and her sister were not strangers to murder. They had killed three men and cut off their penises. In comparison, what she was asking for was a walk in the park.

As the conversation between the two of them progressed Alex allowed herself to enjoy the warm feeling of triumph that was building inside her. Every strand of her master plan was coming together.

Her thoughts drifted to Kim. She couldn't help wondering if she'd visited her mother yet. It was only a matter of time. If she had, would Kim have had the courage to speak to her? How had she reacted to seeing her mother after so many years? How much of her had come undone already? How fresh were the memories of Mikey now they were being dragged to the surface?

Was she thinking about him every single minute? Was she waking up in the middle of the night, sweating, screaming, crying as she lived again through the torture of those days?

How was her brain dealing with the fact that in just a few short days her mother, her tormentor, her torturer would probably be walking free; her liberty returned?

All of these questions swirled around in her mind as she relished the fact that she was the one who held the power to loosen the woman's grip on sanity again.

Alex enjoyed the fact that Kim knew that it was she who had discovered Patty's deception. She who had uncovered the fact that a violent episode always preceded an opportunity for release. It was her who had learned that Patty did this as the only gift she could offer her daughter.

And Alex had taken that gift away.

By pretending to be Kim she had offered her mother forgiveness and encouraged her to try for parole, assured her there was no hatred left.

Oh, the permutations of all these harmful thoughts running around Kim's head were just too delightful to imagine.

But her imagination was not enough. She needed to see the detective inspector again. She needed to prod the hurt, massage the anguish.

'What are you doing now, you nasty evil bitch?'

Alex was disturbed from her happy place by Natalya Kozlov. This poor woman followed her around like a lovesick puppy.

Alex tipped her head and smiled up into the long, thin horse face before her. 'Don't be jealous, sweetheart, just because I've found another friend.'

'You have no friends,' Natalya whispered, moving closer. 'You destroy everything you touch.'

Alex met her hate-filled gaze as Natalya placed her hands on the wall either side of Alex's head. Alex's eyes were drawn to the surplus skin that hung from the long, gangly arms.

'Look, darling,' Alex goaded, 'our time together was very special but I've moved on. I've found someone else I like more than you.' She leaned in closer to Natalya. 'And Tanya takes a wash now and again.'

She wrinkled her nose in distaste and ducked her head under Natalya's arm.

'Move on, Natalya. It's done,' she said, turning away.

'Hey, Alex. We are both here for a very long time. I will kill you.'

'Get in line, sweetheart,' Alex said as Katie, the guard, came into view.

Natalya slunk from the room.

Some people just didn't know when to let go. Alex had sought the woman out, befriended her, complimented her and then got her to do exactly what she wanted and then she'd dumped her. Simple.

Her attention returned to Tanya, who stood and moved away from the table. The woman headed in her direction, her face a mixture of anguish, despair and rage.

Alex tipped her head waiting for the words she wanted to hear.

'It's done,' she said, brushing past her.

Alex smiled to herself. Of course it was.

There had never been any doubt.

CHAPTER FIFTY-SEVEN

Stacey sent the final two emails to the Lancashire and Cheshire forces. She had begun with the closest of West Mercia and Staffordshire then worked her way out to Derbyshire, Gloucestershire and Warwickshire. Later she would spread the catchment further north, south and into parts of Wales. If any other police force had any similar crimes, she'd know about it.

And now while she waited for a response she laid out the three sets of phone records for both Deanna and the surviving members of the Brightman family. She had twenty-eight days for all of them.

Someone at Dudley Council was currently trying to track the number from historic records for Deanna's second phone, but she didn't hold out much hope seeing as Deanna had transferred the number over to her personal account.

She had spoken to Mitchell Brightman, who had promised to look through his wife's belongings to see if he could find an old bill. She was expecting the records for the family of Maxine Wakeman and her family any time soon but for now she would have to focus on the ones she had.

For Sylvie that was eight pages. For Mitchell it was twelve pages and for Rebecca a whopping twenty-two sheets.

Stacey began on Deanna's eleven pages. She ruled out calls to and from work, Sylvie, Mitchell and a couple of friends.

That left three mystery numbers unaccounted for.

Stacey immediately rang the first one and got the call menu for a car insurance company. She crossed it out.

The second call was answered by an automated recording for a restaurant booking service. She crossed it out.

The third number, the one that had called Deanna on the night of her death, went straight to generic voicemail. Stacey called it again, and the same thing happened.

She wrote the number on a Post-it and tacked it onto her computer. She wanted to see if that same number turned up anywhere else.

She turned next to Sylvie's and began by putting a ruled line through Sylvie's hairdressers, best friend, daughter and local takeaways. There was little left to analyse.

She reached for Mitchell's and ruled out his work place, friends, gym and was left with a slightly longer list than Sylvie. She ruled out the numbers of friends that were shared with Deanna and was left with four numbers that didn't match up.

Stacey couldn't help feeling in her element when interrogating pages of data. She knew that some people thought she was battle shy, too scared to be out in the field, but she wasn't. That was Dawson's passion and this was hers.

Right now, just in these phone records, lay a mountain of data. Any one of these phone numbers could mean something. Any text message could offer her a clue. It was the proverbial haystack but she knew that somewhere in here was a needle and that she would find it.

Already there was a rogue number tacked to her computer screen. A single number that did not fit in with the rest. It could be nothing, but it could be something. For all she knew it could be everything.

As she started a task like this there was always a feeling that she was looking at a solid brick wall but her methodical mind addressed the problem one brick at a time. Dawson would run at the wall continually until one of them broke. Bryant would try and talk it into submission, and her boss would most likely try and climb over it. But she would dissect it and enjoy every minute.

Again, her gaze lifted to the number tacked to her screen. It was the only call received by Deanna on the night of the murder. It had to mean something. She had learned a long time ago from her boss that everything meant something. And for some reason that number was important.

She returned her attention to the most recent page of Mitchell's call list. Two of the four outstanding numbers had been called on the night of Deanna's murder.

One of the numbers looked familiar.

She picked up another set of records and frowned.

Something was glinting from the haystack and it looked very much like a needle.

CHAPTER FIFTY-EIGHT

'Bloody hell, it's not like we're trying to murder her or anything,' Bryant moaned.

'Someone might be,' Kim said, as they showed their identification for the seventh time. The BBC had spent many years at the Pebble Mill studios but in 2004 had relocated to the brand new site at The Mailbox complex beside the canal in the centre of Birmingham.

They had called ahead and were still jumping through hoops.

'We'd have been quicker booking to come on the tour,' Bryant moaned.

'The what?' Kim asked, as they were asked again to wait at a set of double glass doors.

'You can book to come and have a look behind the scenes at some of the sets and stuff.'

Kim ignored the useless piece of information and tapped her foot impatiently.

The show that Geraldine guested on was an hour-long magazine programme that went out around the same time as Jeremy Kyle, twice a week. It had suffered in the ratings for a few years but was now growing a loyal following.

A young girl came and hurried them through another corridor. They had now been told three times that Geraldine was due on the set in less than fifteen minutes.

They followed the girl into a windowless room barely bigger than The Bowl back at the station. She mumbled something and then disappeared.

Two swivel chairs were placed before salon mirrors surrounded by lights.

Geraldine smiled into the mirror as a thin red-haired man dusted something onto her forehead.

'Come in, come in,' she said.

Both she and Bryant edged against the wall, heading towards the empty chair.

'Sorry to interrupt you at work,' Kim said, sitting in the seat beside her.

'No problem,' she said. Her eyes reddened; Kim saw reflected on her face how her mind carried out the process of association back to their reason for being here: Maxine, her daughter, was still dead. 'Anything I can do to help.'

Kim saw the make-up artist frown at her eyes, and instantly swap to a different brush.

'I wasn't coming in today, but Mother thought it would take my mind off things.'

Of course, Kim thought.

'And Belinda?'

'Told me to make my own decision on what was right for me.'

'I just wondered if you'd had any further thoughts on any of Maxine's friends. Did she ever bring anyone to meet you, a boyfriend?'

Geraldine shook her head.

Kim preferred the look of the woman they'd met yesterday. This one had hair curled, tonged and sprayed into submission. The make-up was heavy and dense; Kim was sure it worked for the cameras but not in real life. Yesterday she had looked like a glamorous mother who had lost a child suddenly. Today she looked like a television star: polished, manufactured.

'I didn't meet her friends. It took a while to get her to open up about relationships but she hadn't had a boyfriend for more than six months.'

'Was there anyone in particular she bonded with during her time in rehab?'

This time Geraldine smiled, and the make-up guy tutted again and reached for yet another brush.

'I don't think so, Inspector. Max thought they were all losers. She was convinced she was different to the druggies and loons, as she used to call them. I don't think she made any lasting friendships in there.'

'Why did you give her up?' Kim asked suddenly.

This woman had so much love for a child she had not raised. Every word, every expression dripped with affection. Kim wouldn't have been offended if Geraldine had told her to mind her own business but somehow Kim suspected she would not.

'I was twenty-six and about to leave medical school. I was going to be working long hours, ridiculous schedules. The father was long gone and I had no one.'

'Your mother?'

'Did not want to relive that part of her life. I had already chosen a career that was not in my mother's master plan,' Geraldine said, leaving her in no doubt that she knew just how controlling the woman was.

She turned from the mirror and faced Kim squarely. 'But I stand by the decision, Inspector. If I had to, I'd do it again. Maxine had a mother who loved her very much.'

There was sadness but no regret.

'She had two,' Kim offered.

Geraldine smiled. 'Thank you for that; but I hope I was at the very least a friend.'

Kim appreciated how open and honest this woman had chosen to be with them.

'And the career?' Kim asked. 'Was it everything you thought it would be?'

Geraldine smiled sadly. 'It was no replacement, if that's what you're asking. I spent a few years working for Sandwell Mental Health division. Spent another few years working in private institutions, consulted for the CPS once or twice and got spotted by a BBC producer who thought I had the right 'manner' for a pilot show, and I've been doing this ever since.'

Kim wondered if 'manner' was some kind of code for attractiveness and sex appeal. Geraldine certainly had both.

Kim's mobile broke the silence that had fallen between them.

'Well, thank you for your time,' Kim said, pressing the button. 'Stace,' she said, as she headed out of the door.

'You know, I can't get that last conversation out of my mind,' Geraldine said so quietly that Kim wondered to whom she was speaking.

Kim told Stacey to hang on.

'Why?' she asked, speaking to the woman's reflection in the mirror.

'I wasn't properly listening. It was the last time I was ever going to speak to her and I had to get off the phone. I was distracted, stressed, worried.'

The make-up artist gave up completely as Geraldine's head dropped and she stared into her lap.

'I keep playing the conversation over and over in my head. Did I miss something? Was there a clue? Could I have... ?'

'You can't do this to yourself, Geraldine,' Kim said from the doorway. 'It sounds as though you offered Maxine every opportunity. I doubt that there's anything you could have done to prevent what's happened.'

Geraldine nodded at the meaningless words.

Kim knew that one of the most destructive emotions that came with grief was regret. Other emotions would settle within her over time but regret would always cut like a knife.

Kim stepped through the door, but then paused and turned back to Geraldine.

'If you don't mind me asking, what was so fraught around that time?'

'Oh dear lord,' Geraldine said, quietly. 'Belinda had just been run over and the doctors didn't know if she would walk again, and we were in the middle of having a brand new kitchen.'

CHAPTER FIFTY-NINE

'Go on, Stace,' Kim said, as they were guided back to the outside world. She listened with interest to her colleague before speaking. 'Thanks for that, Stace. We'll head over there now.'

'Back to the Brightman house,' she instructed Bryant as they headed towards the car park. There were a couple of people there who had some explaining to do.

'Slow down a bit, guv,' Bryant said.

She paused.

'I meant in your head. I'm still processing what we just learned in there.'

They arrived at the car and Kim pulled impatiently on the door handle before she heard the tell-tale beep of the unlocking mechanism.

Another couple of questions had established that Geraldine's kitchen had been fitted by none other than Jason Cross. They would have been heading straight there if the Brightman residence wasn't on the way.

'A bit coincidental that the same kitchen guy is linked to both homes.'

Oh yeah. She couldn't wait to see how he reacted to that line of questioning. She might get out one sentence before he was on the phone to his solicitor.

'She's had a bit of bad luck lately, eh?' Bryant asked.

Kim silently agreed. Geraldine's adopted daughter had been murdered, her mother was straight off *Toddlers and Tiaras* and seemed as sensitive to the situation as a toothbrush, and her long-term partner had been in a terrible accident.

And yet there was a quiet grace to the woman that Kim couldn't help but respect. Despite everything she maintained the integrity that another woman had been a better mother to her child than she could have been.

Kim wished her own mother had felt the same way. Perhaps Mikey would still be with her now. He might be married with children and—

'So, what are you gonna say to the Brightman family when we get there?'

Kim closed the lid of the box marked 'what might have been' and refocussed her attention on what she'd just learned.

'Right, when we get there this is what we're going to do… '

CHAPTER SIXTY

The door was answered by Anna, who looked surprised to see them.

She stepped aside for them to enter.

'Is the family in there?' Kim asked, nodding towards the lounge. She had already established that all necessary parties were present.

'Mr Brightman is in the garden. Sylvie and Rebecca are in the lounge.'

Without speaking further Kim headed outside, and Bryant entered the lounge.

The garden was not as big as Kim had expected. Or she had just become too used to the homes of the wealthy over the last few days. She found herself crying out for a tower block interview.

The patio area at the top of the space encompassed the same vista as inside the lounge, but the garden sloped down so that, three steps away from the patio, the view was lost.

The lawn that stretched before her was short and tidy, with two-tone stripes. Fruit trees softened the six-foot fence that embraced the property.

Kim found Mitchell Brightman sitting on a stone seat beside an elaborate fish pond. It was edged with expensive slate positioned perfectly to cover the black pond liner. A water feature at each end dribbled into the pool to provide oxygen bubbles.

The colourful fish swam languidly around the crystal clear water.

She was three feet away from him and he had not heard her approaching.

'Mr Brightman?'

He raised his head and offered a watered-down smile. Someday, she would like to see that smile on full wattage.

'This was Deanna's favourite place in the garden,' he said.

Kim took a seat beside him. She could understand why. The view was at the top but privacy was further down. From this seat Deanna would have been able to see the beauty of the house or gaze at the weeping willow trees and foxgloves.

Maybe the two of them had sat on this seat at sunset, sharing a bottle of wine and the events of their day. She liked to think so.

She regretted that she had to disturb his reverie and force him back to the horror of the present.

'Mr Brightman, I need to ask you something about your phone records.'

Was it just her imagination or had his back stiffened slightly? It occurred to her that he knew this question was coming.

'Your niece, Rebecca, called you at around nine o'clock on the night Deanna was murdered.'

He nodded but didn't look at her.

'She's my niece; that's not unusual, is it?'

Kim tried to think of a tactful way to phrase her next statement. 'Not at all but there were no other calls between the two of you and you don't seem all that close, if you don't mind me saying.'

The suspicion in her stomach was growing by the second.

'Oh, she's a typical teenager. Calls when she wants something,' he said, vaguely.

'But she hadn't called you any time before?' she pushed, gently.

He rubbed at his forehead.

'May I ask what she was calling for on Sunday night, Mr Brightman?'

He appeared to consider for a minute.

'She wanted me to collect her from a concert or something. Her mother was out with friends and the designated driver hadn't turned up.'

A bit too much detail. The first sentence was enough. The elaboration did not add the validity to his statement that he thought it did.

'And did you?' she asked.

'Did I what?'

'Collect her from the concert?'

He shook his head. 'No, I'd already had a couple of drinks and never drink and drive.'

There were many things that Kim detested but being treated like a fool was a personal hate. Especially when she was trying to find the person who had murdered his wife.

She stood. 'Would you mind coming inside for just a minute? There's something I need to ask you all together.'

Kim made sure she strode towards the house in front of Mr Brightman. He entered the lounge, and Bryant offered her a subtle signal with his hand as he turned towards her.

She noted for once Rebecca was not on her phone. Her lower teeth were scraping over her top lip every few seconds.

'Really sorry about this,' Kim said, looking from Mr Brightman to his niece. 'But there seems to be some disparity over the content of the conversation between the two of you on the night Deanna died.'

Sylvie's eyes widened. Clearly, she hadn't known about any conversation.

'It was about the concert,' Mitchell Brightman repeated, staring at Rebecca, urging her to agree. Rebecca had the good sense to realise she had already given a different story. She chose not to compound that error further.

She looked to her mother for guidance, but she could offer nothing. She hadn't known they'd spoken and they'd managed to fill nine and a half minutes on the phone, and yet she was still waiting to see them exchange one single word.

'Folks, we can't help you if you won't tell us the truth.'

Mitchell Brightman sat down but said nothing.

Rebecca's eyes were on him, curious, hopeful, pained.

He stared at the carpet and shook his head.

Sylvie stepped forward. 'He's her father,' she said quietly.

There was little emotion. Just a statement of fact.

Rebecca's eyes had not left her father's head. She was waiting… for something.

'It was only once,' Mitchell Brightman said.

Rebecca's crestfallen expression said that was not what she'd been waiting to hear.

She rose and fled from the room.

Sylvie looked stricken and ran after her.

Bryant coughed, and Mitchell Brightman raised his head. There was no malice in his face just sadness piled upon sadness.

'I'm sorry for not telling you the truth,' he said, flatly. 'I have denied her for so long it is a natural reaction.'

And she has been forced to deny you too, Kim thought, as it was the girl's natural instinct to lie as well.

'I'm assuming Deanna didn't know.'

'God, no. It would have destroyed her. You know she couldn't… '

Kim nodded and his words trailed away.

He stood and walked over to the window.

'It's such a cliché that Deanna and I were not getting along and Sylvie was there. I'm sorry for how that sounds but it's the truth.'

It seemed that now he'd found the truth he couldn't stop telling it.

'I hated what I'd done the second it was over, and I hated Sylvie too. Bad enough I betrayed my wife but she'd betrayed her sister. I felt that one act had deprived Deanna of the two people she loved and trusted the most.

'When Sylvie told me she was pregnant I begged her to have a termination, but she refused. Although, she did agree to keep the identity of Rebecca's father a secret.

'I can't help that every time I look at her I am reminded of what an absolute bastard I was to do that to the woman I loved… love.'

Kim had to respect his honesty but her sympathy was reserved for the girl that had run from the room.

'And the phone call?' Kim asked.

'Both Sylvie and Rebecca had been asking me to admit the truth to Deanna and I had flatly refused.' He moved from the window back to the sofa and stood behind it. 'Rebecca threatened to tell Deanna if I didn't do it.'

'The conversation was heated?'

He nodded. 'Very. It only ended when I cut her off. I made it clear that I would never tell my wife the truth and that if she wanted to break her aunt's heart I couldn't stop her.'

'Did Rebecca threaten your wife at all?'

He thought for a second. 'No. She said some rather unkind things but no direct threat, no.'

It was a possibility she'd had to explore.

Kim felt there was nothing more here to gain at the moment, yet there was something she was compelled to say.

'Mr Brightman, I appreciate you being so candid in your feelings towards Rebecca but you should bear one thing in mind. None of this is her fault.'

He looked at her for a long minute and then nodded.

Kim headed out of the lounge and met Anna in the hallway.

'Where's… ?'

'Sitting on the patio,' Anna said, without breaking her stride.

Kim felt like a weathervane in inclement conditions: inside, outside, inside.

She found Rebecca sitting on a patio chair, her feet up on another. It was clear from the smudged eye make-up that she'd been crying.

'Where's your mum?' Kim asked.

'Making tea. It'll help, apparently.'

She looked beyond the garden.

'I just want to go home.'

Kim sat beside her and stared in the same direction.

'Did you make any kind of threat towards Deanna on the phone that night?' Kim asked, just because she had to.

'No,' Rebecca said.

'But you threatened to tell her about Mitchell being your father?'

She sighed. 'Yeah, I said it but I never would have done it. The point was that I wanted him to do it. And if he had said yes I would probably have told him not to. I didn't want to hurt my aunt. She was a great woman. I loved her a lot. I just wanted… ' She looked to the ground. 'Oh, I don't know what I wanted,' she said, weakly.

Kim understood. 'You just wanted your father to acknowledge you, even if it was only between you both.'

She nodded and looked behind her to make sure they were still alone.

'My mum told me when I was twelve, and I really wish she hadn't. I was happy enough not knowing. The knowledge only brought pain. Before I knew the truth I wasn't hiding anything from anybody. I was just me. I wasn't someone's affair or a reminder of their deceit; I didn't know I was my mother's mascot of a man that would never love her back.

'That's what I got when she told me. I became the dirty little family secret, part of the cover up, and I just wanted to be a kid. All three of us were lying to my aunt, and although I wouldn't have hurt her for the world, some days I hoped and prayed it would get out there just to end the lies.'

Kim felt the girl's pain. Both Sylvie and Mitchell had turned their few moments of lust and passion into a bag load of shit for a twelve-year-old girl.

'As I just said in there, none of this is your fault. Just give it a little time, eh?'

Rebecca smiled tremulously, and Kim felt that despite her demeanour the tears were never far away.

Kim would have liked to say more but Sylvie and the tea appeared at the same time her phone began to ring. She bid them goodbye and started walking towards the front of the house before she answered the call.

'Stace?'

'Guv, yer might wanna goo see Jason Cross again, quick smart,' Stacey said excitedly. 'We already have his DNA. He was arrested eleven years ago and convicted: statutory rape.'

Kim stopped walking. 'Go on.'

'He was eighteen and the girl was fifteen. He said she lied about her age, and she said they were in a relationship. Parents said they dow care which it is: our daughter is a minor and he should have known better.'

Kim had started walking again. Her feet appeared to be directly linked to the speed of thoughts running around her head.

'Thanks, Stace, we're on our way,' Kim said, ending the call as Bryant appeared beside her.

She held out her hand for the keys.

'Time to say your prayers, Bryant. Because it's my turn to drive.'

CHAPTER SIXTY-ONE

Kim tried to quell her anger as she tore through two amber lights.

'Is the word idiot written on my head, Bryant?' she seethed. 'Why do people think they can blatantly lie to us and get away with it? Why can't they just get it all out there? Why not just let us decide what's relevant to the case?'

Bryant said nothing.

'Did he not think we would investigate, you know, like do our actual job?' she asked.

Bryant remained silent.

'Well?' she prompted. She wanted company in her anger.

'Sorry, guv. I thought all five of those questions were rhetorical.'

She sighed loudly. Sometimes his easy-going nature infuriated her. Some days she wanted him to explode.

'Okay. Just answer this one. How did he not think we were going to find out? How stupid… ?'

'Ahem, you're at it again,' he interrupted. 'But, to answer your first question, he may not have felt that something he did years ago had any bearing on events today. And to be fair—'

'It was rape,' she cried.

'Statutory rape,' he clarified.

'Bloody hell, Bryant. It's not called statutory sex with a person under the legal age who may or may not have consented and possibly looked older than her age. It's a conviction of statutory rape.'

'But we know the sex with Deanna was consensual.'

Kim shrugged. 'We have his description of the events that day, not hers.'

'She never reported any kind of assault,' he said.

'Oh yeah,' she offered, sarcastically. 'We all know that every sexual assault gets reported, don't we?'

'Umm… guv, you do know I'm not the enemy here?'

'Well stop acting like it then,' she snapped, even though it wasn't him she was angry with.

Those people were not involved in this case at all. Only they weren't here with her now. Both her mother and Alex were managing to reach her from behind bars.

Kim stayed silent and focussed on not killing people before she got to speak to the man himself.

She pulled into an empty driveway. The house was clearly empty.

'Damn it,' she raged, smacking both palms against the steering wheel. 'How the hell are we going to find… ?'

'Calm down,' Bryant instructed. 'Ring his office and ask where he is.'

'They're as bloody helpful as—'

'Just try,' he insisted.

Kim growled and took out her phone. She scrolled to the number called earlier in the week. It was answered on the second ring.

Kim rolled her eyes as she waited for the greeting to end.

'I need to know the whereabouts of Jason Cross,' Kim said, sharply.

Bryant frowned, groaned and took the phone from her hand.

She narrowed her eyes as he apologised on her behalf and asked politely if the woman could assist them in locating her boss. Her obvious hesitation was met with a plea of how urgent it was that they speak to him.

He ended the call.

'He sometimes eats his lunch at the reservoir,' Bryant said, handing her the phone.

'Information I could have found out if you'd let me finish my conversation,' she said, turning the car in the spacious drive.

Kim used the drive through Amblecote and past the Merry Hill shopping centre to calm down.

Damn those two women in her head who were making her short-tempered with everyone. However much she tried to focus on the case a portion of her mind kept wandering back to them.

'Thanks,' she said, quietly, as she took the turn into Netherton Reservoir.

'For what?' Bryant asked, surprised.

'For knowing when to keep quiet,' she said. 'And for taking the phone away from me,' Kim said as she drove slowly past the changing pavilion.

The place was deserted. She knew that the reservoir hosted water skiing, yachting and scuba diving at times, but there was no activity on the lake today.

'Guv… ?' Bryant said as two things became obvious very quickly.

There was no sign of a white van and a gangly male was running towards them while holding a phone to his ear. His bull terrier trailed behind.

They jumped out of the car at the same time.

'Over there,' the man screamed, breathlessly, pointing towards the water. He lowered the phone from his ear and pointed again. 'He's in there. One minute he was—'

'Who?' Bryant asked, although Kim didn't need the clarification.

She stared hard at the ramp that led into the water. The water was moving in circles but there was nothing there.

'A guy in a white van. One minute he was sitting there and the next—'

'How long?' Kim asked, heading towards the ramp.

'A minute, two… I'm not—'

'Call an ambulance,' she instructed as she met the gaze of Bryant.

'Damn,' he said, as they sprinted towards the water. Their jackets landed somewhere on the ground behind them.

The reservoir had a surface area of sixty-thousand square metres and hit a depth of fifteen metres in places.

The water exploded around them as they hit it together.

Kim blinked five times rapidly to adjust her eyes to the murky green water that had been disturbed and was swirling around them.

Kim knew he wouldn't be too far from the end of the ramp. A car could sink rapidly: anywhere from thirty seconds to two minutes.

Two strokes in and her right hand met with metal. She knew she had reached the back door, and a feeling of dread formed in the pit of her stomach.

She swam around to the front of the vehicle and drew level with the glass.

Jason Cross peered out at her with surprise. The water was up to his neck in the front of the van. She looked for the door handle and so did he.

He pressed down the old-fashioned push lock. She felt the mechanism engage beneath her fingers.

She looked through the glass to see Jason Cross shake his head at her.

Damn it, he was not going to make this easy for them.

She was fighting the instinct to gulp at the water.

She pushed herself up to the surface and coughed the water from her lungs.

Stars were exploding in her eyes, but she saw Bryant's head pop up ten feet to her left.

She knew they were running out of time. Jason Cross was now completely submerged.

By her reckoning she had no more than a couple of minutes to bring him to the surface before there was no point.

But the bastard had locked himself into the van. He was sealed inside his own vehicle, and even if he was capable he would do nothing to help her. If only he hadn't locked the bloody doors.

A thought hit her so quickly she had no time to share it with her colleague.

'Bryant, follow me,' she cried out, then took a deep breath and dived back down. She must have floated around the vehicle. As her hands worked to separate the water she hit the bonnet of the van.

As she'd suspected, the van was now filled with water and the eyes of Jason Cross were closed. His hair was floating around his face as the water continued to move inside the space.

Damn it. Even if her plan worked she could now be rescuing a corpse.

She swam to the back of the van and tried the door handle, praying it was not locked. Tradesmen in and out of their vans all day didn't always lock the door after themselves.

As she'd hoped, the handle moved freely in her grip but the door wouldn't budge. She knew from her old physics lessons that once the vehicle filled with water the doors could be opened.

Bryant appeared beside her. She pointed at the handle and nodded to indicate it was not locked.

He placed his hand over hers and they pulled together, but still nothing.

They were both floating and couldn't use their core strength. Kim used her feet to lock onto the van and crouched against it; her knees bent with her feet resting flat against the metal like a rock climber. Bryant followed her lead.

They tried again, and the door opened.

Kim could see that many of the tools had become dislodged from the metal racking on the side of the vehicle and had fallen to the van floor. She used the rear bumper to add momentum as she launched herself through the back of the van.

The headrests of the two front seats meant that she could not get through to where Jason Cross lay motionless.

She reached around the side of the chair and felt for the lock he had pressed down right in front of her.

Her fingers met with the rubber sleeve and she pulled upwards.

Her fingers slid from the rubber and the button stayed down. She tried again, this time digging in her nails. The button popped up.

Her lungs were throbbing in her chest. It felt as though she'd been holding her breath for hours, but it was probably no more than two minutes.

The shadow of Bryant was already at the door waiting but he would not be able to prise it open alone.

She used the soles of her feet to push against the headrests to propel her towards the rear door of the van.

She swam around to where Bryant was already in place with his hand poised on the handle. She turned herself into position and added her weight to his.

The door exploded open on first attempt.

She pulled the door as Bryant reached in and grabbed the inert form of Jason Cross.

Her colleague laid the form above his own and used his free hand to drive himself and his cargo towards the surface.

She knew his body would be feeling the same level of fatigue as her own but his mind would not allow him to dwell on it.

She swam alongside as they both headed towards the surface.

Their heads broke out of the water together.

They both gasped for air.

Bryant held his hand under the chin of Jason Cross and lowered the back of his own head back into the water as he began to backstroke his way towards the ramp.

Bryant could not see what she could.

She looked at the face of Jason Cross and knew immediately she was looking at a dead man.

CHAPTER SIXTY-TWO

Kim helped Bryant ease Jason Cross out of the water onto the grassy bank before her colleague collapsed on his back. The force of moving his own body weight and the body weight of another grown adult was exhausting. His breathing was deep and laboured and his eyes closed as the pain contorted his face.

'Bryant,' she shouted.

His eyes snapped open and saw the urgent question in her eyes.

He nodded that he was okay.

'Paramedics are coming, mate,' said a male voice behind Bryant. She could hear the sirens in the distance. She nodded at the thin man holding the lead of a bull terrier.

Kim was grateful because neither of them had the spare breath to make the call. She didn't have the time to wait for them to get here either.

The man before her was dead.

She gently eased Cross's head back with one hand beneath his chin and the other hand on his forehead to open his airway. She quickly confirmed that he was not breathing before lacing her fingers together.

She located the area close to his breastbone and lowered the heel of her right hand. She began to pump down around five to six cm at two pumps per second.

She counted to thirty and stopped.

She pinched his nose closed while taking a deep breath. She lowered her face, sealed her lips over his and blew into his cheeks until his chest rose.

By her calculations he had been submerged for three to four minutes. She knew she was fighting a losing battle.

She repeated the breath before lacing her hands again.

'Guv, you're wasting…'

Kim ignored him as she compressed all the way back to thirty. Her muscles began to deaden somewhere around the twenty-third.

'Guv, he's not gonna—'

'Bryant, shut up,' she growled, as she took in a deep breath.

The sirens had stopped beside the clubhouse but she could not stop until someone else was ready to take over.

Everything around her disappeared as she focussed every ounce of energy she could muster on the next round of compressions.

She blocked out the pain that was burning through her thigh and upper arm muscles and concentrated on willing them to carry on.

Each compression felt like muscle was being ripped from her bone. Her shoulders felt like they were going to collapse.

Bryant moved towards her.

'Guv… you need to stop—'

'Yes,' she cried, as a torrent of water escaped from the mouth of Jason Cross.

'Jesus Christ,' Bryant whispered, as Jason Cross continued to cough.

'Fucking hell,' the terrier man said, as an ambulance pulled up twenty feet away.

Kim felt elation surge through her body. She had felt death creeping along his flesh beneath her hands and her mouth.

With every second it had been claiming him, and she had brought him back. There was now breath in his body. Blood pumping through his veins. She had felt his departure and now he was back.

The paramedics moved her gently to the side as they took control of the patient whose eyes were wide within a deathly pallor. That was okay; his colour would come back.

Only now that she sat back would she allow her body to accept the fatigue that was trying to pin her down.

Bryant scooted over. 'You know, guv, sometimes your bloody determination—'

Kim didn't hear the rest of his words as the world suddenly turned black and she fell to the ground.

CHAPTER SIXTY-THREE

Alex admitted to a mild feeling of irritation. It wasn't yet growing to annoyance but the potential was there.

Her plan was twofold. One part of her plan was moving along perfectly. The other, not so much.

She had expected a second visit from the detective inspector by now. Alex knew that Kim's need to know everything would have driven her to try and find out what her mother had. Surely by now she knew her mother actually had nothing at all. This should have catapulted Kim straight back to her, demanding an explanation. And she had not yet appeared.

And this was part of the problem with having a worthy adversary. Now and again you were forced to adjust. Because of their history, Kim had a heightened awareness of her tactics unlike the pathetic people in here with her.

The fools had no clue just how many techniques she'd used on them already.

Alex knew that the key in successful manipulation lay in matching the technique to the victim.

The play of state transference had worked like a charm on Katie, the prison officer. She had easily been able to transfer her emotional state onto the woman and reach the emotional part of her psyche. During their last conversation, when Alex had used the woman's phone, she had managed to destroy the prisoner and guard relationship between them in seconds. They had become two women sitting around a table discussing the health of innocent babies.

The mind was such a vulnerable part of the body. People often had no clue just how much they were being manipulated in everyday life.

A normal person might shudder at the regimes in place in North Korea, where people were forced to listen to patriotic messages regularly. In truth, Alex respected the honesty of the situation. The ruling party made it clear they were going to tell you how to think. No need for veiled, clever, hidden messages designed to bypass the conscious mind and embed itself in the part of the iceberg below the water level.

In the western world the wish to control, persuade and manipulate was no less prevalent; it was just more underhand.

Marketing experts spent millions analysing the effect of para-linguistics, the voice tone, inflection, loudness, pitch. They studied the value of body language, voluntary, involuntary movements.

Luckily for Alex the mind was incredibly susceptible to influence and being controlled.

Alex had learned very early in her psychiatric training that everyone has a semi-fixed set of values and beliefs they have garnered since childhood. Persuading people to question themselves was a technique known as unfreezing; best used when people had suffered a loss or had been fired or were away from familiar surroundings. It was a technique that had worked well for her in prison.

Everyone could be controlled: you just had to find the right method for the right person and the right situation.

Although it was easier to do if the person would actually turn up, she reflected.

The techniques she wanted to use on Kim were burning a hole in her pocket.

'Hey, Alex, you okay?' Katie asked from the doorway.

Her smile was warm and her eyes were bright. Her hair was clean and tidy. She'd had a good night. Never mind.

Alex held out her hand. 'Give me your phone.'

The pretty face creased in confusion.

'I said, give me your phone. I need to use it.'

Katie stepped into the room as two prisoners walked past. 'I don't have—'

'Stop fucking me around, Katie, and pass me your mobile phone.'

Her face began to harden. 'I think you'd better watch how you're speaking to me.'

'And I think you'd better give me your phone whenever I ask for it,' Alex replied.

'I will do no such—'

'Yes, you will,' Alex said, pushing herself up from the bed. 'Or I will tell the warden that you have let me use it already. And then you'll lose your job.'

Katie hesitated, and Alex enjoyed the hatred that formed in her eyes as she realised just how badly she'd been played.

'And then how are you going to feed that little bastard of yours? His father isn't interested and you have no family. Unemployment benefit is not going to cover—'

'Be quick,' Katie said, taking it from her pocket and handing it over.

'Thank you,' Alex said, politely.

This time Katie didn't give her the space to make a private call like the last time.

She stood in the doorway with her arms folded and glared at her.

It made no difference to Alex as she wasn't going to speak.

She keyed in the number she had memorised a long time ago and then keyed in a message. She smiled as she hit the send key. There, that should do the trick.

Alex smiled and handed the phone back. 'There, that wasn't so difficult, was it?'

'Your niece was never ill, was she?'

Alex shrugged. 'Not that I know of. But thank you for your sympathetic words.'

Alex sat on the bed. It was a slow day and entertainment was scarce.

She looked Katie up and down. 'I'm surprised that you worked it out so quickly – what with trying to take care of a child unwanted by its father and trying to stay clean at the same time. It must be quite a challenge.'

Katie opened her mouth to speak but Alex was having too much fun. The floor belonged to her.

'I have the power here now, Katie, and the irony lies in the fact that you offered it to me on a plate the second you handed over that phone. I can say whatever I want to you and you can do nothing about it. You gave me your job, you pathetic cow.'

Alex chuckled as the mouth closed and the cheeks flushed. 'I mean, here you are, stuck in this job now. You probably wanted to be a police officer and you failed. This is the closest you can get, and if you lose your job for gross misconduct you'll probably lose your licence and won't even be able to guard your local off-licence on a Friday night.

'But it's okay because you have this baby at home that makes the destruction of all your dreams bearable. Because it's just the two of you, your love will be squandered all over that child. Over time you will suffocate him with your neediness and efforts for that affection to be reciprocated. Eventually he will grow away from you and leave home, and you'll be left with this shitty little job and a face that grew old while you weren't looking.'

Alex could see a slight trembling of the lower lip. It was gratifying to know she still had the gift.

The doubt and rage fought each other in her face.

She stuck out her chin defiantly. 'It's the last time, Alex. It's over.'

Alex's smile widened. When she spoke her words were quiet but deadly.

'Katie, you should know something about me. I always decide when it's over.'

CHAPTER SIXTY-FOUR

Kim was pleased to feel the fresh clothes warming her skin as she headed back towards the office.

A warm shower soothing her tired muscles had been just the thing to put some distance between her and the blackout at the water's edge.

She had only been out for a few seconds but long enough to see the panic on the face of her colleague when she'd opened her eyes – right before she'd shoved the paramedic away from her.

Bryant often told her she pushed herself too hard, but when there was a dead man lying before you, how hard was too hard?

She couldn't help the sliver of pride that surged through her at the knowledge that Jason Cross was still alive. The gnawing ache in her muscles would remind her of that fact for the rest of the day.

She was aware of Bryant's watchful gaze falling upon her as she stepped back into the office.

She didn't normally conduct evening briefings but today had been that kind of day.

'Okay, I'm sure Bryant has updated you on the fact that Mr Cross today tried to take his own life.'

'Admission of guilt?' Dawson asked.

Kim shrugged. She'd wondered the same thing herself as a hundred needles of water had rained down on her.

'Or was it 'cos he knew we'd uncover his charge of statutory rape?' Stacey asked.

'Could be,' Kim said. 'I'm betting his wife doesn't know, and I'm pretty sure he wouldn't want her to.'

'Never even got to ask him about that second kitchen,' Bryant said.

'The what?' Dawson asked, sharply. He hated not knowing everything. It sometimes irritated Kim but she was the exact same way. It would serve him well later in his career.

'Geraldine recently had a new kitchen fitted but couldn't remember the name of the guy. The physical description she gave us matched.'

'You're thinking Jason Cross?' Dawson asked.

'A bit coincidental,' Kim said. She didn't like coincidences.

'DNA should be back tomorrow,' Stacey said. 'I think if I chase them any more they'll block me and teck out an injunction.'

Kim turned to Dawson. 'Anything on the friends and acquaintances of Maxine?'

'Nothing yet, guv. It is starting to look a bit like she sometimes turned to prostitution to fund her habit, so I don't know if people I'm talking to are friends, customers, pimp or what. And this Flem guy is a homeless wanderer that splits his time between here and Leeds.'

'Any whisperings about her relationship with her m— with Geraldine?'

He shook his head. 'No one seems to know anything about that. It seems our Maxine kept her business private.'

'Anything else?' Kim asked.

'Still cor trace this phone number,' Stacey said, nodding towards her computer screen. 'The caller had a two-minute conversation with Deanna a matter of hours before she died but the call just goes to voicemail.'

'Contact the family and her colleagues and see if it's a number they recognise,' Kim advised. 'But do it tomorrow. We'll start fresh in the morning.' She looked pointedly at Bryant. 'And that means all of you.'

He nodded his understanding, and stood. He'd managed to blag a pair of plain black trousers and a black T-shirt from the uniform stores.

He picked up the carrier bag containing his wet clothes and headed out behind the other two.

She stepped into The Bowl and saw that the red light on her mobile phone was flashing receipt of a message.

One swipe and she saw the number attached to the speech bubble.

The number was not one she recognised but when she tapped into the text she was left in no doubt as to who had sent her the message.

The words made her blood run cold. She grabbed for her jacket and ran.

CHAPTER SIXTY-FIVE

17 December 2007

Dear Diary,

Oh, where to begin?

I lay awake all night picturing what I would do to her next, imagining all kinds of ways I could torture her and pleasure myself.

The ideas and fantasies were like flashes of delicious colour in my mind as I thought through the detail of every single one. All day I was barely able to contain myself.

Today I helped with the search.

Over a hundred people were there. I was impressed with the turnout in such cold, nasty weather. A lady brought flasks of tea. Another brought sandwiches. There was an air of camaraderie. Individuals together for a purpose, a goal. People who hadn't seen each other for months met and shook hands, hugged, shared a joke and then quietened as they remembered where they were. And why.

Her mother, father and brother were surrounded by black uniforms. Their eyes were red as they looked around, as though she may just magically appear before them. As though the effort that was being expended by everyone turning up would be enough for her to materialise. I ached to tell them that she wouldn't.

They were hoping she'd be found and yet praying she wouldn't.

And then there was me. I knew exactly where she was. Every single person, police, family members, volunteers, voyeurs were all searching for one thing only. And I knew exactly where it was. I could hardly contain my smile at my own cleverness. Seriously.

Twenty minutes in and I left just as soon as my entertainment waned.

I was too excited to get home and begin. I had too much to do.

When I opened the door she seemed almost pleased to see me. There was relief and then fear and then hope and then fear. I offered her no response. I no longer had any interest in her face. She was not a person to me. She was a thing. She was my thing.

And I could do with her exactly as I wished.

CHAPTER SIXTY-SIX

Kim tapped on the door and waited. She could hear the collection of male voices that sounded from the room immediately to the left of the property. A single familiar voice reached her as he moved through the hallway towards the front door.

'Don't worry, I'll get it,' he called.

Kim knew the voice well and smiled as the door opened.

'Kim,' he said, looking puzzled.

'David,' she acknowledged in return. He stood still looking at her.

She stared back. 'Umm… now the introductions are complete, may I come in?'

'Of course,' he said, stepping back, allowing her room to enter.

Her presence at Hardwick House was not a totally alien occurrence. Since meeting during the earlier investigation into Alex she had visited a couple of times. At one time there may have been an ember of a spark between the two of them, but it had quickly died once they had spent hours talking about their shared love of motorcycles. Being friends had been the best thing for both of them. And as Bryant had pointed out – David Hardwick was far too nice for her.

David was the housemother for a privately funded facility that housed males released from prison and attempted to reintegrate them into a world that had moved on in their absence. The average stay was around six months.

Alexandra Thorne had offered her services as a psychiatrist free to the facility as an apparent act of benevolence. In truth it had been the perfect arena in which to sharpen her manipulating skills to get what she wanted. By her own admission she had used the occupants of Hardwick House as target practice.

Some people had survived her manipulations and some had not been so lucky.

Kim followed David through to the kitchen. He pointed to the coffee machine and looked at her.

She nodded.

They also shared a love of good coffee.

His fair hair was even lighter than the last time she'd seen him. She realised it had been bleached by the sun and that it had been more than six months since her last visit.

She opened her mouth to apologise and closed it again. No apology was needed between them.

'So, what brings you—?'

'David, where is Shane?' Kim asked, unable to hold the words in any longer.

David looked stunned. 'Sorry… why would you ask… ?'

Kim took out her phone and showed him the text message. It read simply, *'How is Shane?'*

David stepped back against the counter. 'Is that from Alex?'

Kim nodded. He understood her power much more easily this time. The first time she had come to him, he had struggled to understand why a person like Alex did not have red horns and a pointy tale. The fact that she was beautiful and charming had always assisted Alex in her endeavours. Although she had never quite managed to get her claws into David.

Initially, he had been disbelieving of her motivations and capabilities despite the fact he had sensed that something just wasn't quite right with the psychiatrist who was so generous with her time to a bunch of ex-convicts.

'He's still in prison, as far as I know. You remember—'

'Of course I remember,' Kim said, as David turned back towards the coffee maker.

Shane was perhaps the person most damaged by Alex. She had manipulated him into doing unspeakable things and had cruelly sent him straight back to prison once he had served his purpose.

David had tried to visit him, attempted to find out what had happened for Alex to lodge an assault charge against the young man, but Shane had refused to see him and requested that David never visit him again.

David had enough to do with the men that wanted his assistance than to continually chase after people who did not.

'Have you seen her?' he asked.

Kim nodded and sighed.

'Is that a good idea?'

She laughed. 'Of course not but you know how she works.' She pointed to her phone. 'She knows I would want to know what's happened to Shane, another one of her damaged souls.'

David didn't turn when he spoke. 'You weren't responsible, Kim,' he said. 'She was experimenting here on Shane way before she crossed your radar. I was the one who missed it here, not you.'

He said the same thing every time but she still felt responsible. If only she could have stopped the woman before she left the trail of carnage that she had.

'Okay, enough of the guilt party,' Kim said. 'There's only you and me here so it's just plain sad.'

He nodded his agreement but she knew that, just like her, he would question why it took so long for him to spot the type of person she really was and mourn for the people she had destroyed in the meantime.

David took out his phone. 'Let me call Stephen,' he said, referring to the welfare coordinator who matched prisoners with Hardwick House.

As he put the phone to his ear Kim sensed a presence in the doorway behind her. She didn't need to turn to know who it was. A smile began to spread across her face.

'Hello, Dougie,' she said, gently.

Dougie didn't fit the Hardwick House criterion. He was in his early twenties, autistic. He had been thrown out of home aged twelve and had somehow survived out of skips and bins until David had caught him out back. As David always said, 'Dougie's room was for life', and, as he and his brother shared the foundation responsible for Hardwick House, it was a claim that he could safely make.

She heard his trainer-clad feet shuffle into the room behind her. She stood and reached up to place her palm against his cheek. His eyes didn't move from their fixed point on the ceiling but a small smile rested on his lips. His palm found her cheek. Initially, it was the way she had shown him that she was no threat. It was the way she had shown him that she was trying to save his life at the canal side, and it had been their form of greeting ever since.

'Kim... o... o... o... ok?' he asked. He blinked on each 'o' that sounded.

'I'm fine, Dougie, and you look very well too.'

He nodded and continued nodding as he turned and left the room. Kim felt a rush of affection as he left. That young man would never understand just how instrumental he had been in helping her to get Alexandra Thorne behind bars.

She looked back to David, who was listening intently to his contact. The frown on his face lit the anxiety in her stomach. The conversation was taking far too long for a simple confirmation.

'Thanks, mate, appreciate it,' he said, ending the call.

David shrugged. 'He's going to do some checking and ring me back.'

'Damn,' Kim said, as a suspicion started growing in her mind.

'Is it really so bad if he's out of prison, Kim?' David asked. 'We both know that place is going to kill him.'

'Depends on why he's out, doesn't it?' she answered, before voicing what they were both thinking. 'And if she's managed to get to him again.'

CHAPTER SIXTY-SEVEN

Kim had just kicked off her boots when the sound of the door startled her. Even Barney's head shot up and then looked to her for guidance. Normally, the only person that knocked her door was Bryant, and she tended to have a sixth sense about when he would appear.

She pulled the door open and was surprised to see Gemma standing there.

It took Kim a few seconds to catch up, which was long enough for the girl to see the confusion.

'You forgot,' she stated moodily as she turned to walk away.

'No, no, it's just been a long day,' Kim said, finally recalling their conversation the previous night. In her mind it had taken place two weeks ago.

'I was just about to throw in a pizza,' she said, as the girl took another step away.

Gemma paused.

'It's nothing fancy,' Kim said, feeling terrible that she'd forgotten her offer of a meal.

'Well, I don't wanna be any fucking trouble,' she said caustically.

Kim couldn't help the smile that played around her lips. Oh, she already knew this kid well.

She also knew that she could do with a good meal. Unfortunately, for that the girl would need to go elsewhere but for one night Kim could make sure she wasn't out doing anything dangerous in order to eat.

Barney sat in the doorway to the kitchen. His tail was tensing as though it wanted to wag but there was doubt in his eyes.

'It's okay, boy,' Kim said, as Gemma followed her through.

Barney headed towards Gemma cautiously. Gemma held out her hand.

'I remember you from the other night,' she said, smiling at the dog.

Barney accepted one stroke of the head and walked away.

Other than herself Barney appeared to prefer men. When Bryant visited, the dog wouldn't leave him alone.

'I didn't think you'd come, to be honest,' Kim said, opening the freezer door.

'I wasn't fucking gonna, to be honest, but there was a gap in my social calendar.'

Kim wished she couldn't almost quote what was going to come out of her mouth next. If not the exact words then the attitude and the tone.

Kim was about to respond when her phone sounded from behind her. She saw immediately that it was David.

'Gotta take this,' Kim said, reaching for the phone.

'Fuck this,' Gemma said, standing up.

Kim skidded the pizza box across the breakfast bar towards her. 'How high and for how long?' she said, switching on the ignition to the oven.

'You fucking kidding me?' Gemma asked.

'About what?'

'You don't know how to cook a pizza?'

Kim shrugged. 'Pretty much like everything else: wallop it in on the middle shelf and take it out when it's brown, or some other colour,' she said, pressing the answer button on the phone.

'Hey,' she said as a greeting.

'Shane's out,' David said, without preamble.

Kim closed her eyes for a second. She'd suspected as much. 'How?' she asked.

'Case review, prompted by new information.'

'What new information?' she asked, glancing at Gemma, who was trying not to listen to a conversation she couldn't fail to overhear.

'An admission from Alex that she may have overreacted to the incident at her office. His parole was revoked because of the incident with Alex. With her retracting her statement and a very expensive lawyer on the case—'

'Don't tell me, Alex's lawyer?' she asked.

'Bingo. He was released three months ago.'

'Shit, shit, shit,' Kim said. The woman had got Shane thrown back in prison and released again just because it suited whatever sick game she was playing this time. Alex's willingness to manipulate people's lives to her will should not have surprised her anymore. And yet it still did.

Kim turned towards the window. 'You know she's controlling him again, don't you?'

David sighed heavily before speaking, signalling his agreement.

'I'm going to see if I can find out where he was released to,' he said.

Kim could hear the concern in his voice. Neither of them believed Shane deserved to be in prison but was being tied to Alex any better fate?

'Thanks, David. Let me know,' she said, ending the call.

Her first instinct was to get on the bike and ride the streets looking for him. Although they'd never met she had seen his photograph in the newspapers when he'd been returned to prison on Alex's instruction. If she hadn't had a green-haired kid in her kitchen, staring at her dolefully, it's what she probably would have done.

She had no idea what she would do if she found him but the first part of the plan was good.

'You're not joking, are you?' Gemma asked, frowning. 'You really can't cook?'

'Look, I'm no Nigella but I can manage a bloody pizza,' she said, defensively.

'Well… ' Gemma said, reading the back of the box.

Kim opened the freezer again realising that one pizza was not going to go very far.

'What about these?' she asked, holding up a bag of frozen burgers.

Gemma looked at her like she was mad. 'Got any chips, fries?'

Kim delved further. 'Potato wedges?'

'More like it,' Gemma said, sliding the pizza box towards her. 'Pizza needs thirty-five minutes from frozen on gas mark five.'

'Okay,' Kim said as she unwrapped it and threw it onto the top shelf.

She emptied half the bag of wedges onto a baking tray and put them on the middle shelf.

'You're proper clueless, aren't you?' Gemma asked, shaking her head. 'How the fuck did you get to be bacon?'

Kim held up her hands. 'What?'

Gemma got off the stool and came around to the cooker. She took the oven glove and opened the oven door.

'You're cooking dough on the top shelf and potato on the bottom. Heat rises so the top shelf will be cooked way before the middle shelf.' She shook her head with disgust. 'Seriously?'

Kim shrugged.

Gemma swapped the baking trays over and closed the door.

'Now they have a fighting chance of being cooked at the same time.' She stepped back to the stool and eyed Kim suspiciously. 'You sure you're a copper?'

Kim smiled. 'Yes.'

'You any good at it?' Gemma asked, suspiciously.

'My boss seems to think so,' Kim answered. Well, maybe not her temporary boss, but Woody certainly had no complaints. Okay, not many.

'Hmm… fucking shocker.'

'My ability to solve crimes does not depend on my ability to cook a pizza,' Kim explained.

'Good fucking job.'

Kim tipped her head. 'Do you have to use that word in every sentence?'

She thought for a moment then nodded. 'Yeah.'

'Did you get all your stuff sorted?' Kim asked.

'Stuff?'

'From having your bag taken.'

Gemma rolled her eyes. 'What's to fucking sort? Luckily my f… stocks and share certificates were in the Hermes bag I left at home.'

Kim laughed out loud. Sarcasm was a humour she had always enjoyed. She appreciated the fact the girl pronounced it 'her mez'.

'Drink?' Kim offered.

Gemma's eyes lit up.

'I don't keep alcohol. I was thinking coffee or I have tea… somewhere.'

'Tap water,' Gemma said.

Kim took a glass and filled it.

Gemma nodded towards the oven. 'You gonna check on them?'

Kim followed her gaze. 'Why, are they going to do a trick?'

Gemma sighed and again came around the other side.

'Thanks for offering to cook me a meal,' Gemma mumbled as she opened the oven door.

She took out the tray of wedges. 'Do you have a spatula?'

Kim shrugged. 'Unless it came attached to a 1600 cc engine, I don't have the first clue.'

'Do you even have knives and forks?' Gemma asked incredulously.

'Somewhere.'

Gemma checked a couple of drawers.

'This is what I'm after.'

She held up a tall utensil with a wide flattened end. Kim suspected it had come free with something. She certainly couldn't remember walking into a shop and thinking that she needed one.

Gemma turned the potato wedges and shook the tray around.

She reached for the salt and offered a light sprinkling of the condiment before putting the wedges back in the oven.

'So, what are you doing to earn money to eat?' Kim asked.

'Whatever I need to,' Gemma answered honestly.

Kim had now lost count of the sentences that had not contained the 'F' word.

'Your mum… ?'

'Is a bit busy right now.'

'You get on?'

Gemma thought and then nodded. 'She loves me and I love her and once I learned to lower my expectations we got along just fine.'

'Sometimes—'

'Boring subject. Can we talk about something else, like why you made a motorbike reference?'

'You interested?'

Gemma shook her head and smirked. 'Not really. Just changing the subject.'

Kim appreciated her honesty. She nodded towards the garage door. 'Take a look, anyway.'

She had asked the girl over for the purpose of giving her a meal not a reforming session. It was her life to live.

'Why, what's in there?' Gemma asked, trying to look beyond Kim.

'Go and see.'

Gemma hopped off the stool and stepped over Barney to stand in the doorway.

'Shut the fucking door… oops, sorry,' she said, stepping over the scattered bike parts on the floor and stopping at the Kawasaki Ninja.

Kim smiled as Gemma gingerly touched the polished metallic paint on the petrol tank.

'It's even better in the light and your cool points just jumped up a level,' Gemma said, now stroking the black leather seat.

'Oh good, 'cos that was really beginning to worry me.'

Gemma frowned. 'Be careful, someone might be planning on having this away.'

'Huh?'

'There was a guy… over the road, earlier, when I came. Just standing and watching—'

'Was he watching my house?' Kim asked, urgently.

Gemma shrugged.

'What did he look like?'

'Tall, thin, mousy hair,' Gemma answered.

'Where exactly?' Kim asked.

'Behind the lamp post.'

'Wait here,' she said, as she sprinted through the house and out the front door. Her eyes locked on the lamp post. A grey-haired lady was walking two white Westies but there was no other soul in sight.

Kim paused for a moment, examining every inch of the street. She found nothing out of the ordinary.

Her heart was beating wildly even though she was not exerted in the slightest.

Calm down, Stone, she told herself as the weakness in her legs developed into a tremble.

She leaned back against the wall that fronted her property.

Her head was trying to take control and was insisting that it could have been nothing to do with her at all. It could have been something completely innocent.

But her gut disagreed. Her gut said that the stranger was Shane and that he had definitely been sent by Alex.

CHAPTER SIXTY-EIGHT

For some reason Shane got comfort from watching her. There was a beauty that he hadn't expected to find. He wasn't thinking of the natural beauty of her unmade face but of what he saw beyond that. There was a grace, an elegance, to her movement that was poetic yet unapologetic. He felt he could watch her for the rest of his life and not get bored.

There was a vulnerability when she thought no one was looking. When her face fell into normal repose her default expression appeared to be studious. There was always something running around that busy little mind.

Watching her had provoked something he had never felt before. It wasn't in his trousers; he felt nothing for her sexually. He felt nothing for anyone sexually.

But the feeling was in his stomach. As though somewhere in the ball of darkness was a pinprick of light.

And it went when he moved away from her house.

Years ago he may have cherished the feeling, fanned it. But not anymore. Joy and light were now lost to him.

It was like the delicious torture of a flame against your fingertips, right before it went out.

It wouldn't have lasted. It couldn't have lasted. And she would have disappointed him in the end.

No one could make him clean.

He stepped back as her front door opened. The young girl came out, turned right and disappeared from view.

But she stayed in the doorway. Her eyes looked to the right and then to the left and then right towards where he was standing.

His breath caught in his throat. She was looking right at him. But she couldn't be. He had stood in that very spot she stood now and knew his hiding place was secure.

But her face. Her expression. It was soft, gentle, concerned. A slight frown and drop of the mouth held a question.

She looked left and right once more before sighing and stepping back inside.

The door closed behind her, and Shane let the breath escape from his body.

He would swear she had been looking for him.

But none of it mattered anymore, he thought, as he took out his phone.

There was no new message.

That meant it was time to activate plan B.

CHAPTER SIXTY-NINE

Kim found herself eager to get on with the morning briefing.

Since learning of the person watching her house the previous night she had not wanted to stay in one place. A restless energy had taken over her body and was propelling her forward. Her gut told her that the mystery man Gemma had mentioned was Shane, and he was not watching her for any reason she would like.

She paced the walkway between the two sets of desks as she spoke.

'Stace, go,' she instructed.

'The DNA for Jason Cross is a match. It was definitely his hair in Deanna Brightman's car.'

Kim was not surprised by this news. She wondered if their relationship had exceeded that one fumble when his clothes had got dirty.

She would be stopping by the hospital later to clarify the reason for the man's suicide attempt. Her earlier call had confirmed that he was alive and conscious if not very communicative.

'Keep at that phone number,' Kim said, nodding towards the yellow Post-it note. 'Whoever made that call may have been the last person to speak to Deanna before she died.'

Stacey nodded. 'Already sent chasing emails to the networks.'

'Good work,' Kim said. She turned to Dawson. 'Kev?'

'Getting nowhere quick,' he said. 'But I'll stay on the Maxine angle. I'm gonna check on the local hostels and drop-in centres,' he said. 'Although Maxine wasn't officially homeless she must have been eating and sleeping somewhere.'

Kim agreed. 'Good idea, Kev.'

Kim ran through her head the things they had learned yesterday and a sudden thought came to mind.

'Stace, find out about the accident that involved Geraldine's partner. That family is sure having a lot of bad luck recently.'

'Gotcha, boss,' Stacey said.

Kim was happy that all parties knew what they were doing. 'And we are heading over to the hospital to see our kitchen...'

'No, we're not.' Bryant said.

Kim's head snapped around.

'Yes, we are.'

Bryant shook his head. 'Not unless you want to go against the direct instruction of Baldwin, who states quite clearly in this email that Jason Cross is not to be approached.'

'What the...?' Kim came to stand behind Bryant, who scrolled to the top of the message for her benefit.

She took out her phone and dialled Lloyd House. His assistant, Martha, informed her he was in meetings all morning and could not be disturbed.

Oh yeah, I'll bet, she thought, ending the call. She'd see about that.

She scrolled to the email on her phone and began typing in a reply.

'Guv, what are you doing?' Bryant asked. 'This instruction is about as clear as it gets.'

She half smiled and carried on typing. She read back the text:

> 'Sorry, Sir, didn't see your message, am about to enter the ward right now. Will only keep him a minute.'

She pressed send and counted backwards from ten.

She got to three when her phone rang. She stepped out of the squad room and into The Bowl.

'Stone, do not enter that ward,' Baldwin said, without preamble.

'May I ask why not, sir? I'm right here and—'

'This is a direct instruction, Stone. Jason Cross, via his lawyer, has filed police brutality charges against you. He has three broken ribs.'

Kim's mouth fell open. 'I saved his damn life.'

'We know that, Stone. There is not a question that this will be dismissed but right now that piece of paper is a brick wall between you and Jason Cross. Got it?'

Kim shook her head with disbelief but she knew to ignore this instruction would cost her her job.

'Got it, sir,' she said, ending the call.

She shook her head disbelievingly as she recalled the effort she'd put into saving his life. Her shoulders were still holding onto the memory now.

She knew it was not a serious lawsuit but it had served its purpose as far as Jason Cross was concerned. It had put him beyond her reach.

She stepped back into the general office and was greeted by a wall of silence. Dawson's head rested in his hands, Stacey stared at the computer screen, and Bryant looked as though he was about to throw up.

'What is it?' she asked, looking from one to the other.

'Just heard back from Staffordshire Constabulary. They've got another one,' Stacey said, still not looking at her.

She looked to Bryant for clarification.

His eyes were filled with sadness and his voice was barely a whisper.

'And this one was a child.'

CHAPTER SEVENTY

The house they sought lay in a place called Bramshall on the outskirts of Uttoxeter.

The journey on the M6 had been made in silence. Kim's aggravation at Jason Cross had paled against the horror of what they'd learned about the death of a seven-year-old boy named Tommy Howard nine months earlier.

For Kim, the case had taken a dark, sinister turn. Until now the victims had been adult females: different in just about every way possible but fully grown adults. That they were dealing with someone who could coldly murder a child had both shocked her and chilled her to the bone.

She had detected a definite lack of emotion in the murder of Deanna Brightman and Maxine Wakeman but perhaps she had been wrong. How did one drive a blade into the flesh of a child?

'Have we underestimated our killer?' Bryant asked.

His voice was a sudden intrusion into the solitary rumblings of her mind.

'I don't know, Bryant, but I know one thing for sure: we certainly don't understand him.'

A pall had fallen over them all since Stacey had received the email. She knew that the two colleagues she couldn't see would be carrying around the weight of young Tommy's death. And it would stay with them until they found the person responsible. She had left Stacey trying to contact the DI heading the case.

Herself and Bryant had wasted no time in heading towards the family residence.

'Not sure where this house is, guv,' he said, driving past a single storey chapel for the second time. 'The only thing here is—'

'It is the chapel,' Kim said, peering closer at a numbered sign to the right of the door.

They didn't even consider their normal 'guess the house price' game. By silent agreement this was a meeting they wanted to conduct as swiftly as possible.

The door was opened by an attractive female wearing a floral dress and a short pink cardigan. The white hair was cut in a stylish bob with a blunt fringe. The ageing face held a touch of foundation and powder. A single pearl hung around her neck.

Kim held up her identification as Bryant introduced them.

Her expression changed from neutral to hopeful.

'Have you found the person responsible for Thomas's... ?' her words trailed away as Kim quickly shook her head. She didn't want the woman to get false hope.

Her face settled back to neutral as she stepped aside. 'Please, come in,' she said.

Kim did so and was suddenly hit by the desolation of the property. The furnishings were beautiful and expensive. The stained glass windows had been expertly preserved. She could almost choke on the good taste. But the silence was deafening.

'Beautiful house,' Bryant observed.

'You think so?' Barbara Howard asked, surprised. 'Personally, I hate it,' she said honestly. 'Much too big for just me,' she said, traversing the stone hallway.

Kim followed, noting the limp that signalled, most likely, a recent hip operation.

'I have a cleaner five days a week and a gardener three days a week, and they care for it much more than I do.'

'But why do you stay?' Bryant asked, conversationally.

'Memories, officer. Many of my memories are here. I have no wish to restart my life again. I've done that already. I'm happy to live amongst the dead until it's my time.'

There was no self-pity in the words. Simply facts. This lady was waiting to die.

'Thomas was your grandson?' Kim asked as they reached a kitchen that would have been lighter and airier if not for an elm tree right outside the window.

Mrs Howard took the easy chair that faced away from the tree.

'Yes, Inspector. We took custody of Thomas when our daughter died in childbirth.'

'The child's father?' Bryant asked.

'Killed in Afghanistan three months before his son was born.'

Kim nodded her understanding.

'And your husband?'

Mrs Howard offered her a smile. 'Inspector, why are you here?' she asked. 'Forgive my bluntness but at my age tact and diplomacy matter less.'

Kim smiled in return. She appreciated directness. It was a trait she possessed herself. She only wished she had Mrs Howard's grace.

'We are from West Midlands Police, and we are taking a fresh look at the case of your grandson,' Kim answered.

'Why?' she asked, simply.

'Because we feel we may have something to add to the current investigation,' Kim responded.

'I can see in your face that you will reveal nothing more and I shall respect that,' she said. 'And as I've already explained that I don't like to waste time, continue with your questions.'

'Thank you,' Kim said. 'You were saying about your husband?'

'He died four weeks after our grandson was murdered. He adored that child to distraction, just as he had adored Jennifer.'

'May I ask how your husband died?' Kim asked. Some of the families were meeting with a lot of bad luck.

'A heart attack, Inspector,' she said, before glancing outside.

Kim felt a growing admiration for this stoic woman who had faced more loss than the average person in the last eight years of her life, and there was no plea for sympathy in sight.

'Of course, I loved the child too. He was my grandson but I'm honest enough to admit to some bitterness when we first lost Jennifer.'

'Really?' Kim asked.

'Oh yes, Inspector. This was supposed to have been our time. My husband worked hard all his life. I feel like the majority of mine was spent wishing away years until retirement so I would finally have my husband to myself for a few years.

'When Jennifer died it almost killed us both, but having Thomas gave us a reason to go on. I suppose he became our reason to live, to help us through the pain and loss of our only child.

'But eventually, as my heart healed around the loss of Jennifer, I found myself yearning for my husband. Unfortunately, my husband didn't share my view. He retired and poured every ounce of love and attention into Thomas.'

Kim appreciated the woman speaking so candidly.

'I understand how painful this must be but may we ask about the day Thomas—'

Mrs Howard held up her hand and nodded. Nine months and she still couldn't hear certain words in the same sentence as his name.

'It was a school trip to a petting zoo in Uttoxeter. One moment he was there and the next they found his backpack discarded a hundred metres from the picnic area. It was chaos. The zoo was closed down after the initial search proved fruitless. No one knew how to do a full search of the area. Nothing like this had ever happened before. It was thirty minutes until the police were called and another forty-five until a full search was coordinated. Members of the public, zoo staff and teachers were all trampling over the same area.'

She shook her head. 'His body was found an hour later in a ditch that served as a border on the other side of the farm.'

Kim accepted the woman's silence. It was a day that would play through her head for ever.

'I saw him, you know,' she said, suddenly. Her eyes were now fixed on the wall ahead. 'His body seemed smaller than it had when I'd kissed him goodbye no more than three hours earlier. I saw the wound too. So much blood for one wound.'

She suddenly turned to Kim. 'Do you know what I remember from that day?'

'What?' Kim asked, hoarsely.

'The stain on his crisp blue shirt. It was the proportion. The size of the stain to the size of the shirt. Everything about him was small. His body, his clothes, his feet, his arms, his hands. Everything except that stain.'

Kim felt a shudder run through her. It was not a memory to cherish.

Kim felt that the link between these murders was getting further and further away. The disparity between her victims was really churning her gut.

'I mean, he was just a little boy. What could he possibly have done to hurt anyone?'

Kim felt a pang of sympathy for this woman who had so many painful, unanswered questions and no one to share them with.

'Do you not have any other family here, Mrs Howard?' Kim asked.

She shook her head. 'There is only my husband's sister, and she lives down in your neck of the woods. We're not close.'

Kim frowned. 'I'm sorry, Mrs Howard, I assumed this was the area you'd always lived,' she said. There was no trace of any accent in the woman's speech.

'Not at all, Inspector. We are originally from Kidderminster and only moved here following my husband's retirement last year. In fact, I'm surprised that you didn't meet my husband during the course of your work.'

Kim looked again at the grandeur of the house as a feeling began to build in her stomach.

'And what was your husband's job, Mrs Howard?'

The woman smiled. 'I would have thought you would have known that, Inspector. My husband was a Crown Court judge.'

CHAPTER SEVENTY-ONE

Kim walked slowly to the car. The thoughts were coming thick and fast.

'Damn it,' she cried, slapping Bryant on the arm.

'Bloody hell, guv,' he said, startled.

She stopped and turned as the realisation dawned on her.

'Mrs Howard asked what Tommy could have done to hurt anyone. The answer is nothing. He couldn't possibly have done.' She shook her head, angrily. 'We've been looking in the wrong direction for the link. It's not the victims that are the same, Bryant, it's their bloody loved ones.'

He frowned as he considered her words.

She ploughed on. 'Look at Deanna, Maxine and little Thomas Howard. They have nothing in common: one male and two females, no similarity in age, sex or background.'

She felt the stirrings of discovery in her stomach alongside the disgust. Finally, something about this case that made sense.

She got in the car. 'The link is the family members.'

The thoughts were coming thick and fast. She took out her phone. Stacey answered immediately.

'Stace, drop what you're doing. Focus on the families. Mitchell Brightman is a prosecutor; Geraldine is a psychiatrist who occasionally testified for the CPS; Harold Howard was a judge. I need to know if there is any case that involved these three people.'

The line went silent for a second, and Kim could picture her colleague looking at the board.

'The family members,' Stacey breathed.

'Get Kev back to help,' Kim instructed. If these people were all linked to one case there was the possibility that it wasn't over yet. More people could be in danger.

Kim ended the call, as Bryant headed through the tree tunnel.

'Think about it, Bryant. How better to make your enemy suffer when you feel that death would be too simple?'

Bryant still looked doubtful.

'Look at Geraldine. Her long-term partner was involved in a hit-and-run. As the person closest to Geraldine, Belinda could have been first choice but she's been housebound ever since. Our killer can't get to her so he went for the next best thing.

'He's going for the people that mean the most to his real victims. He wants them to suffer loss and heartbreak. Death is just too simple.'

Bryant said nothing. She could feel his doubt through his silence, but she knew she was right. It explained why the murders had lacked the emotion normally present. The killer wasn't angry with the victim. He was angry with the family. But he had planned to kill a child and actually been dispassionate enough to carry it out. An innocent child who had done nothing wrong. Only to hurt someone else.

The knowledge that they now had a clear direction invigorated her while sickening her at the same time.

Only one thing stood between her and total focus.

A vision of Shane drifted into her mind. She needed to know whether or not he was a danger to her, and there was only one way she could find out.

She made a sudden decision.

'Bryant, take a left, we're going on a little detour.'

CHAPTER SEVENTY-TWO

Ruth felt there had been a strange atmosphere in the gym hall that morning. Occasionally, she had felt that some of the women were whispering behind her back. She hadn't caught anyone looking directly at her. In fact, the opposite. It was as though people were trying not to look at her.

She shook her head at her own paranoia and remembered a saying she'd heard. 'Just because you're paranoid does not mean they're not out to get you.'

She smiled at her own thoughts as she stood up to brush her hair.

She caught a reflection of a shadow passing by the doorway. Her heartbeat increased. In prison you didn't ignore shadows.

She paused with her hand in mid-air. A form appeared in the doorway.

Ruth turned.

The woman blocking the doorway was staring at her with a strange look in her eyes.

Ruth felt her heart begin to hammer against her chest.

She knew of this woman, had seen her around. Ruth knew that people didn't mess with her.

'Hey there, I hear you murdered your rapist.'

Ruth nodded slowly.

The woman stepped further into the room, and Ruth found herself involuntarily stepping back.

'Yeah, you and me both,' she said, taking another step forward. 'My name's Tina, and I'm pleased to meet you.'

CHAPTER SEVENTY-THREE

Bryant eased the car into a parking spot right next to the front gates of Drake Hall Prison.

'Guv, are you sure this is a good idea?' he asked. 'And getting déjà vu with that question,' he added as they got out of the car.

'Why now?' Kim asked, as two men in suits separated to allow her through the entrance doors. She hadn't told him about Shane's release or the fact that someone was watching her house. He would have insisted she report it.

'Does it matter?' Bryant asked, wearily.

'Of course it does,' she snapped. 'When did Alexandra Thorne ever do anything that wasn't calculated and conniving? She's been inside for over a year. Why has she contacted me now?'

'Come on, guv. You know how she likes to play with people, mess with their heads.'

'I know how she works, but why not do that months ago? She could have written to me at any time, but why has she waited so long?'

'Guv, if you think I've got any chance of being able to answer any question relating to the workings of any woman's mind, never mind Alex Thorne or you, you can think again.'

'Are you likening her to me?' she asked, glancing sideways.

'See, I got in trouble and I didn't even answer the question,' he moaned.

'She's up to something,' Kim said as she reached the front desk.

She took out her warrant card. 'I need to know who has been to visit Alexandra Thorne… please,' she said. Occasionally, that had helped her cause in the past.

The male behind the desk was early thirties with a small scar above his lip. He was the kind of man you'd walk past in the High Street as Mister Average, but in a place full of incarcerated women he would be the object of at least half of their fantasies.

'May I ask why you… ?'

'It concerns an ongoing investigation. I'm sorry, but I can't divulge the details.'

She heard Bryant's intake of breath and ignored it.

The guard looked doubtful. 'I'm not sure that's enough—'

'If you can't help me, please get me someone that can,' she said, favouring the direct approach.

He opened his mouth to speak.

'I'm not moving until you do,' she added.

He whipped up the phone receiver with a smug expression. 'I'll check with the warden but he'll confirm what I've already said.'

Kim nodded. Fine. And when he did she would ask to speak to him.

Kim watched as the guard straightened up and spoke deferentially to the person on the other end. 'Sorry to disturb you but I have a police officer who wants access to visitor information on one of the inmates.'

The guard looked at her as a slow smile began to rest on his face.

'That's what I said to the—'

He frowned as the voice continued to speak. 'The inmate concerned is Alexandra Thorne.'

The frown deepened. 'But you just said… '

He listened some more as his cheeks reddened. 'I understand. Thank you.'

His expression was no longer triumphant, and Kim couldn't help but wonder what had caused the warden to change his mind and bend the rules once he had known that it concerned Alexandra Thorne.

The guard tapped a few keys on the computer to his left. 'Other than her solicitor she only has two other visitors. One man, one woman.'

Kim leaned forward as he continued to scroll.

'Yeah, here it is. The woman has only been twice.'

'Her name?' Kim pushed.

'Yeah, Yeah, her name is Sarah Lewis.'

Kim didn't hide her surprise. 'You're sure?'

He looked again. 'Yep, that's her name.'

Kim had met Alex's sister only once but from what she had gathered Alex had been torturing her younger sister her whole life. Kim could not correlate the image of the woman she had met visiting her sister in prison.

Perhaps she had needed to come and see for herself that her sister was safely locked away. That would take one visit, not two. Kim pushed the thought aside.

'And the man?' she asked.

His eyes scanned down the page. 'Oh yeah, here it is. His name is Michael Stone.'

Kim stared at the guard for a full five seconds. She felt an unfamiliar weakness enter her knees.

Bryant moved closer. 'Come on, guv, let's get—'

'No,' she said, forcing strength into just one word.

What the fuck was that bitch up to? Kim wondered. She fought the nausea down. How dare she use Kim's own dead twin in that way.

'Guv, a word,' Bryant said, grabbing her elbow and guiding her to the side of the room. 'Seriously, we need to leave. You're being sucked in.'

She pulled her arm away. 'She knew I'd ask about her visitors. That's why she's used Mikey's name. She knew how—'

'I know,' Bryant hissed. 'That's why I want you to leave. She knows you far too well and that's dangerous for you.' His eyes bore into hers. 'I'm asking you, begging you, Kim, to walk away.'

His use of her first name during work hours was a slip that had never happened before. It jolted her back to reality.

She could feel how strongly he felt, and the logical, sensible part of her mind knew he was right. There was every chance she could not survive another battle with Alex.

Her actions so far had been damaging enough.

She knew that Bryant was right. Alex was too much for her.

She took a step towards the doors.

She had to know when to walk away.

CHAPTER SEVENTY-FOUR

Stacey couldn't help but marvel at the workings of her boss's mind. To link the crimes back to the relatives was a conclusion she wasn't sure she'd ever have reached. She knew the focus of her boss was never far away from her current case, regardless of whatever else was on her mind.

Never warm and fuzzy, there had been a distance to Kim this week. Just now and again, a second or two longer to respond than the usual light-switch speed.

Once or twice she had caught Bryant eyeing the boss with a concerned expression that he probably wasn't aware of.

But that was her forte. Dealing in data, it was always the small things.

Her boss was distracted by something, and Stacey couldn't help but wonder what.

If she'd have thought for a minute her boss would share her demons she would have offered her help immediately, but she knew better.

There was only one way she could help her boss and that was by doing her job.

She eeny-meeny-miney-moed over the names of the relatives and ended on the name of Harold Howard.

She googled him and got over seven thousand hits. She reduced it to news items, which cut it by half. The first few pages were the news items surrounding his death. By page six, the death articles were mixed with the news reports on the murder of his grandson.

Stacey found her jaw tensing as she speed read the articles. It was despicable enough that a child had been murdered but to do it to get back at someone was beyond sickening.

By page seventeen the headlines were focussing on his cases. It was clear that some of his decisions had been controversial.

She read a sexual assault case where the sentence passed down was a paltry two months because the judge thought the crime was hardly surprising given the actions of the victim. The nineteen-year-old had been into town, had a few drinks and made the mistake of walking the last quarter of a mile home on her own. Fourteen people testified that she had been loud and raucous in two nightclubs and an Indian restaurant. Not one of them had witnessed her being raped two hours later.

A second set of headlines were for a GBH case where a three-month custodial sentence had been given to two men who had beaten and permanently scarred a gay man, because the judge felt the victim should expect his lifestyle choices to have consequences.

Stacey felt the blood throbbing through her veins but the cases went on and on.

She sat back and continued to scroll.

CHAPTER SEVENTY-FIVE

Ruth hadn't yet stopped trembling even though her visitor had left more than fifteen minutes ago.

Nothing untoward had been said. They had conversed about very little, as tended to happen in prison, Ruth realised.

The whole world, the whole existence, boiled down to and revolved around the activities within the confines of these walls.

The fact that one of the guards was out of sorts could spark conversations aplenty. That the TV had gone on the blink again could fill hours. The fact that the carrots had been hard at dinner time would do the rounds. And any news, any real news, would entertain them for days.

Tina had not said anything wrong but her presence had been unnerving. People like Tina didn't speak to her. Ruth knew she was a 'grey'; a nobody. Someone that just fades into the background. Tina kept company with women whose sentences were close to her own. She didn't mix with the 'noobs' nor the 'greys'. And that had suited Ruth just fine.

A figure at the door caused another temporary twittering of her heart. She smiled at her friend and student.

'We read?' Elenya asked, holding out her book.

Ruth shook her head. 'Not right now, maybe later.'

Elenya hesitated, nodded and stepped away.

Truthfully, Ruth would like nothing more than to sit on the bed and listen to her friend traversing the challenge of the English language but Tina had told her that a few of them were meeting up in the library and that it would be good if she came along.

For some reason Ruth had the nagging sensation that she hadn't really been given a choice.

She brushed her hair, took a deep breath and headed off to the library.

CHAPTER SEVENTY-SIX

Kim was two steps away from the double doors when she stopped. She offered Bryant her best stab at an apologetic smile and turned back.

She had not listened quickly enough to her gut about Alex Thorne in the past and people had died.

She had allowed other people's opinion of the charming, enigmatic sociopath to sway her conviction that all was not well. She had bent to their disbelief and it had cost a few people dearly.

She would not make that same mistake twice.

'What sort of prisoner is she?' Kim asked, startling the young man behind the desk. 'She ever give you any trouble?'

He shook his head. 'Quite the opposite. Quiet, cooperative. She's helped us calm down a few situations, talked other prisoners around, sometimes.'

Kim felt her heart sinking with every word. The woman was working her bloody magic again. Kim was unsure which orifice of hers the sun shone from in this guy's opinion.

She recalled the exact same situation a year ago when there had been only one person who had felt about Alex the same way she had. A sweet, young, intelligent autistic man had seen through the façade.

It had to be worth one more try. Just for Dougie.

She was aware of Bryant's form beside her. If she was going to stay, then he would stay with her.

'No strange friendships, unlikely alliances?'

Kim knew prisons held intelligence on that kind of detail. If Alex was up to something here she had no hope of getting it out of him.

'Nope, nothing,' he answered.

Damn it, perhaps Bryant was right after all. Maybe she was imagining—

'Even refused to press charges against her old cellmate,' he said, shaking his head.

'What was that?' Kim asked. Her senses started to align like the planets, ready to absorb every word.

'Her cellmate lost the plot the other night. Nice girl, or so we thought, went crackers,' he said, making the looping at the temple sign that Kim detested. 'She just started punching Doctor Thorne for no reason at all.'

Aah, thought Kim, that explained the scratches.

But her buddy here had no clue just how much he had just revealed.

A previously calm and nice inmate had suddenly, for no good reason, opened up and started punching her cellmate.

Oh no, this was not some simple coincidence. Kim would have liked to think this cellmate had actually seen through Alex and given her what she deserved, but she doubted it.

Alex was a master at deceit. She had always known what she was. Other people had to be watching very closely to find out.

'How long had they shared a cell?' Kim asked.

'Dunno, a few months,' he said, looking down to the desk, indicating he had other work to do.

'And you didn't wonder why she suddenly "went psycho" that one time? You just accepted it?'

'Look, lady, the proof was there. I saw it myself.'

Kim leaned forward. 'Firstly, I'm not a lady.' She realised how that sounded and decided to stick with it. 'I'm Detective Inspector, and secondly, what exactly did you see?' she demanded.

He began to sneer. 'Is this official?'

'It can be,' Kim shot back.

Bryant coughed. She got the message. Her hostility was not going to win her any prizes, but more importantly, it was not going to get her what she wanted.

She offered him a smile to defuse the tension.

'All I'm after is a bit of assistance. Just a couple more questions and I'll be out of your hair.'

He appeared somewhat appeased.

'What was the cellmate in for?'

He shrugged. 'Not my business to tell but she is… was due out in a week or so. Not anymore, obviously.'

Kim looked to Bryant, whose perplexed expression told her he was beginning to agree.

Why would a woman who was due to be released any day flip out?

It didn't make sense.

'What was her explanation?' Kim asked.

'Swears she didn't do it, but there was no one else in the room and the marks didn't get there on their own.'

Are you sure? Kim wanted to ask, recalling how Alex had engineered Shane's return to prison.

Her mind was screaming. This was far too coincidental. An awful lot appeared to have happened to Doctor Thorne in a few short days.

What had the guy said? That Alex had chosen not to press the matter. That would be most unlike the woman. That meant she had to already have achieved what she wanted. Yet another unsuspecting innocent appeared to have become a victim of Alex. The thought made her sick to her stomach.

Come on, think, she told herself. *Think like Alex.* She took the steps in her head.

'So, what did she ask for?'

'Look, Inspector, I really do have things—'

'I understand, but this could be really important.'

'She asked to be housed with a particular prisoner.' He smiled. 'She's got some balls, I'll say that. Not many people want to live with the most vicious woman in the place.'

Kim felt her stomach turn. Now she was getting somewhere. She knew it.

'What's her name?' Kim asked.

'Tanya Neale,' he said.

Bryant took out his phone and googled the name.

'What's she in for?' Kim asked.

The guard pursed his lips. 'As I said before, I'm not discussing—'

'Murder: three men,' Bryant answered.

She could see his eyes travelling quickly from left to right. He scrolled and then lifted his eyes and looked at her.

'Shit, guv,' he said, handing her the phone.

Kim scanned briefly. Her eyes danced from the name of the sister to the place she was being held.

Her eyes met Bryant's and she saw her own fear reflected there.

She nodded. He turned and rushed from the building.

She turned back towards the guard.

'I want to see Alex Thorne, and I want to see her now.'

He began to smile. 'No offence but what if she doesn't want to see you?'

'Oh, she will,' Kim said confidently. 'Just tell her that Kimmy's here.'

CHAPTER SEVENTY-SEVEN

Ruth walked along the corridor towards the door to the library.

There was an anxiety in her stomach that she could not think beyond.

She hesitated for a moment, and again thanked Alex for her indecision. The woman had destroyed her trust in people. In her mind, everyone had a motive for something. Alex was supposed to have been helping her, healing her. Guiding her through the pain to the other side. But she hadn't. She had only been using her for her own sick games.

She fought down the hesitation and continued on her journey. Tina had done nothing to provoke this distrust. She had spoken pleasantly.

Ruth tried to ignore the voice that questioned why she had spoken at all.

That was Alex speaking, not her, and she was sick of it. She added momentum to her step, hoping to outrun the sound of Alex in her head.

She would not view the world with such bitterness and distrust. She would not allow Alex to shape the rest of her life.

She would not suspect every person that spoke to her of hidden agendas and ulterior motives.

She fixed a smile to her face as she entered the library.

The first blow caught her to the back of the head. She stumbled forward with confusion. Had something fallen on her?

And then she saw Tina before her.

She knew that the blow to the head had affected her peripheral vision. There was activity to the left and to the right of her but she could only see straight-ahead.

A fist or foot slammed into her right kidney. The impact sent her reeling forward. The world turned to slow motion as she felt her body pitching forward, and yet, perversely, it was happening so quickly she could not think.

She wanted to cry out that they had made a mistake. They had the wrong person; but a foot caught her in the throat as she tried to get onto her side to curl up.

She choked and spluttered as blood filled her mouth.

Another blow landed between her shoulder blades.

Ruth wondered how she could use just two arms to protect her whole body.

Her mind was trying to understand what she'd done wrong. She had never spoken to Tina, never crossed her. It had to be a case of mistaken identity.

A foot landed in her stomach. Her hands moved to try and cover it as the sickness rose inside her.

She tried to scoot around to face Tina; to explain that she'd done nothing wrong.

She looked up into a face that held no hate, no anger, no rage.

Ruth tried to speak as Tina stepped forward.

'Wh… at… why… ?' she spluttered past the pain in her throat.

'Nothing to do with me, mate,' Tina said.

Ruth's head was spinning with both pain and confusion. The woman beating the living daylights out of her was calling her mate.

Ruth cried out as a foot embedded in the small of her back. Fresh new pain sites were springing up all over her. A blackness was trying to fall. She welcomed it, and yet she wanted to understand.

She summoned all of her energy. 'Tina… please… '

She held out her hand.

Tina kicked it away. 'Bitch, we got instructions. Not my business but you gotta die.'

Ruth tried to understand the words through the pain that was wracking her body. She hadn't done anything to offend Tina? She was doing this for someone else.

Realisation hit her like a thunderbolt through the pain. It was Alex. Somehow this was because of Alex.

Despair took any residue of fight from her muscles. She couldn't reason with them because it wasn't their fight.

Ruth suddenly knew she was going to die.

She made no sound as the blows continued to rain down on her. The blackness was approaching, and she welcomed it. She couldn't fight anymore.

'Get out,' said a familiar voice.

Fists and feet stilled all around her.

'What you say, bitch?' Tina asked, with attitude.

'I said, get out.'

Although the voice was familiar, it was different somehow.

Activity recommenced and feet began to move. Ruth readied herself for a further onslaught, but they were moving away. Leaving the area.

Relief flooded through her.

'It's all right,' said the reassuring voice as it came closer.

Ruth felt the tension leave her body as a soft hand gently stroked her cheek. They had stopped, and she wasn't dead. Despite the pain she wanted to laugh, to cry.

'It's going to be okay, Ruthee,' Elenya said, before the blade plunged into her stomach.

CHAPTER SEVENTY-EIGHT

By the time Stacey had read through the fourth controversial case of Judge Harold Howard she thought her blood was going to burn right through her veins.

Her phone rang, and she took the opportunity to stand.

'What?' she said.

'Bloody hell, Stace, who pissed on your Imp?' Dawson asked.

She rolled her eyes. He never missed an opportunity to take a swipe at her online gaming. Some days it was funny but mainly not.

'Are yer on yer way?' she snapped. She had called him an hour ago and passed on the boss's instructions.

'Kind of,' he answered.

Stacey frowned. His voice held the tone of a child who was about to put his hand into the fire to see how it felt even though he knew it would hurt.

'Kev…?'

'How's the research on Harold Howard going?' he asked, sweetly.

She stood up and stretched her legs. 'Harold Howard is a knob,' she said.

He chuckled. 'Oh yeah, I could have told you that. Before my first court appearance I went and observed a case at Birmingham. He was the judge, and he was a complete knobchop.'

'Thanks for that, Kev. But why are we not having this conversation across the desk?'

'Stace, are you pacing?'

'A bit,' she said, turning around at the coffee machine.

'What's wrong?'

'We can safely assume he wor the president of the minorities club,' she snapped. 'But how the hell did he ger away with it?' Stacey asked, shaking her head.

'How does anyone, Stace?' he asked, quietly.

She turned at the door and walked back. 'Kev, I'm gonna keep asking why you're not here yet.'

'Just for clarification, Stace. Jason Cross has filed a complaint against the boss, right?'

'Yeeeaah,' she said, getting a feeling of what was coming.

'So, I mean, maybe other members of the police could happen on by the hospital.'

'Don't even think about it,' Stacey said, coming to a halt. 'If the boss thought for even a minute that was a good idea she would have asked you to do it.'

'Yeah, but sometimes—'

'No, Kev, no times is it a good idea to go against the boss's wishes, and after the newspaper episode I would think yow might know that.'

'But strictly speaking she never said not to.'

'She never says specifically dow go throwing yourself in front of fast moving vehicles but yer dow do it.'

'It's not really the same—'

'Kev, if you've called me to get permission, I'm the wrong person, and if you've called me to get encouragement, see above. And if yowm still willing to do it after the shit you've had this week, then I'm gonna look into getting yer certified.'

'Aww... Stace, you're no fun—'

Stacey shook her head and ended the call.

She wasn't in the mood to be her colleague's enabler.

As she sat back at her desk, Kev's nickname for the racist, bigoted bastard she was researching was at the forefront of her mind.

She moved on to the next case on the list, and her eyes widened. It wasn't so much the screaming headline that got her but rather a name in the third line down.

CHAPTER SEVENTY-NINE

Kim had been handed over to a young, slim female prison guard who she followed to the visitors' room. She idly wondered if the officer had had a long day. The elastic band holding her ponytail was not as tight to her head as it had probably started the day and a few tendrils of hair had broken free. A small stain coloured the back of her sleeve and there was a distinct weariness to her walk.

Kim worked hard to fix a nonchalant expression to her face as they passed the vending machine.

Alex was already seated with her back to the door. Two cups of coffee had been placed on the table. Her demeanour said she was not eager for the meeting, as though she could take or leave this interruption into her busy day.

Everything about the woman was a play of some kind. Kim wondered how exhausting it must be to have your mind constantly plotting and planning, devising scenarios and possibilities.

And she'd bought coffee as though they were two old friends catching up.

And this was what people didn't understand about Alex. The devil was in the detail. You had to catch the small things before they could grow up.

Kim's thoughts briefly went to Bryant outside. She knew a part of him felt she was overreacting to the tenuous link between Alex and Ruth. That Tanya's sister happened to be in the same prison as one of Alex's former victims was a leap of faith too far for her colleague. And for once she hoped he was right.

'Kim, how are you?' Alex said, as she sat down. 'Such a lovely surprise.'

'No it isn't,' Kim answered, drily.

Alex smiled, accepting the words as a compliment of her victory.

'You sent me a message. Where is Shane?'

Alex attempted to look surprised but the enjoyment danced in her eyes. 'Why would I know where he is?'

'You know,' Kim said.

Alex began to shake her head. 'I assume you've checked at Hardwick House. Doesn't your friend, David, know where Shane is?'

Kim cursed herself for doing exactly what Alex expected of her. She would have known that's the first place she'd check. Just as she'd known Kim would try and find out.

'How is my little friend, Dougie? Has he taken any more swimming lessons?'

'You fucking—' Kim snarled, before catching herself. The memory of Dougie flailing helplessly in the canal lock was not a vision that would ever leave her.

The guard stood just inside the door watching closely.

'Dougie is perfectly fine, Alex,' Kim said, trying to keep her voice even.

Alex leaned forward. 'Come on, who would have actually missed him if you hadn't pulled him out?'

Kim ignored the question. It was designed only to rile her. Dougie's name on her tongue had no other purpose than to get her fired up. She resented the fact that it had.

'I want you to tell me about Shane,' Kim pushed.

Alex rolled her eyes with boredom. 'I really have no idea, and I could not care less. He was a disappointment to me. Why are you always so focussed on the waifs and strays, Kim? What is Shane to you?'

'So, he's not the visitor listed as Michael Stone?'

Alex laughed out loud. 'Oh, Kim. It is so much fun seeing you again. I have missed you so much. And while we're playing catch up, how is your dear mother?'

'She sends her love,' Kim said, sarcastically.

Alex chuckled. 'Oh, you went to see her?'

Kim said nothing but thrust her hands into her front pockets.

'You did, didn't you?' Alex said, as her eyes widened. 'After all these years you went to see your mother. Oh I'm so happy for you. It must have been such fun to catch up on all the years that—'

'Alex, shut the fuck up.'

Kim could see the amusement dancing in the woman's eyes. She hated all of Alex's faces but this giddy schoolgirl act was just too much. 'Why did you want me to see her?' she asked.

'Because I thought it would be good for you,' she said, too quickly, leading Kim to the assumption that it was the rehearsed response: meaning it had no connection to the truth.

But hell, she'd play along: she had a few moments to spare.

'Why would it be good for me?'

'Oh the future tense you just used would indicate you didn't speak to her yet. Oh Kim, that disappoints me.'

Kim wouldn't let that keep her up at night. 'But what does it matter to you?'

'It doesn't, but I care about you. I think you're ready to take that next step on your journey. I think you're ready to forgive her. I think you have to forgive—'

'You know nothing, Alex,' Kim spat, realising that she had played right into her hands. Again. Once more she had exposed her underbelly to the predator.

Surprisingly, Alex allowed it to pass. 'Did you see her?' she asked.

Kim nodded, absently, while still reprimanding herself for the slip up.

'Oh Kim, that was a mistake,' Alex said, smiling. 'You were just thinking about something else. Your mind was distracted, and I saw exactly what you don't want me to see.'

Kim gathered herself back together. 'Alex, stop pretending you know—'

'I know there is a small part of you that doubts the strength of your conviction. Your eyes hold a question about your mother.'

Kim said nothing and worked hard to keep her expression neutral.

'You saw her, didn't you? You looked at the woman she is now and you can't correlate that with the woman you remember. The woman that painstakingly planned the torture and murder of you and Mikey.'

She wanted to rip the name of her brother from the bitch's mouth but that would offer Alex enough ammunition to shoot at her throughout eternity.

'She's not the same woman, is she? The woman you see now is calm, contented, sane, possibly even nice. So how are you going to reconcile the two pictures that are in your head?'

'Alex, you have no clue how I feel about—'

'The picture will never go away, now, Kim. You can't un-see her as she is now and return to that one expression you recall on the day she left you and your twin to die.'

Kim tried to rise above the words that were trying to find a space to land in her consciousness.

'I'm sure we've had this conversation before,' she said.

Keep moving, Kim thought. It was the only way to avoid the tiny little darts of poison being aimed her way.

Alex sat back and shook her head. 'No, Kim, I don't think we did. We talked a lot about Mikey and the guilt you feel for not being able to save him. We talked about how you torture yourself every single—'

Kim bristled. 'Didn't you just say we'd already done this?'

She needed no reminders of her feelings on that score. She fought with them daily.

Alex chuckled. 'Oh, Kim, we've barely scratched the surface of your feelings about Mikey and you know it. Those feelings are the motivations behind just about everything you do. It's what drives you at work. You want to save everyone.'

Kim's fingers tightened around her phone. She willed it to vibrate against her hand. Every passing minute terrified her.

'You want to save everyone you meet from pain, despair, loneliness, loss, all the things you felt yourself. You want to save the world, Kim, because you couldn't save him. You forget that I'm the only person that truly knows you.'

Kim's phone vibrated in her pocket. She took a quick look at the prison guard, whose eyes were burning into the back of Alex.

She whipped the phone into view, opened the message and began to read.

'Looks important,' Alex said, smiling in her direction.

Kim continued to stare down at the phone, trying to absorb the message from her colleague in the car park.

She didn't raise her head to meet Alex's smug, triumphant expression.

When her voice came it was deep and quiet and devoid of emotion.

'You'll be pleased to know that they got her,' Kim said, finally raising her head.

A slow smile began to form on her face as the victory showed in her eyes. 'I have absolutely no idea what you're talking about.'

'But luckily, she's not dead. The guard got there just in time.'

Kim was rewarded by the confusion that contorted her face. Alex had wanted her here when the news came through about Ruth's murder.

Too bad.

'Oh, and your contingency plan didn't work either. Neither Tina nor the foreign girl were successful.'

Kim enjoyed the rage that filled Alex's eyes despite her attempts to hide it.

Kim stood. She no longer had any cause to be here.

'You forget, Alex, that I'm probably the one person that knows you, too,' she said, walking away.

She tried to leave the things Alex had said at the table.

Kim could feel the rage travelling like a tsunami towards her. Alex had failed, and her anger had to find a target. Kim knew she had to get out before it hit.

'I know why you'll never forgive her, Kim. You can't. Because if you forgive your mother then you will have to forgive yourself, and you will never do that.'

Keep moving, Kim told herself, trying to close her ears to the poison.

'It's not her you can't forgive. It's yourself. You should have saved him. You know you should have saved him. You were stronger than he was. You could have done more.'

Kim felt the emotion gathering in her throat. She had to get out. She forced herself to keep moving forward.

'I have a photo of you and Mikey.'

Kim's heart stopped for just a second. There was no such thing.

'You've forgotten, haven't you?' Alex said.

Kim could hear the strength entering her voice.

'There was only one photo of the two of you ever taken. One single school photograph, and I have the only copy.'

Kim steadied herself against the last remaining table as a vague memory came back to her. A double seat, a big blue background of sky.

She had nothing of her dead brother; she carried his picture in her heart but some days she couldn't quite recall the curve of his chin or the light freckles across the bridge of his nose.

'I have the last remaining copy of that photo. And I'm happy to give it to you.'

The thought of seeing the face of her brother clearly again was overwhelming.

'If you just come back to the table.'

Kim didn't turn. She couldn't. The emotion was attacking her from every direction.

To see Mikey again would be like a hundred Christmas wishes but in her weakened state she could not return to the battle.

She knew that if she walked through that door the photo would be destroyed. Mikey's face would be lost for ever but the alternative was worse.

It was just too high a price to pay.

The tears were pricking at the back of her eyes as she felt she was failing her brother all over again.

She gathered her strength and continued her journey to the doorway.

She heard her name being called behind her.

But Kim made sure she didn't look back.

CHAPTER EIGHTY

Alex walked back to her cell slowly. The meeting had been a semi success on the one hand, but a total disaster on the other.

How the hell had she learned of the attack on Ruth, and how the fuck had she stopped it?

That woman should be dead right now. Part of her problem should be resolved.

She would have to devise another plan, and she would, but right now she wanted to focus on Kim.

So far their interaction had been a positive one from her point of view. She had manipulated the woman to visit her mother, which had stirred up all kinds of emotion, and now Kim knew of the existence of the photo.

Alex could almost feel sorry for the victims of Kim's current case. They had no chance of getting a conclusion. With all the thoughts floating around her head, banging into each other, colliding, the woman's brain must be turning to mush.

Alex knew that Kim's weakest points were her unending hatred for her mother and the guilt of not being able to save Mikey. Start playing with those two fireworks and the result was Chernobyl.

The thoughts would burrow into her mind and fester like an abscess. She had made a choice. She could have walked away with the photo, but she had been weakened to a state whereby she had been forced to concede the battle. Triumph was mixed with disappointment.

'You really are a despicable person, aren't you?' Katie said quietly from beside her.

'Oh sorry, didn't see you there. You are so inconsequential to me that your presence barely registers.'

'What pleasure do you get from torturing people?'

'More than you can ever imagine,' Alex said cheerfully.

Time for a little light relief to chase away the disappointment.

'Look at you. You're nothing. You have no dreams, no ambition. You will eventually exit this world as you entered it: silently. You will leave no mark anywhere. Your greatest achievement will be producing that child or even a whole gaggle. That is no achievement, it is simply breeding.

'You will sleep with any man that finds you remotely attractive and you will call that love. Your gratitude for their attention will be pathetic as you try to find a substitute father for your children.

'With little else to occupy your mind you will absorb every bit of negativity from this job, and the incidents, hatred and despair will weave themselves into your clothes and follow you home. The negativity will eat at your table and sleep in your bed until one morning you will wake up bitter and old, consumed by regret.'

Alex stopped as she reached the doorway to her cell.

The woman was pale and clearly trembling.

'Did that answer your question, officer?'

Katie took a deep breath and fixed her with a look of pure hatred. 'Thank you for the warning. Doctor Thorne. You may well be right but at least now I know what to look out for.'

Alex viewed her dispassionately. She had been hoping for something more.

Katie smiled. 'Now, please step aside, Doctor Thorne. I've received intelligence that there may be contraband in your room.' She took a pair of latex gloves from her pocket. 'And so I'm going to be taking a look.'

Alex opened her mouth to argue. *Damn, the bitch had surprised her.*

As she watched the guard advance towards the bedside cabinet and the book, she knew there was nothing she could do.

But she consoled herself that all was not lost.

Alex's silence had already activated plan B.

CHAPTER EIGHTY-ONE

'Bloody hell, guv. You look like you've just seen a ghost,' Bryant said.

Almost, she thought, as she leaned against the bonnet of the car. She needed a minute to breathe the fresh air into her lungs.

'How's Ruth?' she asked, finally.

'On her way to the hospital. She's in a bad way. She's been beaten badly but it could have been worse. Tina Neale and her buddies were doing a good job on her when it appears her friend, some Russian girl, came to finish the job.'

'Two separate attempts?' Kim asked.

Bryant nodded and blew out air. 'Jesus, if you'd listened to me when I was asking you to leave, she'd be dead right now. Possibly twice,' he added.

'You were only thinking of me, Bryant. I can't hold that against you, and on that score you were probably right,' she admitted.

'Damn it, I knew if you went in to see her—'

'It was worth it,' she said, holding up her hand. 'Ruth is alive, and I'm not hurt,' she said, with a weak attempt at a smile.

'Are you sure?'

Kim tried to silence all the voices in her head.

'I'm sure; now let's get back to the station quick smart.'

'Inspector… Inspector… wait… ' Kim heard a shout, as she opened the car door.

The prison guard was heading towards her at speed.

And in her hand was an envelope.

Kim stared at the woman hard. It couldn't be.

Bryant looked between the two of them, confused.

'I think… I think this is what she was talking about.'

Kim dared not look down at the envelope.

'But how, I mean… ?'

'Cell search,' she said.

Finally, Kim looked down at the envelope. Emotion gathered in her throat as her hand reached out to accept it.

This envelope contained her world.

She shook her head as the envelope was safely placed into her hands.

'I don't have the words to thank you. There is nothing I can say.'

'Please, say nothing. Consider it my own act of revenge.'

'Thank you,' Kim said, sincerely.

The woman smiled and turned away.

Kim looked down in wonder at what had been gained, lost and gained again in the space of fifteen minutes. As she watched the guard walk away she recalled the hatred in the woman's eyes during the visit.

Maybe there was something she could give her after all. She recalled the warden's willingness to hand over information about Alex. Had he been bitten too?

'Officer, hang on,' Kim called, and closed the gap between them.

'Whatever she has on you, stop it now. Take away her power. Go to your boss and tell the truth, because if you don't you will be her prisoner for life. I promise you.'

'There isn't anything,' the guard said.

Kim touched her forearm lightly. 'I don't think that's true. Whatever you did she will continue to use. Tell the truth and explain the circumstance. If you've learned from it, I think they'll understand.'

The guard weighed her words carefully before an expression of relief rested on her face.

She smiled weakly. 'I'll go there right now.'

Kim nodded and their gaze held for just a second before the guard turned and walked away.

'What's that?' Bryant asked, appearing beside her.

A smile formed on her face. 'It's a Christmas present, Bryant. A very late Christmas present,' she said, hugging the treasure to her chest.

'Well hang on to it tightly; we're heading off at speed. Stacey wants us back at the station. Now.'

CHAPTER EIGHTY-TWO

'Okay, Stace, what have you got?' Kim said, entering the squad room.

She noted the absence of Dawson and assumed he was on his way.

They had made it back in record time. She suspected Bryant may have broken the speed limit once or twice. She wondered if Woody would ever realise that influence could work both ways.

She took the treasured envelope and placed it in her desk drawer. Now was not the time.

Her full attention was needed elsewhere right now.

'I've gor a case here, guv. It involves all three of our victims' loved ones. It could be totally coincidental but Harold Howard was the judge. Mitchell Brightman was the prosecutor and Geraldine Hall was an expert psychiatric witness for the CPS.'

'Where's Kev?' Kim asked. She would prefer a full house so that whatever Stacey had learned only had to be said once. But she couldn't wait for ever.

Stacey shook her head. 'He's not back yet.'

She had requested his return to the office to assist Stacey a couple of hours ago. It appeared that she and the sergeant were going to be having another conversation.

'What was the case?' Kim asked, sitting down.

Stacey swallowed, and Kim tried to ready herself for what was to come.

'Luke Sweeney was fourteen years old in December 2007 when he abducted a fellow classmate, Casey Rudd, on the way home from school. The rest of his family was away, and he was under the loose care of an aunt that lived down the road. He was almost fifteen,' Stacey explained.

Kim nodded for her to continue.

'He kept her prisoner in the garden shed for five days and even assisted in the search. It was actually an undercover police officer that noticed his behaviour at the search gathering and decided to investigate further. Had this smug expression on his face and just kept staring at the parents. Didn't listen to the search instructions and disappeared after about twenty minutes.'

It was a known process to have officers in plain clothes amongst the volunteers, observing any strange or erratic behaviour. It was also known that some criminals liked to remain close to the action to feed their ego and sense of achievement.

Stacey continued. 'The victim was found on the fifth day.' Stacey paused and closed her eyes for a second before continuing. 'She had been violently raped, and medical staff counted over one hundred and fifty separate injury sites around her body.'

Kim could feel the horror growing inside her. Bryant stared at the wall ahead.

'There was no shortage of torture tools in the shed. He sawed off her little finger, crushed her wrist in a vice and hung a pair of pliers from her eyelid.'

Kim held up her hand. The bile was rising to the back of her throat.

Stacey got the message. 'Other injuries sustained included pinch marks, bite marks, bruises and knife-inflicted cuts. She was dehydrated and close to death.'

'I remember it now,' Bryant said, still not looking towards the screen. 'She didn't live for long.'

Stacey nodded in agreement. 'She spent five weeks in hospital fighting both her injuries and infections from the dirty tools. Her identity was outed on social media, and despite what she'd suffered she received the usual trolls and hate messages, not to mention the sick and disgusting jokes. Her news feed was full of pictures of tools and severed fingers.'

Stacey raised her gaze from the screen, and Kim already knew what was coming.

'She committed suicide before the case went to trial.'

Kim shook her head wondering at the use of lifelong anonymity in this day and age.

She felt her hands clench of their own volition. Another innocent life lost.

She took a deep breath. Regrettably, they could not help her now. 'What about Luke Sweeney?'

Kim was doing the calculations in her head. Nine years. Could he be out now?

'He was sentenced to a term of no less than fifteen years. He died of pneumonia three years ago.'

Kim struggled to find one bone in her body that was sorry about that. Her mind was still with the teenage girl who had been terrorised physically and mentally for days.

Stacey continued. 'Geraldine Hall testified that he was of sound mind and that there were no extenuating circumstances. She didn't find him to be psychologically incapacitated in any way.'

'So, we know it's not him,' Bryant said, stating the obvious.

Kim frowned. 'What about his family?' she asked.

'Well, the parents and two other children – a boy and a girl – were hounded out of town. Luke's details got out and his family became the focus of disgust and rage from the local community. The kids were beaten up, and the parents were egged and abused everywhere they went. There were seventeen phone calls to the police during the first month after Luke's arrest. Complaints included faeces through the letterbox, two broken windows, and lit fireworks down the chimney.'

'So, the family members suffered?' Kim asked.

They all fell silent for a moment, processing the catalogue of horrific events.

Kim spoke first. 'We have the DNA of Jason Cross at the scene of the first murder, and we can tie him to the family of the second. Damn it, we really need to speak to him.'

Dawson tore into the office, flushed and breathless.

'If you're talking about Jason Cross, ain't nobody going to be talking to him. Sorry I'm late by the way, boss.'

'Good of you to join us, Kev,' she snapped. 'Now what the hell is this about Jason Cross?'

'I stopped by the hospital to try and speak with him.'

Bryant swore under his breath.

'What the hell are you playing at?' Kim raged. 'You know he's off limits.'

Only Stacey appeared unsurprised. She was too busy frowning at the computer screen.

Dawson nodded. 'Yeah, I know, I'm sorry, boss, and I'm happy to take my bollocking later. But the guy is gone. Discharged himself this morning and even his solicitor doesn't know where he is.'

'Damn it,' Kim said. 'Our main suspect has been back in circulation for bloody hours and who knows who's next on the hit list.'

'You thinking he's a family member, guv?' Bryant asked.

'It could be bloody anybody,' Kim answered with frustration. They had the link and it brought them no closer to identifying the actual killer.

'Shiiiiit,' Stacey said.

All eyes turned her way.

'Boss, you're not gonna like what I just found.'

Kim didn't like the tremor in her colleague's voice.

'I carried on looking at the key personnel in the case thinking it might give us a clue as to who might be next.'

Stacey stared at the screen as though she still couldn't believe whatever it was that was right in front of her.

'Stace, what's wrong?' Kim asked.

'It's the investigating officer, boss. The person who arrested Luke Sweeney was Woody.'

CHAPTER EIGHTY-THREE

'Martha, I don't care who he's in a meeting with,' Kim shouted. 'I need to speak to him now.'

'I'm under strict instructions not to disturb the Super—'

'An officer's life is in danger if you don't.'

Kim realised she was now speaking to the hold music.

Three seconds later, Baldwin's irritated voice sounded in her ear. 'Stone, what the hell—?'

'Sir, I have reason to believe that the lives of either DCI Woodward or his granddaughter are in danger. I need to know where he is.'

She knew she had his attention.

'Summarise,' he instructed, curtly.

'We've been working a case whereby the families of the victims are linked. Our guy is killing the people his intended victims loved the most. He is torturing the people who were left behind. He doesn't want them to die. He wants them to hurt. We've identified the case involved and, so far, we have the prosecutor, the expert witness and the judge. The arresting officer was Woo—DCI Woodward.'

'Okay, Stone. Case made. The DCI is in Wales, close to Welshpool. He has a caravan there. I'll contact the local force and get them over to check. I'm assuming you've called his mobile.'

'Appears to be no coverage, sir,' she said, glancing at Bryant, who was still trying constantly to get through.

'Yes, that's why he likes it there. I suggest you and your team get going. I'll assemble a team to follow you but start heading towards.'

'Yes, sir,' she said with surprise. He had been more accommodating than she could have hoped. She hadn't needed to be rude once.

'Okay, guys,' she said, grabbing her coat. 'If you've got plans tonight, you should cancel them. We're going for a ride to the country.'

Everyone followed her out the door and she was pleased to have her back to them.

She only hoped the flippancy had covered the fear.

For once, she was pleased they were sending backup.

Because right now she had no idea who or what she was heading towards.

CHAPTER EIGHTY-FOUR

Baldwin put down the phone and smiled. Martha sat poised with her ballpoint pen at the ready.

'Sir, should I… ?'

'No, Martha it'll be fine,' he said, heading towards his office.

DCI Woodward had never worked out how to control that woman, even after managing her for a few years. He had worked it out in just a few short days: tell her what she wanted to hear, humour her.

'Sir?' Martha questioned.

'Oh, ring local police and ask them to take a look and then send the address to Stone.' He felt his lips turn up. 'Woodward should get quite a surprise when his entire CID team turns up on the doorstep of his holiday home. Serves him right. He should have learned how to control his stray dog a little better.'

Martha had picked up the phone, ready to dial. 'What about the support team?' she asked.

He laughed. 'On the back of what she just told me I wouldn't send her two PCSOs and a special constable.'

Martha looked at him questioningly.

'That woman costs us a fortune every year. I'm not dispatching a support team on this wild goose chase. Her motive for the murders appears to be one step removed and she has no idea who she's chasing. It's going to be a lot of fuss over nothing and from Monday morning she will be Woodward's problem again.'

His assistant did not appear convinced. 'But you told her—'

'Martha. There's nothing there. Stone has no more than a vague theory of a killer murdering the next of kin of his intended victim. It's so thin I could pick my teeth with it.'

He hesitated. No. He had made the right decision. He was happy with the instruction he had given.

He returned to his office and closed the door. Preparation for the budget meeting next week still awaited him.

Now that the inspector had been told everything she wanted to hear, he knew she would not be disturbing him again.

CHAPTER EIGHTY-FIVE

Alex lay down on the bed. There was a sense of loss creeping over her.

It wasn't loss born of emotion, attachment or love. It was the kind of loss when you decide to get a new car. There is a sense of loss when you remember how the old car once made you feel.

There was disappointment in knowing she would never see Kim Stone again and, as much as she enjoyed the relationship they had, her freedom must come first.

Her lemons had turned into lemonade during the last few hours. So what if the photo was gone. The woman would barely have a chance to enjoy it. And although Ruth wasn't dead, as she should have been, the woman was probably too terrified to speak out against her in an appeal. Good enough, she supposed.

The only other obstacle to her freedom was the detective inspector. And that would be resolved soon enough.

She felt the stirrings of a tear start somewhere close to her eyes.

Was she going to cry for the loss of her dearest friend? She smiled and wiped at what appeared to have been an itch.

Of course not. She was a sociopath and she only ever had tears for herself.

CHAPTER EIGHTY-SIX

The squad car dispatched by Dyfed-Powys Police entered the site at 8.47 p.m.

Both police officers wound down their windows and listened.

'What exactly are we looking for again, Sarge?' asked PC Jones.

He shrugged. 'Any activity around caravan twenty-seven. I don't know. Some vague idea that someone might be looking for someone.'

'Good job it's a quiet night then, eh?'

'Not for long.'

PC Jones growled. It was Friday night and they were on countdown to the calls to the town centres. The local small towns were nothing like Cardiff or Swansea but if there was a pub or a club there was often trouble. It didn't need to be real trouble or enemies or people fighting over something tangible. By the end of a heavy night two best friends could be kicking seven shades out of each other.

'These are even numbers,' PC Jones said as the sergeant brought the car to a halt and switched off the engine.

They both listened and then looked at each other.

'Job done?' PC Jones asked.

Sergeant Hunter opened his car door. 'May as well just check the property while we're here.'

An occasional globe light offered basic illumination but the sergeant switched on his torch and shone it with sweeping movements left and right.

PC Jones sighed behind him. Being sent on random excursions by other police forces was not the highlight of his night. If he was honest, he was spoiling for a scuffle.

'This the one?' Sergeant Hunter asked.

He stepped forward and searched for the number. He nodded.

The sergeant shone the torch around the facia of the caravan.

No lights illuminated the inside. He walked the length of the caravan and shone his torch behind.

PC Jones moved around the other side and bent down to shine his light beneath. Nothing but a couple of folded-up deck chairs and some old planters.

'Nothing here, Sarge,' he said.

'Yeah, we'll just knock the door and then call it in.'

PC Jones took the two metal steps to the doorway and knocked.

The sound travelled through the silence of the caravan. PC Jones took a step back, marvelling at the futility of this exercise.

He looked to the sergeant, who wrinkled his nose and shook his head.

'Enough time-wasting. I'm thinking West Midlands called this one wrong.'

He took out his radio and called it in as nothing to report.

CHAPTER EIGHTY-SEVEN

Detective Chief Inspector Woodward was unable to move from his position on the floor.

He had seen the torchlight pass over the windows. He had felt like crying with relief. He had no clue how anyone knew what was happening but he was just thankful that someone had come.

He pulled again on the plastic ties that were available in every hardware store. They were colourful, cheap and nasty and they were also bloody strong.

The one that tied his ankles together had also been looped around the leg of the cooker, and his hands were shackled behind his back. He knew noise carried from inside a caravan and tried to kick out so that whoever it was might hear him. Any small sound would alert them to his presence.

Another torchlight shone through from the small bedroom at the back. Lissy's room. The thought of her made him buck his body again like a demented worm.

The sodden cloth wedged into his mouth prevented him from crying out.

The torchlight dimmed.

Don't go, his mind was screaming. *They have my grandchild. Please, don't go.*

He still wasn't sure exactly what had happened. Lissy had been watching a cartoon on the TV, and he had been cleaning away the supper dishes. He had only stepped outside to put the rubbish into the bin.

The next thing he knew he woke to find himself gagged and bound.

He strained against the ties once more as he pictured seven-year-old Lissy in her butterfly pyjamas. The only grandchild he would ever have. Everything to him since the death of his son.

She had been taken and he was powerless to protect her. His dear sweet Lissy who had inherited her father's passion and her grandmother's grace. He saw them both every day in the child.

They had grown even closer in the two years since his wife had passed. And on that day, when Marion had succumbed to her five-year cancer battle, Lissy had climbed onto his lap without speaking, snaked her arms around his neck and offered him the warmest and most comforting hug he could ever have wished for. His generous daughter-in-law enjoyed the special bond between Lissy and him and actively encouraged it. Outside of his work she was all he had left.

He struggled to contain the emotion and again tried to break the ties.

His body shook with frustration, rage and fear when he heard the car driving away.

As the noise of the engine faded he knew he would never see his granddaughter again.

CHAPTER EIGHTY-EIGHT

Kim could feel herself growing frustrated at the speed. It felt as though they had been in the car for hours.

Bryant had carefully negotiated the dark, winding narrow lanes to Bridgnorth. He had opened up towards Much Wenlock and then hit the traffic on the Shrewsbury ring road.

Stacey was trying to track down Jason Cross, and Dawson was ringing Woody's phone every few minutes.

She was in the process of deciding how best to vent her frustration when her phone rang.

'Stone,' she answered.

'Detective Inspector, it's Martha. I have the address of the campsite. Are you ready?'

Kim called to Stacey behind and then recited it as Martha read it to her.

'Have the local force attended?' Kim asked.

'They confirm nothing to report,' Martha answered.

Kim shook her head. How hard had they looked?

'Is there a team on the way?' she asked.

'I have carried out all of the superintendent's instructions,' Martha confirmed.

'Thank you, Martha,' Kim said.

There was a pause.

'Detective Inspector. Be careful,' Martha said before ending the call.

Kim frowned at the phone as she put it in her pocket. There was a tone to the conversation she couldn't define. She shook her head. Her imagination was running riot with her.

'Bryant, where the hell are we?' she asked.

'Just about to exit the Shrewsbury ring road,' he answered.

'Miles, Bryant?'

'Twenty, twenty-five miles.'

'Pull over,' she said, unbuckling her seat belt.

'Guv, seriously, not a good idea.'

'Bryant pull over or I'm gonna move across and sit on your lap.'

'Guv, I'm doing the speed limit. It's not safe—'

'Bryant, pull over now or you can tell that to Woody at his granddaughter's funeral.'

CHAPTER EIGHTY-NINE

Woody saw the beam of headlights pass across the glass panel. The engine of a car died right outside. Car doors slammed together. He couldn't tell how many. His first thought was that his earlier visitors had returned. He tried to think quickly as he strained at the ties. His head was only a few inches from the door. If he could bang his head against the glass whoever was outside might hear.

He tried again, but the tie wraps around the leg of the cooker would not budge.

'I'm here,' he cried against the gag that caught and blocked every syllable.

He didn't care who it was as long as they could help him. Every moment took Lissy further away from him.

He would never forgive himself if anything happened to her.

A light shone around the windows again. He tried to follow it with his eyes to see where the person was going. Another torch shone through from the other side. The beams crossed each other in the darkness.

Don't give up so easily this time, he pleaded silently. *I'm here and my grandchild is in danger.*

He heard a voice.

More than one.

There was an urgency in their tone that gave him sudden hope. If it was the same people that had been before maybe this time they knew something was wrong. All he needed was to be freed from these damn ties so he could go and find his granddaughter.

Ironically, right now, there was only one person he wanted it to be but believing in miracles was not the behaviour of a detective chief inspector.

And then he heard her voice.

CHAPTER NINETY

'Kev, I don't care how the fuck you get me in there, just do it,' Kim snapped.

The caravan stood in total darkness, silent, until all four car doors had slammed shut. Lights were illuminating in other caravans but not in this one.

Dawson kicked hard at the door, but it didn't budge. Bryant stepped up beside him and they kicked it together, but nothing.

Bryant sprinted back to the car and returned with a crowbar.

He forced it between the door and the frame and prised it open.

Kim shone her torch into the darkness. It landed on a banquette seating area on the opposite side of the space.

She cast the light around.

'Oh Jesus,' she cried, as the light landed on the bound hands of her boss.

She stepped inside and felt to her left. She clicked on the light switch and then fell to her knees.

Her team filed into the caravan as she ripped the gag from Woody's mouth.

'Stone, how the hell—?'

'Does he have her, sir?' she asked urgently.

Woody nodded, and only then did she see the blood seeping from behind his left ear.

'Stace, you got a signal?'

'Just about, boss.'

'We need an ambulance here straightaway.'

Dawson took a knife from the kitchen drawer and began cutting the ties.

'What happened, sir?' Kim asked.

'Hit from behind,' he said, trying to stand.

Of course he had been. With Woody's height and girth he would be a formidable opponent from the front.

'Stay where you are,' she said, putting her hand on his arm. 'No disrespect, sir, but you can't help us.'

'Stone, get me out of these ties right now. My granddaughter—'

'Sir, please. You've suffered a head injury. How long has Lissy been gone?'

'Twenty minutes, maybe a little more.'

She looked around. Until the backup team arrived it was just the four of them.

Her options were limited.

'Stacey, stay here with the DCI and put a chase on the support team. Call it in to the locals as well. They may be able to help.'

'Got it, boss.'

Dawson reached for some kitchen roll as Bryant helped the DCI to his feet.

His bulk swayed but Bryant managed to hold him steady to the sofa.

Kim thought quickly. The killer had not taken young Tommy far from the snatch point.

'Right, Bryant, I want you knocking on every door you can find. If they're still here, they're not getting out. Use the residents to form a makeshift perimeter around the entrances and exits. They will know strangers on the site better than us.'

She wondered whether the site had any level of CCTV but there was nobody spare to go and check. She needed backup right now.

'Stone, I need to help find my granddaughter.'

'Sir, please don't make me restrain you,' she said, only half seriously. 'Now, can you tell me what Lissy is wearing?'

'Butterfly pyjamas and pink furry slippers.'

'Sir, you know the layout of this site, please brief the support team when they get here. We'll need their help in conducting a search.'

She turned to her colleague. 'But for now, Kev, it's just you and me.'

CHAPTER NINETY-ONE

From what Kim could work out the campsite was divided into two parts. The top half, nearest the main entrance, comprised caravans sitting side by side with a gravel road separating the rows.

A single track tarmac road headed to a lower part of the site.

'Where the hell are we going to start, boss,' Dawson asked as they reached a fork in the tarmac road.

The lighting was much less obvious around this part of the site. There were still globe lamps but the distance between them was much further.

They had left behind the manicured lawns and the uniformity of equal spacing.

They were now entering a vast area that contained log cabins built into banks and separated by thick, dense trees. All the dwellings appeared to be in darkness, making them more difficult to spot. The inquisitive chatter of the occupants at the top of the site had long since been left behind.

'Boss, look to the left, over there.'

Her eyes were still adjusting to the darkness, but the moon had peeked out a quarter to light up a dense wooded area at the bottom of the road.

The site owner had mentioned a lake to the right of the woods

Kim could see that the fork in the road took a circular route to the same place at the edge of the woods.

'Okay, Kev, you go right and I'll go left, and we should meet somewhere in the woods.'

'Boss, for safety, shouldn't we stick together?'

'He already has too much of a head start,' Kim said. 'And don't forget to shine your torch all the way around the lake. Remember what she was wearing?'

Dawson swallowed and nodded. It was a thought neither of them wanted to entertain, but a child had been murdered and they might already be too late for Lissy.

They turned and headed off in different directions.

Each step forward took her further into the darkness. She shone her torch left and right and all around her. The road cut through cabins on either side. To her left they were cut into a gently sloping bank. To her right they were surrounded by trees, their frontages looking on to the lake.

Kim paused as something darted past her feet. She hunted it with a torch until she found the white tail of a rabbit disappearing into a row of dense green laurels.

She continued heading towards the woods. Every instinct in her wanted to run but a seven-year-old girl could be anywhere, lying injured or worse.

The last cabin on the edge of the woods had a double lantern that illuminated the entrance into the trees. Kim knew that once she stepped into the opening she would have only her torch.

She swung it around her feet as something made a noise on the debris of dried twigs.

A tree branch slapped her around the face. She smacked it away angrily.

She was following the trodden path through the middle of the woods but she was aware that there were searchable areas on both sides.

An owl sounded its warning from somewhere above, and Kim cursed out loud.

Jesus, give her the West Midlands any day. The Black Country didn't offer a lot of nature which, for Kim, was a good thing. It was nowhere near as frightening as the countryside.

Kim felt something soft beneath her foot. For a brief second she wondered if she'd stepped on a rabbit. She shone the torch down expecting to see a pair of ears and a fluffy tail.

She gasped when she saw that it was much, much worse.

She was looking down at a blood-covered pink slipper.

CHAPTER NINETY-TWO

Dawson's torchlight reached her before he did.

'Jesus, boss, you okay?'

She had shouted his name as loudly as she could.

If the killer was still here, they weren't going to be able to leave the site. Right now, her only concern was for Lissy.

'She's in here somewhere,' Kim said, holding the slipper tight.

'Right now, I'm wishing we had a sniffer dog,' Dawson said.

Kim agreed.

'Okay, I want to carry on moving through these woods but slowly. And I'm going to call her name. You shine left and I'll shine right.'

They took two steps forward.

'Lissy,' Kim called.

They halted and listened for any response. Nothing.

Three more steps. Dawson jumped as something scooted past him.

'Calm down. It's rabbits,' she said, as though she was some kind of expert.

'Lissy,' she called again.

Nothing.

Kim felt the nausea rising in her stomach. Every passing moment told her she would be taking Woody the dead body of his grandchild.

'Boss,' Dawson said.

'I know,' she whispered. The hope was dying in both of them.

They took four more steps and stopped. Kim could see they were about twenty feet from the end of the woods.

'Lissy,' Kim called.

Nothing.

'Boss, should we—?'

'Shush,' she said, grabbing his arm. She had heard something. It was low and faint but it had been a sound.

'Lissy,' she called again.

A whisper sent Kim's heart soaring.

'Lissy, we're here,' Kim called. 'We're going to find you.'

Another whisper sounded from her left. She stepped off the path and used her torch to whip at the bramble that was trying to capture her legs.

She raised her feet higher and trampled it down.

'Lissy, we're coming, sweetheart.'

No response.

Kim felt the panic take its rightful place in her stomach. If the child was in and out of consciousness she must be in a bad way.

'Shine that way again, Dawson,' Kim said urgently.

His torch had swept over something lighter than the foliage around it.

'Lissy,' Kim said, heading towards it.

Dawson aimed his torch towards the shape.

'Oh Jesus,' Kim exclaimed. Her hand covered her mouth, as her eyes registered the sight on the ground.

CHAPTER NINETY-THREE

'Sir, please sit back down,' Stacey said, uncomfortably. On the hierarchical food chain Woody had to eat at least two ranks before he got to her. She couldn't recall one direct conversation they'd had. And now she was trying to keep him calm.

'I'm an extra body, Constable. I can help,' he snapped.

'Sir, we need to get you checked over by the paramedics.'

'I'm perfectly fine,' he said, reminding her of another one of her bosses.

His gait and colour didn't agree: his step had faltered twice and the whites of his eyes were bloodshot.

'Sir, I just want to say that I ay comfortable with trying to tell you what to do but you were asked to stay here for your own sake… and Lissy's,' she said. She expected a torrent of rage and a few choice words ending in 'disciplinary hearing'.

'Where the hell is this backup?' he snapped.

Stacey took out her phone. Perhaps she could contain him for a few more minutes while they progressed the support team.

She heard Bryant giving instructions to residents outside the door and suddenly wished he'd been given the task of babysitting the big boss.

She dialled into the station. She quickly identified herself and asked for a progress report on the operational order.

She heard the tap of keys. A pause. A second tap of keys.

'Nothing noted here about a support team.'

Stacey frowned. Normally they would have given her the information within seconds. She clarified the incident number to the operator.

'I have the incident, Constable,' the operator responded, shortly. 'I can see exactly where you are and what you're doing but there is no operational order in place for backup.'

Stacey swallowed and realised that Woody was watching her very closely.

'What is it?' he asked, before she'd ended the call.

'There's no order, sir,' she answered.

His expression gave in to confusion.

'Did Stone request it?' he asked.

'Of course,' she said.

'She went directly to Baldwin?' he asked, swaying to the left.

'Yes, sir,' she confirmed as she entered what had to be one of the most awkward conversations she'd ever had.

The realisation seeped into his eyes and was followed by rage. 'If anything happens to Lissy I will kill that bastard myself.'

He forced himself to a standing position, and Stacey had to reach out and steady him.

She could hear an ambulance siren growing closer. Just a few more minutes and she'd have some help keeping him out of danger.

'I have to go and help. There's no one looking for Lissy.'

Stacey understood his panic and compulsion to be out looking, and her boss was now in a vulnerable position. She wanted to let him go and make sure that everyone was safe. Yes, the boss and Kev were out searching alone but Stacey could not imagine any situation whereby a concussed DCI would help her boss at all.

But she was rapidly running out of options. 'Do you trust her, sir?' she asked, quietly.

His expression gave her the answer.

'Then please will you sit back down.'

CHAPTER NINETY-FOUR

The bloodstain coloured the front of the pyjama top, and Kim was reminded of little Tommy and what his grandmother had said. Blood glistened on the leaves.

Her pretty little face held no expression beneath the curly black hair that had been gathered into two bobbles on top of her head.

Dawson knelt down and put two fingers to her neck.

'Faint, but alive.'

Kim leaned down and touched her cheek gently. 'It's all right, Lissy. We're here now and you're safe.'

Kim gently lifted up the pyjama top. A knife wound an inch long was still seeping blood slowly. Kim had nothing with which to stem the blood flow, but if she didn't do something the child was going to die. She had to get her the quarter-mile to the top of the site as quickly as possible, apply pressure to the wound site, and keep the child warm.

Kim took off her jacket and laid it on the ground. She gently moved the child on top of it and wrapped the arms around her waist. She focussed the knot to land on top of the wound, while the back of the jacket offered some warmth. Her own body would have to do the rest.

Once the jacket was fixed in place, she scooped the child up into her arms. It was like holding a large ragdoll.

'Follow me up, Dawson,' she said.

'I'll take a look around first,' he said. 'There might be something left behind.'

Kim nodded her understanding. There could be vital clues around the immediate area that might not still be present when the techs arrived. Dawson was a professional; he knew not to disturb the crime scene too much.

Dawson shone the torch in the direction of the entrance to the woods. Her own torch was in her pocket.

As she hit the tarmac she began to walk quicker. After a couple of seconds, she began to sprint as quickly as she could.

'It's okay, sweetheart, you're going to be fine,' Kim said as the long incline to the top began to wind to the left.

She increased her speed again. The muscles at the top of her thighs burned but she couldn't slow down. She prayed that the movement was not causing the ooze to turn to a gush but knew that she had to get her to the medics at the top.

Kim could feel no movement against her and she had to wonder if the child was still with her, but she didn't have the time to check. Doing so would cost her valuable seconds.

Every second seemed to add a kilogramme of weight to Lissy's frame.

'Nearly there, sweetheart,' Kim gasped as she saw the flashing blue lights ahead.

The hill increased in gradient as she neared the top. Something ran in front of her and caused her to stumble. She pitched forward but managed to stop herself falling to the ground.

As she rounded the corner she cried out in pain as the muscles in the top of her arms cramped.

Bryant was still updating the residents but he was the first to see her.

'Medic,' he screamed into the caravan as he sprinted past. He placed his arms beneath hers.

'Let her go, guv. I've got her.'

Kim slid her arms out and as soon as the weight was gone they wanted to rise above her head. Her legs buckled but she grabbed onto the steps at the entrance to the caravan.

Two green uniforms came hurtling out of the holiday home.

'Single stab wound to abdomen: approximately one inch. Heavy blood loss,' she managed to say.

The one at the back nodded and headed towards where Bryant was carrying her to the ambulance.

She heard him reassuring the child: it gave her hope that Lissy was still alive.

She stepped into the caravan as Woody was pushing himself to stand. His face held more emotion in that one second than she'd seen in three years.

'We have her, sir,' Kim said.

She followed his eyes to the bloodstain on her top.

'She's alive, barely,' she said honestly.

'He began to shake his head. 'Stone—'

'Ambulance, sir,' she said, pointing outside.

She was keeping words to a minimum until her lungs returned to normal.

Stacey reached out to help him as he walked across the room.

He offered her a look that was not unkind but definite.

Stacey nodded and stepped back.

He reached her position by the door. He paused and locked her gaze. She held it for just a second before smiling.

'I understand, sir. This changes nothing. You like me no more today than you did yesterday.'

An almost smile touched his lips.

'You've got that right, Stone,' he said before rushing off to find his granddaughter.

Kim collapsed onto the chair beside Stacey.

'Please tell me someone has briefed the support team on the search?'

'There isn't one, boss,' Stacey said, quietly.

'What, a search?' Kim asked, confused. There was still a killer out there somewhere.

'A support team,' Stacey clarified.

'What the hell?'

'I called dispatch,' Stacey said. 'There was no instruction issued. There's no support team coming.'

The bastard had lied. He had humoured her to get her off the phone.

Kim stood and headed for the door.

If their killer was still on site, Dawson was down there alone.

CHAPTER NINETY-FIVE

Dawson could see that the torchlight was dimming.

His training had included the basic crime scene investigation steps and, despite the conditions, they had to be followed.

First, he had to protect the area. There was no one around yet, but once backup arrived he would place officers at both entrances to the woods. Next he had carried out a preliminary survey and determined the scene boundaries. These were often expanded later by the techs.

The lighting had prevented him exercising the next step effectively. He had used his torch to illuminate the area of blood loss and taken photographs on his phone. He would leave the next stage of sketching the scene to the professionals.

Unfortunately for him, many of the search protocols required more than one person. Line searches were conducted with bodies in a row moving steadily forward. A grid search needed two or more people to overlap separate line searches to form a grid. At one scene he'd witnessed a wheel search where techs began at the centre and worked out in straight lines to the boundary.

As he was alone he had opted for the spiral. He had begun at the point of blood loss and started moving slowly in a circle around it, moving further out on each rotation.

He knew there would be something of the killer here. It just had to be found amongst the foliage, elements and wildlife; it had to be found now. The team being sent by Baldwin would not include techs. They would come later.

Yes, the boss had wanted him to follow her up the hill but this was his moment. He was still trying to claw back ground for his mistake earlier in the week. And the only way he could think of doing so was to do his job. Only better.

Ideally, he would find some single piece of evidence that would prompt the light bulb in his head to illuminate and put it all together. And he could present it neatly to his boss. Now, he just had to find it.

The torch suddenly flickered and died. The total darkness of the woods felt suffocating around him. He shook the torch, trying to bully it into one last burst.

It illuminated an area the size of a football at his feet.

He could hear the boss's instructions as though she was right beside him. *Leave the woods now while you still have enough light. Safety first.*

And he knew he should listen but the killer was long gone, and he had a rough idea of the direction of travel to the opening.

He wondered if the killer had been spooked by the sound of the police car engine at the top of the site and had bolted before checking that Lissy was dead. He had probably thought he had done enough to finish her off.

The torch faltered again.

'Damn it,' he growled into the darkness as he shook it again.

The torch flickered to life once more as it was knocked clean out of his hands.

CHAPTER NINETY-SIX

Kim jogged away from the caravan, ordering her body to do as she bid. Running uphill, holding a seven-year-old girl, had found muscles she didn't even know she had.

She tried to shake off the anger at her boss's boss. Woody would never have done anything so low. He would have said no at the outset and left her to deal with it. She wouldn't have liked it but she would have formed operational decisions based on the truth.

She would have left Stacey with the occupants and the DCI and brought Bryant to help search, because then her colleague would not now be down there alone.

For all she knew Jason Cross was right there with him. Her stomach reacted the way it always did when her brain linked Jason Cross to the crimes. It reacted against the evidence, and yet it was there. She couldn't ignore it.

Her speed increased the more she thought about Dawson alone in the woods.

But was it Jason Cross? It was all too neat, all too tidy, and what was his link to the Howard family?

And what about the phones? Who the hell had called Deanna on the night of her murder, and why had the killer taken Deanna's old phone but not Maxine's. Who the hell would be prepared to kill innocent children?

And yet she could not explain the fact that Jason Cross's hair had been found in Deanna's car.

Suddenly, she slowed as a curtain began to peel back in her mind. Her legs braked to an almost stop as her brain quickened and began fitting pieces together.

'Oh shit,' she said into the darkness.

Her legs gathered speed and broke into a full run.

Because now she knew who it was.

CHAPTER NINETY-SEVEN

Dawson felt the nausea rise and burn the back of his throat. The wind had been punched from his body as the form had exploded and thrust him backwards. The searing pain reminded him that he had hit something hard which had momentarily knocked him out. He didn't know for how long but his hands were now tied behind him.

And his feet were being placed together. Instinct caused him to kick out violently.

'You should have left when you had the chance.'

He heard the words, as something hard cracked against his right ankle.

He cried out in pain at a voice he didn't recognise.

The form shone the torch upwards and illuminated the face he had seen taped to the incident board.

'Anna,' he said, placing her in the Brightman household.

For a moment he was stunned. His gaze had passed over her unassuming face a hundred times and never once had he considered this. Thoughts began to occur to him.

'You worked for the families,' Dawson said into the darkness. 'That's how you got close to them all.

'You called Deanna that night, told her something… ' His words trailed away as a memory fought its way through his fuddled brain. The phone. 'You rang Deanna from her own phone. You stole the old one she kept and you called her from it, telling her you'd found it. She met you and dropped you off in Colley Gate. She'd dropped you off there before… '

'Deanna was a very generous woman,' she said.

He blinked in the darkness as though that would clear the fog from around his brain.

'You were fond of her,' he said, shocked. 'It was genuine grief you felt—'

'Of course it was,' she said, cracking his left ankle with the torch.

The pain shot up his leg.

'I'm not a monster,' she said. 'Deanna was lovely and I'm sorry she's dead, but it had to be done.'

Dawson thought about one dead child and a possible second. Oh, she was a monster all right.

'Why the relatives?' he asked, trying to keep her talking. The support team had to be close by now.

'Because that's who suffer the most. The victims are dead; their pain is gone. Nothing hurts like losing the person you love the most. And you have to carry on living. You don't get the easy way out. You suffer. Truly suffer.'

'Luke Sweeney was your son,' he said.

'We were vilified for what our boy did. Somehow it was our fault he did it. We didn't raise him right. Or we should have known what he was going to do. Or we should have stopped it somehow.

'Our children were taunted and beaten up by the other kids. Our house was bricked every other night. We had dog shit put through our letter box. Everything you could think of and more. Our lives were hell.'

'He died in prison,' Dawson said.

No answer but no crack to the ankles.

Dawson knew he had to keep her talking. The support team would be closing in and the place would be crawling with police. She had no hope of escape. He just had to not die in the meantime.

'He should never have been there,' she spat. 'He was clearly ill. Mitchell Brightman painted the picture of a monster and then in her statement that girl had exaggerated everything my boy had done.'

Stacey had briefed him in the car of what she had found, had described the girl's injuries, and he could not believe what he was hearing but he couldn't react. The fact that the case had relied on the victim's statement instead of her testimony didn't seem to affect her at all. The girl's suicide didn't even register. But he couldn't let his anger show now. He had to try and keep her focussed.

'And with Geraldine. She testified that Luke was fit to stand trial. You tried to kill her partner first, didn't you? She was the person Geraldine loved most in the world but you couldn't get to her again.'

'I got her daughter instead,' she said, triumphantly. 'It was her child and she will never recover, just like I will never get over losing mine. Stupid bitch testified that my boy was fit to stand trial and that disgusting judge sent him away.'

'But you murdered a child,' Dawson said.

He could tell she was moving around his body in the darkness. He heard the crack of the twigs close to his left ear.

'Wasn't a particularly nice child,' she said, without emotion. 'But Howard adored him. It was going to be his wife until I saw how he looked at that little boy. It was a change of plan. Nothing more.'

Dawson listened intently. He wished he could hear activity in the distance.

She was pacing around him in the darkness.

The crack of leaves and branches to his left ear; two steps – crack to his right ear. Six steps – crack to his left ear.

It occurred to him she was trying to decide what to do with him. He had to keep her attention. He knew she had a knife. He couldn't use his hands, but maybe he could use his feet.

'You met Jason Cross at Geraldine's house, didn't you? And you recommended him to Deanna Brightman? You had the perfect opportunity to set him up when he slept with Deanna. His clothes turned up washed and dried. You took that hair and placed it in the car.'

He turned his foot to see how much movement he had within the confines of the ties. His foot met with no resistance. He recalled the kick out when he'd regained consciousness. It must have prevented her securing the tie wrap properly.

She chuckled. 'Just a distraction, officer. A bit of misdirection.'

Dawson suddenly knew what he had to do to get out alive.

He had to count the steps.

'And what about DCI Woodward. What—?'

'I was there when that bastard turned up and took my son away.'

Crack to the left

'That was an easy one,' she said.

Two steps.

Crack to the right.

'I enjoyed killing that child,' she said.

Three steps.

He swallowed the shock and horror of her words and concentrated on the count.

'She's not dead,' he said.

A pause. Halfway. Level with his feet.

'What are you talking about?'

He raised his legs up so that his knees almost touched his chin.

And kicked.

Pain ripped through his ankles as his soles made contact with her shins, and her squeal of shock and pain covered his own as she fell backwards.

The stars were exploding in his eyes but he knew he had to make the most of her confusion.

He launched himself to a sitting position and brought his bound hands underneath his behind. He cried out loud as he swept his hands beneath his ankles but with his hands now in front of him he scrabbled around on the ground, feeling for any part of her.

His hand touched a shoe. She had fallen directly backwards.

He knew he couldn't stand quickly enough to maintain the few seconds' advantage he'd gained. There was only one thing he could do, but if that knife was in her hand he was fucked.

He launched himself forward and landed right on top of her.

She made a sound as the air was pushed from her stomach. He used his hands to turn himself sideways and throw his bulk across her body.

'Get... off... me,' she cried.

Dawson knew that his weight not only held her in position but confined her hands. He mentally checked himself over and could feel no fresh pain sites.

He knew he was no longer in danger from the knife.

She spluttered beneath him.

There was only one thing that was still confusing him and it had been their one key reason for ruling her out immediately. 'Your phone, your alibi, it all checked out that you—'

'She posted it, Dawson,' said his boss from the darkness.

He blinked rapidly as a torch illuminated the area like a stage spotlight.

His boss stepped forward.

'She posted it to herself so it tinged to the mast closest to Wolverhampton. She used Deanna's lost phone to call Deanna's new phone, and she had her own phone back the next morning when we came to question her and the family.'

His boss took another step closer to the head of the woman on the ground.

'Sometimes, it's the simple things,' she said, taking another step. She was now as close as she could be, except his boss didn't stop walking.

The toe of her boot met with the side of the woman's head.

'Oops, sorry, but that was for the children.'

The woman cried out and then struggled to break free.

'You okay there, Dawson?' Kim asked as she bent down and offered her hand.

'Yeah, what took you?' he asked, accepting her offer of help.

She smiled. 'Hey, gotta give you guys a little fun now and again.'

He cried out when his standing weight rested on his ankles. He stumbled but his boss's arm snaked around his waist and steadied him.

The irony of that simple gesture was not lost on him.

He smiled and so did she.

They stood together looking down at the spent form on the ground.

His boss spoke first.

'Okay, time to get her up.' She paused and looked at him. 'You up to doing the interview?'

He felt the slow smile spread across his face at the trust she was prepared to place in him after everything he'd done.

'Oh yeah, boss, I'm up to it all right.'

CHAPTER NINETY-EIGHT

Kim pulled onto the drive at ten minutes to two in the morning.

What her tired body wanted more than anything else was a cuddle from her furry best friend.

Unsurprisingly, Charlie's lights were all out. She would go and fetch Barney in the morning.

She would have to be content with a hot shower and bed.

She turned the lock and opened the door.

The absence of the whooshing tail and paws on the laminate was unnerving, but there was something else. Something in her home was out of kilter, off balance.

She sharpened her senses and listened keenly. There was no sound.

The light from the outside street lamp and familiarity of her own home enabled her to negotiate the living room with ease.

The kitchen was in total darkness.

She switched on the light and stopped dead.

Shane stood on the opposite side of the breakfast bar.

In front of him was a terrified Gemma. A kitchen knife poised at her throat.

The room swayed before her slightly as her brain computed that this was not some nightmare scenario but actual real life. She swallowed deeply as she made eye contact with the tortured young man.

She tried to inject strength and calmness into her voice, but she didn't dare move towards him.

'Shane, put the knife down.'

He returned her gaze and shook his head.

'I can't,' he said.

Kim nodded. She did not break eye contact for a second. She couldn't offer the terrified girl any reassurance. If she looked away it would only take a second.

'You can,' she said.

'You don't understand,' Shane said, casting his eyes down to the top of Gemma's head.

She waited for his gaze to lift again.

'Yes, Shane, I do,' she said, meaningfully.

He blinked, and then she saw understanding dawn in his eyes.

Alex had a plan. It was the same as before. Only two things had stood in the way of an appeal: Ruth and her. She had tried to have Ruth killed by two separate people. And again, she had tried to loosen Kim's grip on sanity.

But she'd also had a contingency plan. And that had been Gemma.

Alex had slipped up when she'd mentioned Kim's habit of picking up waifs and strays. What better person to infiltrate her life than someone who was so much like herself?

'I promise you, Shane, I understand,' she said, softly.

In one swift movement he turned Gemma away from him and pushed her to the ground.

The girl slid across the kitchen floor and landed against a kitchen cabinet.

Kim heard a stunned whimper from the side but she didn't look. She didn't care. The girl had been here to kill her.

There was now only her and Shane.

'She's never going to let me go,' he said, brokenly.

Kim stopped herself from moving towards him even though it was what she wanted to do.

His pain travelled right into her heart.

'Shane, I know how she's made you feel, but I know someone who can—'

'Nobody can beat her. She ruins lives as if they were nothing.'

Kim didn't want to talk about Alex because she knew she could not disagree. She wanted to talk about him.

'But she doesn't have to control you anymore, Shane. Now you know what she is you can arm yourself against her.'

'I believed her, you know. Back at Hardwick House. I believed she could make me feel clean. I believed she could make me feel normal. I believed she would stop the nightmares and that she would take the picture of his face from my mind. But the dirt is still there. He is still there.'

Every fibre of Kim's being wanted to grab hold of this tortured soul and wrap protective arms around him so that nothing could ever hurt him again.

'Shane, I can—'

'He moves around my veins like sludge. He seeps into my organs. I thought killing him would make it stop but in a way it made it worse. It was the worst thing I could ever do, and it still wasn't enough because I could only do it once.'

A tear slid from his eye. 'There's no escape from either of them.'

Kim wanted to take this young man in her arms and try and soothe his pain. The aching lay heavy at her throat.

'Shane, please. Let me—'

'We both know there's only one way I can be free,' he said, raising the knife out front.

The scene before her turned into slow motion as the knife plunged into his chest.

She leapt around the breakfast bar and fell to the ground. The knife had missed his heart but was gushing blood.

'Phone an ambulance, now,' she barked at Gemma.

Gemma scrabbled to her feet and took out her phone.

Kim sat on the floor and pressed a tea towel around the wound. Removing the knife could kill him instantly.

Shane leaned against her.

'Please… stop… ' he said.

Kim felt the emotion choking her.

She continued trying to apply pressure. It was the only thing she could do.

His hand rested on top of hers.

'Please… Kim… no… '

The sound of her name on his lips ripped her heart in two. She knew what he wanted. She knew what he needed, but she didn't know if she had the strength to do it.

'It's on its way,' Gemma said.

'Good, now get out,' Kim cried.

Gemma hesitated.

'Get out,' Kim screamed, and didn't watch as the girl headed out the door.

She looked back to Shane's face, cradled in her lap.

His eyes beseeched her. 'I have… to… be… free… let… go… '

Kim stared into his eyes and saw the truth.

She slowly removed the pressure from the wound.

The tears blurred her vision but she wiped a lock of hair from his eyes.

She saw the peace start to come as she stroked his forehead and temple.

'You're… only… one… knows… her,' he whispered.

Kim nodded.

'Tell… something… from me?' he asked.

'Of course,' she spluttered, as the tears fell onto his face.

His eyes locked with hers. 'For a moment... clean... right now... happy... '

She nodded. 'I'll tell her but, Shane, you were always clean.'

By the time she finished the sentence she knew he was gone.

She howled and sobbed as though her heart was being torn in two but she lay still and caressed his head.

And that's where she was when the paramedics finally arrived.

CHAPTER NINETY-NINE

Kim stepped into the prison meeting area for what she knew would be the last time.

She had passed the young female officer in the corridor. A smile and a nod had told her all she needed to know.

Kim took a moment to get two coffees from the machine and sat at the table she'd occupied with Alex the other day.

As soon as the cups were placed onto the table she dug her hands back into the trouser pockets. No matter how many times she'd washed them she could still see Shane's blood all over her hands. There had been no sleep.

She had cried and she had cleaned and then she had cried some more. She mourned for the little boy that had suffered but his last words would stay with her for ever.

And that was the message she had come here to give.

She had managed to grab a moment with the warden before being shown through to the visitors' room. Alex's previous cell-mate, Cassie, would now be released on the intended date and be with her family early the following week. Kim had recounted to Mr Edwards how Alex had harmed herself to send Shane back to prison. He had listened in bewilderment but he had listened and he had believed.

It hadn't taken much digging to find out that Alex's previous cellmate to Cassie had been Gemma, who had donned a blonde wig to visit Alex under the name of Alex's sister, Sarah Lewis.

Kim guessed rightly that Sarah would never have visited Alex in prison and the solicitor, Barrington, had admitted to bringing in the letters from Kim's mother from the P O Box.

The fate of Tanya and Tina was yet to be decided while the prison, police and CPS wrangled over the appropriate charges and action to be taken.

Alex had also blackmailed Natalya – Elenya's mother. She had unearthed the fact that Natalya had another daughter who had been involved in the armed robberies but had not yet been caught. She had gained Natalya's trust and established where her second daughter was hiding, and then she had threatened to turn her in if Elenya did not carry out her wishes.

Natalya had been forced to consider sacrificing the daughter who was already in prison to ensure the safety of the one that was not. And so she had sent the instruction to Elenya to kill Ruth.

Ruth herself was now out of danger but would remain in hospital for a while longer until a safe place was established. Two attempts on her life dictated she would not be returning to Eastwood Park.

'Kim, I wasn't expecting to see you,' Alex said, taking a seat.

'Yes, I'm sure,' Kim said, smiling. 'But plans change, don't they?'

She saw Alex note the coffee cups which she then pointedly ignored.

She tipped her head at Kim. 'You looked a little peaky when you left the other day. Are you okay?'

Kim smiled. 'Yes, just a virus. But it's almost gone now.'

'Glad to hear it. So what brings you here?'

'Shane is dead, Alex. He is finally free of you. You can't hurt him anymore.' She did not expect to see any emotion from the woman, but was rewarded with a flash of annoyance. 'But he wanted me to give you a message. He wanted you to know that he died in my arms and he felt clean. For just a few moments he felt happy. He wanted you to know that.'

Kim pushed down the emotion that rose in her throat at the memory.

The news had no effect on the woman's expression at all. Kim could imagine that her only thoughts were for herself and wondering where it had all gone wrong.

Kim continued. 'Your little puppet, Gemma, was all poised to carry out your contingency plan and kill me, but Shane saved my life.'

Kim saw the confusion that entered her eyes. That eventuality had not occurred to her at any time.

'But you didn't even know him,' Alex said.

'Yes, but he knew me. He'd been watching me, Alex. And that's what you never allow for in your plans. Emotion. Because you have none you can't even begin to understand how they affect people's actions.

'He knew Gemma was supposed to kill me, and he couldn't let it happen.'

Alex said nothing. Her look was filled with hatred.

'And you'll be pleased to know that Ruth is out of danger and an enquiry has already been launched. Obviously I have offered my full assistance,' Kim clarified.

'How is your mother, Kim? Isn't it her parole hearing today?'

Kim laughed out loud at the woman's desperation in trying to undermine her composure.

'I really don't see how that has anything to do with you. It's not your business, Alex, but I would like to thank you for the gift.' Kim smiled widely. 'It is going to give me so much more than you planned.'

Alex looked close to exploding.

'And now that I've delivered the message Shane wanted me to, I'm afraid I must be going,' Kim said. She looked hard into the eyes of the woman whose calculating brain was still trying to come up with a sum that would work.

Kim shook her head. 'All in all, this week has been one epic fail for you, hasn't it?'

'You know you can't just walk away, Kim. There is a bond.'

'Oh Alex, only in your own head; I've already told you that your obsession with me will be your downfall. Had you not chosen to involve me at this time there is every chance that one of your plans with Ruth would have worked, but you just couldn't leave me alone, could you?'

'Don't pretend there is no bond, Kim,' Alex said confidently. 'You think of me at times.'

'You're right, Alex, I do think about you but I'm not consumed by you,' Kim said as she stood. 'You, better than anyone, know what I do with things I don't like. I put them in a box and pack them away.'

Alex smiled. 'But I have a box.'

Kim made a gesture holding her thumb half an inch from her forefinger. 'A small one, Alex, only a very small one.'

'You can't just pretend I don't exist. There will always be something there between—'

'Yes, Alex, it's called prison walls.'

She smiled one last time and moved behind the woman. She was struck by a sudden memory. She remembered it as a kind of victory dance Alex had bestowed on her when she'd felt she was winning.

It was time to return the favour.

She leaned down and kissed Alex on the left cheek.

'Goodbye, Alex, and this time it's for good.'

CHAPTER ONE HUNDRED

Kim would have liked to stay and chat longer with Alexandra Thorne but she had somewhere else to be.

She had cut it fine and walked into the Grantley Care facility two minutes before the hearing was due to start.

'I thought you weren't coming,' Lily said, holding a thick folder to her chest.

'Wouldn't miss it for anything,' Kim said honestly.

She followed Lily along the corridor into a meeting room at the end.

Two men and one woman were already seated at a round table. Three separate piles of paperwork sat before them.

Kim knew the parole board was an independent body charged with conducting a risk assessment on each individual case. Their primary goal was in establishing the likelihood of the prisoner reoffending. They would also be carefully observing her mother's behaviour.

Lily took a seat at the table and motioned for Kim to sit beside her.

Instead, Kim headed to a single seat that had been placed out of the way in the corner.

Kim put her hand into her pocket and felt the reassuring presence of the envelope she'd been given. She hadn't yet opened it but the memory of that day and its implications were now fresh in her mind.

Lily introduced Kim and then made a quick call from a phone that sat in the centre of the table.

Two minutes later the door opened and in walked the woman she had seen the other day.

Her mother looked around the room and finally her eyes rested in the corner.

'Kim… ' she whispered.

Kim continued to stare straight-ahead.

When the woman sat, Kim was treated to a profile shot and here she saw some resemblance to the mother she had known.

Once the formalities were spoken for the purpose of the meeting notes the young woman that sat in the centre of the three officials leaned forward.

'So, Patty, could you begin by telling us why you think you're ready to be released?'

Her mother took a deep breath. 'I think being here at this facility for so long has been the right thing. I've had time to get better properly.'

'So, you think you're cured?' asked the woman.

Patty smiled. 'Oh no, of course not. I will always have schizophrenia, but with the correct medication and continued support I feel that it is now under control.'

Damn, she's good, Kim thought, watching her closely.

Her mother's hands were set demurely in her lap. Her face was poised and relaxed, her voice regular and calm, and she made eye contact with everyone that spoke to her.

'And how do you feel about the events that led to your incarceration?' asked the portly man on the left.

Kim wanted to scream at the tact being employed. Use the words, she wanted to say. *Ask her how she feels about murdering her own child.*

She stopped herself from leaning forward. This she wanted to hear.

Her mother swallowed deeply. 'I've had a very long time to think about what I did.'

You and me both, bitch.

'And I can never turn back the clock to undo what I did.'

Say it, bitch. Say you murdered your own child.

'I have to live with Michael's death for the rest of my life.'

I'll rip his name from your mouth, woman. And we called him Mikey.

'I will never forgive myself for his death.'

Neither will I.

'But I now fully understand the consequences of my actions and, although I was mentally unstable at the time, I do take responsibility for the death of my son.'

Too fucking right.

Kim watched in amazement as more questions were asked with that same gentle, inoffensive tone and answered with that sickening, rehearsed response.

Every single person around the table was buying it. Every face looked back at this pleasant, nicely dressed, calm, measured woman and believed in the strength and validity of the system.

Kim could feel the words bubbling in her throat. She wasn't sure how much longer she could bear this charade.

Everyone was silently patting themselves on the back for a success story in rehabilitation. The female official leaned forward with a smile.

'Lily here thinks you'd have a good chance at adjusting to life on the outside. She feels—'

'Do you remember the camera?' Kim said, cutting the woman off.

Every face in the room turned towards her, but Kim looked only at her mother.

Kim knew it wasn't yet her turn to speak. Except she had decided it was.

Slowly her mother turned to face her.

'I'm sorry, Kimberly, I don't recall—'

'The camera, Mother. That big instamatic with the giant flash. You stole it from a chemist, with rolls and rolls of film.'

The face before her began to close down.

'Do you remember how frightened Mikey was to have his photograph taken at school?'

Her mother said nothing.

'I remember, Mother. It's because you would pin him down on the bed taking close-up shots of his eyes until he couldn't even see. You would set off that flash a dozen times a minute, convinced that just one photo would show you that your son really was the devil.'

Kim's eyes bored into those of her mother. There was no one else in the room.

'And when you couldn't see it you slapped him, didn't you, Mother? For hiding the devil inside. He couldn't win, could he?'

The whole room awaited her response. She had brought events to them. They had read the family history. They knew what Patty had done but now, in this room, a little boy was screaming as his mother pinned him to the bed searching for the devil inside him.

They wanted to see evidence that her mother had learned from what she'd done. That she was sorry but, most importantly, that she understood that she'd been wrong and that nothing like it would ever happen again.

And that's what Kim was waiting for too.

'You just wouldn't leave him alone, would you?' her mother asked as the face began to drop into one that Kim recognised. 'You wouldn't believe me when I told you the truth.'

'What truth, Mother?' Kim asked.

'That your brother was the fucking devil. I saw it in him every minute. It taunted me and laughed at me. I could see it as clear as day,' she cried, as her face became an angry snarl. 'I told you he had to die, and you wouldn't get out of the way. You hung on to him every minute, and only I knew the truth. He was possessed,' she cried, only at Kim. 'And there was no choice. He had to die.'

Kim sighed, as embarrassment took a seat at the table.

She stood. 'You will never be fit to walk free again. You will never understand that you murdered your child, and you will never be sorry for what you did.'

Kim stepped right up to her mother and drew level with her face.

'And for that may you burn in hell.'

She straightened and looked at no one as she left. Her job was done.

Her mother would not be released today.

She took a breath outside the door as voices crossed each other across the meeting table. There was no triumph in her heart, not even satisfaction that she had achieved what she had come here to do. What she felt was vindicated: justified in what had been a solitary opinion about the woman's ability to function in the outside world. If, after all these years, her mother still believed that the devil had lived inside her six-year-old son, then Kim felt sure that she would never be released.

As she moved slowly along the corridor Kim felt a loosening of emotion inside her. She would never let go of the anger towards her mother. She would never offer an inch of forgiveness but she would carry away with her the knowledge that she could face her mother – and survive.

She walked out of the building into the freshest air she'd ever tasted, and to a car she instantly recognised.

She laughed out loud, feeling the tension ease from her body.

'Really?' she said to Bryant who was leaning against his Astra.

'I was just passing and saw your bike parked—'

'Bryant, honestly?' she asked, shaking her head. The building was two miles from the nearest road and almost seventy miles from home.

'Well?' he asked.

'I think "requires further treatment" will be the official response.'

He smiled and then frowned. 'Would life get any easier for you if she just died?'

Kim shook her head. 'I don't want her to die,' she said simply.

'Bloody hell, Kim, that surprised me. You hate—'

'Not for her,' Kim clarified. 'She could rot in hell for me. But what if there's an afterlife, Bryant? I don't believe in it, but what if I'm wrong?'

'Not been known to happen before, has it?' he said, smiling.

'But what if I am wrong and Mikey's there and she gets there before me. It's a thought I just can't bear.'

Bryant was silent. He had no answer and neither did she.

'Everything okay at the station?' she asked. Woody had refused to allow her any part of the questioning following the trauma of the incident with Shane.

She knew that Lissy had responded positively to surgery and was conscious. The little girl was going to make it. Woody had not left her bedside and wouldn't, Kim suspected, until Lissy left the hospital.

Whatever Woody was going to do about Baldwin's failure was not yet known to her but her boss would take action. She knew that. And she would be right there to support him.

'I assisted Dawson on the questioning, just as you asked,' he said.

'Thank you. He does need a bit more freedom. He's earned it.'

'He was actually very good,' Bryant said. 'I think after their conversation in the woods he had a good idea of the questions to ask. Within twenty minutes she'd coughed to the lot.' He chuckled. 'Much to the despair of her brief.'

'Why now?' Kim asked, wondering what had prompted the murders nine years after the fact.

'Watching and waiting,' Bryant answered. 'Anna wanted to make sure that she murdered the person closest to the object of her hatred. She didn't only want a person close to Mitchell, Geraldine, Harold and Woody. She wanted the closest person to each of them and that took patience.'

'Anything on Jason Cross?' she asked.

'He disappeared to his mother's house in Norwich. Cried on her shoulder, came home and told his wife the truth, the whole truth, and they are now temporarily living apart.'

Kim couldn't summon any feeling for the man at all. She neither liked nor disliked him but he was now paying the price for dishonesty. Fair enough in her eyes.

'Families all informed?' she asked.

Bryant nodded. 'Barbara Howard confirmed that Anna worked for the family for only three months when they lived in the Midlands. She left their employment when they made the move to Uttoxeter. Anna knew where they were moving to and just followed Tommy to school one day, got chatting to one of the mothers and found out about the school trip. She wasn't a stranger to the child so he happily went with her when she lured him away.'

Kim shuddered. 'How is Barbara?'

'Content that the killer has been found but is relieved that her husband isn't here to witness the connection to him and his job. He would not have borne that, she said.'

Kim understood.

'Had a similar conversation with Geraldine, who is doing a special piece next week on the programme about drug addiction. She will publicly acknowledge her daughter and then resign.'

'I'm not surprised,' Kim said. It was the job her mother wanted her to do.

'And she's been in touch with Maxine's birth mother and they will be attending the funeral together.'

For some reason that fact brought a smile to Kim's face.

'Saved the best until last, though, guv. Mitchell Brightman is taking his daughter for coffee later today.'

'No way,' Kim said, surprised.

'Way,' Bryant said, smiling.

Kim offered an invisible air punch for the teenager.

'Not one of them could believe Anna was behind it. She played the respectful, deferential employee brilliantly.'

'Devious piece of work,' Kim said, wondering again how Anna had got past her radar. And she suddenly reached a conclusion. The woman's grief had been genuine. She felt no rage or bitterness towards the people she had killed. Her grief for Deanna had been real.

'What about her real family?' Kim asked. Anna had once had a husband and two other children.

'Emigrated to New Zealand without her six years ago. She wouldn't leave. It was more important to her to seek revenge than continue with the rest of her life.'

'Bloody hell,' Kim said.

'Don't even think about wasting a moment's emotion on that twisted woman, Kim,' Bryant said. 'There was not one bit of guilt for murdering a child and trying again,' he said.

He had a point. She would give the woman no more thought. But she would offer a silent prayer for her victims.

'You okay?' he asked, seriously. It had been a long few days.

She nodded and meant it.

'You know I'm always gonna be here to help whether you want it or not.'

'Oh yeah, I know it,' she said, drily.

'Because that's what friends are for,' he said.

She put two fingers in her mouth and retched.

He laughed and turned to the car door.

She threw her leg over the bike and reached for her helmet.

Yes, it had been a very long few days and, as usual, Bryant had been with her every step of the way. Even here the strong arm of his friendship was ready for her to take if she needed it.

She felt a sudden wave of gratitude that this man was in her life, although she would never find the words to tell him.

'Oi, Bryant,' she shouted with a lopsided grin. The envelope still nestled in her pocket. 'Meet me in town. I need your help choosing a frame.'

Because that's what friends were for.

LETTER FROM ANGELA

First of all, I want to say a huge thank you for choosing to read *Blood Lines*. I hope you enjoyed the fifth instalment of Kim's journey and the return of her nemesis, Alexandra Thorne.

If you did enjoy it, I would be forever grateful if you'd write a review. I'd love to hear what you think, and it can also help other readers discover one of my books for the first time. Or maybe you can recommend it to your friends and family...

After writing Evil Games I knew that the story between Kim and Alex was not finished and I wanted to show the power of a true sociopath even when confined. Even from prison Alex manages to affect the lives of those around her and to spread her venom and also to affect Kim Stone again. I also wanted to explore Kim's relationship with her mother in further detail to offer a better understanding of the woman Kim is now.

As the characters and storylines began to reveal themselves to me, this became a story that I did not want to finish.

I hope you will join both Kim Stone and me on our next journey, wherever that may lead.

If so I'd love to hear from you – get in touch on my Facebook or Goodreads page, Twitter or through my website.

And if you'd like to keep up-to-date with all my latest releases, just sign up at the website address below.

Thank you so much for your support, it is hugely appreciated.

Angela Marsons

www.bookouture.com/angelamarsons

www.angelamarsons-books.com

 angelamarsonsauthor

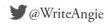 @WriteAngie